D1444670

Born with the Dead

Books by Robert Silverberg

Born with the Dead

THREE NOVELLAS

Robert Silverberg

VINTAGE BOOKS

A Division of Random House

New York

FIRST VINTAGE BOOKS EDITION, June 1975
Copyright © 1971, 1972, 1974 by Robert Silverberg

Library of Congress Cataloging in Publication Data

Silverberg, Robert.
  Born with the dead; three novellas.

  CONTENTS: Born with the dead.—Thomas, the Proclaimer.
—Going.
  I. Title.
[PZ4.S573Bq4] [PS3569.I472]   813'.5'4   74-17406
ISBN 0-394-71447-4

For Brian and Margaret Aldiss,
who live too far away

Contents

Born with
the Dead

One

And what the dead had no speech for, when living,
They can tell you, being dead: the communication
Of the dead is tongued with fire beyond the language
    of the living.

Eliot: *Little Gidding*

Supposedly his late wife Sybille was on her way to Zanzibar. That was what they told him, and he believed it. Jorge Klein was at that stage in his search when he would believe anything, if belief would only lead him to Sybille. Anyway, it wasn't so absurd that she would go to Zanzibar. Sybille had always wanted to go there. In some unfathomable obsessive way the place had seized the center of her consciousness long ago. When she was alive it hadn't been possible for her to go there, but now, loosed from all bonds, she would be drawn toward Zanzibar like a bird to its nest, like Ulysses to Ithaca, like a moth to a flame.

*   *   *

The plane, a small Air Zanzibar Havilland FP-803, took off more than half empty from Dar es Salaam at 0915 on a mild bright morning, gaily circled above the dense masses of mango trees, red-flowering flamboyants, and tall coconut palms along the aquamarine shores of the Indian Ocean, and headed northward on the short hop across the strait to Zanzibar. This day—Tuesday, the ninth of March, 1993—would be an unusual one for Zanzibar: five deads were aboard the plane, the first of their kind ever to visit that fragrant isle. Daud Mahmoud Barwani, the health officer on duty that morning at Zanzibar's Karume Airport, had been warned of this by the emigration officials on the mainland. He had no idea how he was going to handle the situation, and he was apprehensive: these were tense times in Zanzibar. Times are always tense in Zanzibar. Should he refuse them entry? Did deads pose any threat to Zanzibar's ever-precarious political stability? What about subtler menaces? Deads might be carriers of dangerous spiritual maladies. Was there anything in the Revised Administrative Code about refusing visas on grounds of suspected contagions of the spirit? Daud Mahmoud Barwani nibbled moodily at his breakfast—a cold chapatti, a mound of cold curried potato—and waited without eagerness for the arrival of the deads.

Almost two and a half years had passed since Jorge Klein had last seen Sybille: the afternoon of Saturday, October 13, 1990, the day of her funeral. That day she lay in her casket as though merely asleep, her beauty altogether unmarred by her final ordeal: pale skin, dark lustrous hair, delicate nostrils, full lips. Iridescent gold and violet fabric enfolded her serene body; a shimmering electrostatic haze, faintly perfumed with a jasmine fragrance, protected her from decay. For five hours she floated on the dais while the rites of parting were read and the condolences were offered—offered almost furtively, as if her death were a thing too monstrous to acknowledge with a show of strong feeling; then, when only a few people remained, the inner core of their circle of friends, Klein kissed her lightly on the lips and surrendered her to the silent dark-clad men whom the Cold Town had sent. She had asked in her will to be rekindled; they took her away in a black van to work their magic on her corpse. The casket, retreating on their broad shoulders, seemed to Klein to be disappearing into a throbbing gray vortex that he was helpless to penetrate. Presumably he would never hear from her again. In those days the deads kept strictly to themselves, sequestered behind the walls of their self-imposed ghettos; it was rare ever to see one outside the Cold Towns, rare even for one of them to make oblique contact with the world of the living.

So a redefinition of their relationship was forced on him. For nine years it had been Jorge and Sybille, Sybille and Jorge, I and thou forming *we*, above all *we*, a transcendental *we*. He had loved her with almost painful intensity. In life they had gone everywhere together, had done everything together, shared research tasks and classroom assignments, thought interchangeable thoughts, expressed tastes that were nearly always identical, so completely had each permeated the other. She was a part of him, he of her, and until the moment of her unexpected death he had assumed it would be like that forever. They were still young, he thirty-eight, she thirty-four, decades to look forward to. Then she was gone. And now they were mere anonymities to one another, she not Sybille but only a dead, he not Jorge but only a warm. She was somewhere on the North American continent, walking about, talking, eating, reading, and yet she was gone, lost to him, and it behooved him to accept that alteration in his life, and outwardly he did accept it, but yet, though he knew he could never again have things as they once had been, he allowed himself the indulgence of a lingering wistful hope of regaining her.

Shortly the plane was in view, dark against the brightness of the sky, a suspended mote, an irritating fleck in Barwani's eye, growing larger, causing him to blink and sneeze. Barwani was not ready for it. When Ameri Kombo, the flight controller in the cubicle next door, phoned him with the routine announcement of the landing, Barwani replied, "Notify the pilot that no one is to debark until I have given clearance. I must consult the regulations. There is possibly a peril to public health." For twenty minutes he let the plane sit, all hatches sealed, on the quiet runway. Wandering goats emerged from the shrubbery and inspected it. Barwani consulted no regulations. He finished his modest meal; then he folded his arms and sought to attain the proper state of tranquillity. These deads, he told himself, could do no harm. They were people like all other people, except that they had undergone extraordinary medical treatment. He must overcome his superstitious fear of them: he was no peasant, no silly clove-picker, nor was Zanzibar an abode of primitives. He would admit them, he would give them their anti-malaria tablets as though they were ordinary tourists, he would send them on their way. Very well. Now he was ready. He phoned Ameri Kombo. "There is no danger," he said. "The passengers may exit."

There were nine altogether, a sparse load. The four warms emerged first, looking somber and a little congealed, like people who had had to travel with a party of uncaged cobras. Barwani knew them all: the German

consul's wife, the merchant Chowdhary's son, and two
Chinese engineers, all returning from brief holidays in
Dar. He waved them through the gate without formali-
ties. Then came the deads, after an interval of half a
minute: probably they had been sitting together at one
end of the nearly empty plane and the others had been
at the other. There were two women, three men, all of
them tall and surprisingly robust-looking. He had expected them to shamble, to shuffle, to limp, to falter, but
they moved with aggressive strides, as if they were in
better health now than when they had been alive. When
they reached the gate, Barwani stepped forward to greet
them, saying softly, "Health regulations, come this way,
kindly." They were breathing, undoubtedly breathing:
he tasted an emanation of liquor from the big red-haired
man, a mysterious and pleasant sweet flavor, perhaps
anise, from the dark-haired woman. It seemed to Barwani that their skins had an odd waxy texture, an unreal
glossiness, but possibly that was his imagination; white
skins had always looked artificial to him. The only certain difference he could detect about the deads was in
their eyes, a way they had of remaining unnervingly fixed
in a single intense gaze for many seconds before shifting.
Those were the eyes, Barwini thought, of people who
had looked upon the Emptiness without having been
swallowed into it. A turbulence of questions erupted
within him: What is it like, how do you feel, what do you
remember, where did you go? He left them unspoken.
Politely he said, "Welcome to the isle of cloves. We ask
you to observe that malaria has been wholly eradicated
here through extensive precautionary measures, and to
prevent recurrence of unwanted disease we require of
you that you take these tablets before proceeding further." Tourists often objected to that; these people swallowed their pills without a word of protest. Again Bar-

wani yearned to reach toward them, to achieve some sort
of contact that might perhaps help him to transcend the
leaden weight of being. But an aura, a shield of strange-
ness, surrounded these five, and though he was an ami-
able man who tended to fall into conversations easily
with strangers, he passed them on in silence to Mponda
the immigration man.

Mponda's high forehead was shiny with sweat, and
he chewed at his lower lip; evidently he was as disturbed
by the deads as Barwani. He fumbled forms, he stamped
a visa in the wrong place, he stammered while telling the
deads that he must keep their passports overnight. "I
shall post them by messenger to your hotel in the morning," Mponda promised them, and sent the visitors onward to the baggage pickup area with undue haste.

Klein had only one friend with whom he dared talk
about it, a colleague of his at UCLA, a sleek supple
Parsee sociologist from Bombay named Framji Jijibhoi,
who was as deep into the elaborate new subculture of the
deads as a warm could get. "How can I accept this?"
Klein demanded. "I can't accept it at all. She's out there
somewhere, she's alive, she's—"

Jijibhoi cut him off with a quick flick of his fingertips. "No, dear friend," he said sadly, "not alive, not alive
at all, merely rekindled. You must learn to grasp the distinction."

Klein could not learn to grasp the distinction. Klein
could not learn to grasp anything having to do with
Sybille's death. He could not bear to think that she had
passed into another existence from which he was totally
excluded. To find her, to speak with her, to participate
in her experience of death and whatever lay beyond
death, became his only purpose. He was inextricably

bound to her, as though she were still his wife, as though Jorge-and-Sybille still existed in any way.

He waited for letters from her, but none came. After a few months he began trying to trace her, embarrassed by his own compulsiveness and by his increasingly open breaches of the etiquette of this sort of widowerhood. He traveled from one Cold Town to another—Sacramento, Boise, Ann Arbor, Louisville—but none would admit him, none would even answer his questions. Friends passed on rumors to him, that she was living among the deads of Tucson, of Roanoke, of Rochester, of San Diego, but nothing came of these tales; then Jijibhoi, who had tentacles into the world of the rekindled in many places, and who was aiding Klein in his quest even though he disapproved of its goal, brought him an authoritative-sounding report that she was at Zion Cold Town in southeastern Utah. They turned him away there too, but not entirely cruelly, for he did manage to secure plausible evidence that that was where Sybille really was.

In the summer of '92 Jijibhoi told him that Sybille had emerged from Cold Town seclusion. She had been seen, he said, in Newark, Ohio, touring the municipal golf course at Octagon State Memorial in the company of a swaggering red-haired archaeologist named Kent Zacharias, also a dead, formerly a specialist in the mound-building Hopewellian cultures of the Ohio Valley. "It is a new phase," said Jijibhoi, "not unanticipated. The deads are beginning to abandon their early philosophy of total separatism. We have started to observe them as tourists visiting our world—exploring the life-death interface, as they like to term it. It will be very interesting, dear friend." Klein flew at once to Ohio and without ever actually seeing her, tracked her from Newark to Chillicothe, from Chillicothe to Marietta, from Marietta

into West Virginia, where he lost her trail somewhere
between Moundsville and Wheeling. Two months later
she was said to be in London, then in Cairo, then Addis
Ababa. Early in '93 Klein learned, via the scholarly
grapevine—an ex-Californian now at Nyerere University
in Arusha—that Sybille was on safari in Tanzania and
was planning to go, in a few weeks, across to Zanzibar.

Of course. For ten years she had been working on
a doctoral thesis on the establishment of the Arab Sultanate in Zanzibar in the early nineteenth century—stud-
ies unavoidably interrupted by other academic chores,
by love affairs, by marriage, by financial reverses, by
illnesses, death, and other responsibilities—and she had
never actually been able to visit the island that was so
central to her. Now she was free of all entanglements.
Why shouldn't she go to Zanzibar at last? Why not? Of
course: she was heading for Zanzibar. And so Klein
would go to Zanzibar too, to wait for her.

As the five disappeared into taxis, something occurred to Barwani. He asked Mponda for the passports and
scrutinized the names. Such strange ones: Kent Zacharias, Nerita Tracy, Sybille Klein, Anthony Gracchus,
Laurence Mortimer. He had never grown accustomed to
the names of Europeans. Without the photographs he
would be unable to tell which were the women, which
the men. Zacharias, Tracy, Klein . . . ah. *Klein.* He
checked a memo, two weeks old, tacked to his desk.
Klein, yes. Barwani telephoned the Shirazi Hotel—a
project that consumed several minutes—and asked to
speak with the American who had arrived ten days before, that slender man whose lips had been pressed tight
in tension, whose eyes had glittered with fatigue, the one
who had asked a little service of Barwani, a special
favor, and had dashed him a much-needed hundred shillings as payment in advance. There was a lengthy delay,

no doubt while porters searched the hotel, looking in the men's room, the bar, the lounge, the garden, and then the American was on the line. "The person about whom you inquired has just arrived, sir," Barwani told him.

TWO

The dance begins. Worms underneath fingertips, lips
beginning to pulse, heartache and throat-catch. All
slightly out of step and out of key, each its own tempo
and rhythm. Slowly, connections. Lip to lip, heart to
heart, finding self in other, dreadfully, tentatively,
burning . . . notes finding themselves in chords, chords
in sequence, cacophony turning to polyphonous con-
trapuntal chorus, a diapason of celebration.

R. D. Laing: *The Bird of Paradise*

Sybille stands timidly at the edge of the municipal golf
course at Octagon State Memorial in Newark, Ohio,
holding her sandals in her hand and surreptitiously
working her toes into the lush, immaculate carpet of
dense, close-cropped lime-green grass. It is a summer
afternoon in 1992, very hot; the air, beautifully translu-
cent, has that timeless midwestern shimmer, and the
droplets of water from the morning sprinkling have not
yet burned off the lawn. Such extraordinary grass! She
hadn't often seen grass like that in California, and cer-

tainly not at Zion Cold Town in thirsty Utah. Kent
Zacharias, towering beside her, shakes his head sadly.
"A golf course!" he mutters. "One of the most important prehistoric sites in North America and they make a
golf course out of it! Well, I suppose it could have been
worse. They might have bulldozed the whole thing and
turned it into a municipal parking lot. Look, there, do
you see the earthworks?"

She is trembling. This is her first extended journey
outside the Cold Town, her first venture into the world
of the warms since her rekindling, and she is picking up
threatening vibrations from all the life that burgeons
about her. The park is surrounded by pleasant little
houses, well kept. Children on bicycles rocket through
the streets. In front of her, golfers are merrily slamming
away. Little yellow golf carts clamber with lunatic energy over the rises and dips of the course. There are
platoons of tourists who, like herself and Zacharias,
have come to see the Indian mounds. There are dogs
running free. All this seems menacing to her. Even the
vegetation—the thick grass, the manicured shrubs, the
heavy-leafed trees with low-hanging boughs—disturbs
her. Nor is the nearness of Zacharias reassuring, for he
too seems inflamed with undeadlike vitality; his face is
florid, his gestures are broad and overanimated, as he
points out the low flat-topped mounds, the grassy bumps
and ridges making up the giant joined circle and octagon
of the ancient monument. Of course, these mounds are
the mainspring of his being, even now, five years post
mortem. Ohio is his Zanzibar.

"—once covered four square miles. A grand ceremonial center, the Hopewellian equivalent of Chichén
Itzá, of Luxor, of—" He pauses. Awareness of her distress has finally filtered through the intensity of his ar-

chaeological zeal. "How are you doing?" he asks gently.

She smiles a brave smile. Moistens her lips. Inclines her head toward the golfers, toward the tourists, toward the row of darling little houses outside the rim of the park. Shudders.

"Too cheery for you, is it?"

"Much," she says.

Cheery. Yes. A cheery little town, a magazine-cover town, a chamber-of-commerce town. Newark lies becalmed on the breast of the sea of time: but for the look of the automobiles, this could be 1980 or 1960 or perhaps 1940. Yes. Motherhood, baseball, apple pie, church every Sunday. Yes. Zacharias nods and makes one of the signs of comfort at her. "Come," he whispers. "Let's go toward the heart of the complex. We'll lose the twentieth century along the way."

With brutal imperial strides he plunges into the golf course. Long-legged Sybille must work hard to keep up with him. In a moment they are within the embankment, they have entered the sacred octagon, they have penetrated the vault of the past, and at once Sybille feels they have achieved a successful crossing of the interface between life and death. How still it is here! She senses the powerful presence of the forces of death, and those dark spirits heal her unease. The encroachments of the world of the living on these precincts of the dead become insignificant: the houses outside the park are no longer in view, the golfers are mere foolish incorporeal shadows, the bustling yellow golf carts become beetles, the wandering tourists are invisible.

She is overwhelmed by the size and symmetry of the ancient site. What spirits sleep here? Zacharias conjures them, waving his hands like a magician. She has heard so much from him already about these people,

these Hopewellians—What did they call themselves?
How can we ever know?—who heaped up these ram-
parts of earth twenty centuries ago. Now he brings them
to life for her with gestures and low urgent words. He
whispers fiercely:

—Do you see them?

And she does see them. Mists descend. The
mounds reawaken; the mound-builders appear. Tall,
slender, swarthy, nearly naked, clad in shining copper
breastplates, in necklaces of flint disks, in bangles of
bone and mica and tortoise shell, in heavy chains of
bright lumpy pearls, in rings of stone and terra cotta,
in armlets of bears' teeth and panthers' teeth, in spool-
shaped metal ear-ornaments, in furry loincloths. Here
are priests in intricately woven robes and awesome
masks. Here are chieftains with crowns of copper rods,
moving in frosty dignity along the long earthen-walled
avenue. The eyes of these people glow with energy.
What an enormously vital, enormously profligate culture they sustain here! Yet Sybille is not alienated by
their throbbing vigor, for it is the vigor of the dead,
the vitality of the vanished.

Look, now. Their painted faces, their unblinking
gazes. This is a funeral procession. The Indians have
come to these intricate geometrical enclosures to per-
form their acts of worship, and now, solemnly parad-
ing along the perimeters of the circle and the octagon,
they pass onward, toward the mortuary zone beyond.
Zacharias and Sybille are left alone in the middle of the
field. He murmurs to her:

—Come. We'll follow them.

He makes it real for her. Through his cunning
craft she has access to this community of the dead. How
easily she has drifted backward across time! She learns
here that she can affix herself to the sealed past at any

point; it's only the present, open-ended and unpredictable, that is troublesome. She and Zacharias float through the misty meadow, no sensation of feet touching ground; leaving the octagon, they travel now down a long grassy causeway to the place of the burial mounds, at the edge of a dark forest of wide-crowned oaks. They enter a vast clearing. In the center the ground has been plastered with clay, then covered lightly with sand and fine gravel; on this base the mortuary house, a roofless four-sided structure with walls consisting of rows of wooden palisades, has been erected. Within this is a low clay platform topped by a rectangular tomb of log cribbing, in which two bodies can be seen: a young man, a young woman, side by side, bodies fully extended, beautiful even in death. They wear copper breastplates, copper ear ornaments, copper bracelets, necklaces of gleaming yellowish bears' teeth.

Four priests station themselves at the corners of the mortuary house. Their faces are covered by grotesque wooden masks topped by great antlers, and they carry wands two feet long, effigies of the death-cup mushroom in wood sheathed with copper. One priest commences a harsh, percussive chant. All four lift their wands and abruptly bring them down. It is a signal; the depositing of grave-goods begins. Lines of mourners bowed under heavy sacks approach the mortuary house. They are unweeping, even joyful, faces ecstatic, eyes shining, for these people know what later cultures will forget, that death is no termination but rather a natural continuation of life. Their departed friends are to be envied. They are honored with lavish gifts, so that they may live like royalty in the next world: out of the sacks come nuggets of copper, meteoric iron, and silver, thousands of pearls, shell beads, beads of copper and iron, buttons of wood and stone, heaps of metal ear-spools, chunks and chips of obsidian, animal effigies carved from slate and bone and tortoise shell, ceremonial copper axes and knives, scrolls cut from mica, human jawbones inlaid with turquoise, dark coarse pottery, needles of bone, sheets of woven cloth, coiled serpents fashioned from dark stone, a torrent of offerings, heaped up around and even upon the two bodies.

At length the tomb is choked with gifts. Again there is a signal from the priests. They elevate their wands and the mourners, drawing back to the borders of the clearing, form a circle and begin to sing a somber, throbbing funeral hymn. Zacharias, after a moment, sings with them, wordlessly embellishing the melody with heavy melismas. His voice is a rich *basso cantante,* so unexpectedly beautiful that Sybille is moved almost to confusion by it, and looks at him in awe. Abruptly he breaks off, turns to her, touches her arm, leans down to say:

—You sing too.

Sybille nods hesitantly. She joins the song, falteringly at first, her throat constricted by self-consciousness; then she finds herself becoming part of the rite, somehow, and her tone becomes more confident. Her high clear soprano soars brilliantly above the other voices.

Now another kind of offering is made: boys cover the mortuary house with heaps of kindling—twigs, dead branches, thick boughs, all sorts of combustible debris —until it is quite hidden from sight, and the priests cry a halt. Then, from the forest, comes a woman bearing a blazing firebrand, a girl, actually, entirely naked, her sleek fair-skinned body painted with bizarre horizontal stripes of red and green on breasts and buttocks and thighs, her long glossy black hair flowing like a cape behind her as she runs. Up to the mortuary house she sprints; breathlessly she touches the firebrand to the kindling, here, here, here, performing a wild dance as she goes, and hurls the torch into the center of the pyre. Skyward leap the flames in a ferocious rush. Sybille feels seared by the blast of heat. Swiftly the house and tomb are consumed.

While the embers still glow, the bringing of earth gets under way. Except for the priests, who remain rigid at the cardinal points of the site, and the girl who wielded the torch, who lies like discarded clothing at the edge of the clearing, the whole community takes part. There is an open pit behind a screen of nearby trees; the worshipers, forming lines, go to it and scoop up soil, carrying it to the burned mortuary house in baskets, in buckskin aprons, in big moist clods held in their bare hands. Silently they dump their burdens on the ashes and go back for more.

Sybille glances at Zacharias; he nods; they join the line. She goes down into the pit, gouges a lump of moist black clayey soil from its side, takes it to the growing mound. Back for another, back for another. The mound rises rapidly, two feet above ground level now, three, four, a swelling circular blister, its outlines governed by the unchanging positions of the four priests, its tapering contours formed by the tamping of scores of bare feet. Yes, Sybille thinks, this is a valid way of celebrating death, this is a fitting rite. Sweat runs down her body, her clothes become stained and muddy, and still she runs to the earth-quarry, runs from there to the mound, runs to the quarry, runs to the mound, runs, runs, transfigured, ecstatic.

Then the spell breaks. Something goes wrong, she does not know what, and the mists clear, the sun dazzles her eyes, the priests and the mound-builders and the unfinished mound disappear. She and Zacharias are once again in the octagon, golf carts roaring past them on every side. Three children and their parents stand just a few feet from her, staring, staring, and a boy about ten years old points to Sybille and says in a voice that reverberates through half of Ohio, "Dad, what's wrong with those people? Why do they look so weird?"

Mother gasps and cries, *"Quiet,* Tommy, don't you have any manners?" Dad, looking furious, gives the boy a stinging blow across the face with the tips of his fingers, seizes him by the wrist, tugs him toward the other side of the park, the whole family following in their wake.

Sybille shivers convulsively. She turns away, clasping her hands to her betraying eyes. Zacharias embraces her. "It's all right," he says tenderly. "The boy didn't know any better. It's all right."

"Take me away from here!"

"I want to show you—"

"Some other time. Take me away. To the motel. I don't want to see anything. I don't want anybody to see me."

He takes her to the motel. For an hour she lies face down on the bed, racked by dry sobs. Several times she tells Zacharias she is unready for this tour, she wants to go back to the Cold Town, but he says nothing, simply strokes the tense muscles of her back, and after a while the mood passes. She turns to him and their eyes meet and he touches her and they make love in the fashion of the deads.

Three

Newness is renewal: *ad hoc enim venit, ut renovemur in illo;* making it new again, as on the first day; *herrlich wie am ersten Tag.* Reformation, or renaissance; rebirth. Life is Phoenix-like, always being born again out of its own death. The true nature of life is resurrection; all life is life after death, a second life, reincarnation. *Totus hic ordo revolubilis testatio est resurrectionis mortuorum.* The universal pattern of recurrence bears witness to the ressurection of the dead.

Norman O. Brown: *Love's Body*

"The rains shall be commencing shortly, gentleman and lady," the taxi driver said, speeding along the narrow highway to Zanzibar Town. He had been chattering steadily, wholly unafraid of his passengers. He must not know what we are, Sybille decided. "Perhaps in a week or two they begin. These shall be the long rains. The short rains come in the last of November and December."

"Yes, I know," Sybille said.

"Ah, you have been to Zanzibar before?"

"In a sense," she replied. In a sense she had been to Zanzibar many times, and how calmly she was taking it, now that the true Zanzibar was beginning to superimpose itself on the template in her mind, on that dream-Zanzibar she had carried about so long! She took everything calmly now: nothing excited her, nothing aroused her. In her former life the delay at the airport would have driven her into a fury: a ten-minute flight, and then to be trapped on the runway twice as long! But she had remained tranquil throughout it all, sitting almost immobile, listening vaguely to what Zacharias was saying and occasionally replying as if sending messages from some other planet. And now Zanzibar, so placidly accepted. In the old days she had felt a sort of paradoxical amazement whenever some landmark familiar from childhood geography lessons or the movies or travel posters—the Grand Canyon, the Manhattan skyline, Taos Pueblo—turned out in reality to look exactly as she imagined it would; but now here was Zanzibar, unfolding predictably and unsurprisingly before her, and she observed it with a camera's cool eye, unmoved, unresponsive.

The soft, steamy air was heavy with a burden of perfumes, not only the expected pungent scent of cloves but also creamier fragrances which perhaps were those of hibiscus, frangipani, jacaranda, bougainvillaea, penetrating the cab's open window like probing tendrils. The imminence of the long rains was a tangible pressure, a presence, a heaviness in the atmosphere: at any moment a curtain might be drawn aside and the torrents would start. The highway was lined by two shaggy green walls of palms broken by tin-roofed shacks; behind the palms were mysterious dark groves, dense and alien. Along the edge of the road was the usual tropical array of obstacles: chickens, goats, naked children, old women with shrunken, toothless faces, all wandering around untroubled by the taxi's encroachment on their right-of-way. On through the rolling flatlands the cab sped, out onto the peninsula on which Zanzibar Town sits. The temperature seemed to be rising perceptibly minute by minute; a fist of humid heat was clamping tight over the island. "Here is the waterfront, gentleman and lady," the driver said. His voice was an intrusive hoarse purr, patronizing, disturbing. The sand was glaringly white, the water a dazzling glassy blue; a couple of dhows moved sleepily across the mouth of the harbor, their lateen sails bellying slightly as the gentle sea breeze caught them. "On this side, please—" An enormous white wooden building, four stories high, a wedding cake of long verandahs and cast-iron railings, topped by a vast cupola. Sybille, recognizing it, anticipated the driver's spiel, hearing it like a subliminal pre-echo: "Beit al-Ajaib, the House of Wonders, former government house. Here the Sultan was often make great banquets, here the famous of all Africa came homaging. No longer in use. Next door the old Sultan's Palace, now Palace of People. You wish to go in House of Wonders? Is open: we stop, I take you now."

"Another time," Sybille said faintly. "We'll be here awhile."

"You not here just a day like most?"

"No, a week or more. I've come to study the history of your island. I'll surely visit the Beit al-Ajaib. But not today."

"Not today, no. Very well: you call me, I take you anywhere. I am Ibuni." He gave her a gallant toothy grin over his shoulder and swung the cab inland with a ferocious lurch, into the labyrinth of winding streets and narrow alleys that was Stonetown, the ancient Arab quarter.

All was silent here. The massive white stone buildings presented blank faces to the streets. The windows, mere slits, were shuttered. Most doors—the famous paneled doors of Stonetown, richly carved, studded with brass, cunningly inlaid, each door an ornate Islamic masterpiece—were closed and seemed to be locked. The shops looked shabby, and the small display windows were speckled with dust. Most of the signs were so faded Sybille could barely make them out:

PREMCHAND'S EMPORIUM

MONJI'S CURIOS

ABDULLAH'S BROTHERHOOD STORE

MOTILAL'S BAZAAR

The Arabs were long since gone from Zanzibar. So were most of the Indians, though they were said to be creeping back. Occasionally, as it pursued its intricate course through the maze of Stonetown, the taxi passed elongated black limousines, probably of Russian or Chinese make, chauffeur-driven, occupied by dignified self-contained dark-skinned men in white robes. Legislators, so she supposed them to be, en route to meetings of state. There were no other vehicles in sight, and no pedestrians except for a few women, robed entirely in black, hurrying on solitary errands. Stonetown had none of the vitality of the countryside; it was a place of ghosts, she thought, a fitting place for vacationing deads. She glanced at Zacharias, who nodded and smiled, a quick quirky smile that acknowledged her perception and told her that he too had had it. Communication was swift among the deads and the obvious rarely needed voicing.

The route to the hotel seemed extraordinarily involuted, and the driver halted frequently in front of shops, saying hopefully, "You want brass chests, copper pots, silver curios, gold chains from China?" Though Sybille gently declined his suggestions, he continued to point out bazaars and emporiums, offering earnest recommendations of quality and moderate price, and gradually she realized, getting her bearings in the town, that they had passed certain corners more than once. Of course: the driver must be in the pay of shopkeepers who hired him to lure tourists.

"Please take us to our hotel," Sybille said, and when he persisted in his huckstering—"Best ivory here, best lace"—she said it more firmly, but she kept her temper. Jorge would have been pleased by her transformation, she thought; he had all too often been the immediate victim of her fiery impatience. She did not know the specific cause of the change. Some metabolic side-effect of the rekindling process, maybe, or maybe her two years of communion with Guidefather at the Cold Town, or was it, perhaps, nothing more than the new knowledge that all of time was hers, that to let oneself feel hurried now was absurd?

"Your hotel is this," Ibuni said at last.

It was an old Arab mansion—high arches, innumerable balconies, musty air, electric fans turning sluggishly in the dark hallways. Sybille and Zacharias were given a sprawling suite on the third floor, overlooking a courtyard lush with palms, vermilion nandi, kapok trees, poinsettia, and agapanthus. Mortimer, Gracchus, and Nerita had long since arrived in the other cab and were in an identical suite one floor below. "I'll have a bath," Sybille told Zacharias. "Will you be in the bar?"

"Very likely. Or strolling in the garden."

He went out. Sybille quickly shed her travel-sweaty clothes. The bathroom was a Byzantine marvel, elaborate swirls of colored tile, an immense yellow tub standing high on bronze eagle-claw-and-globe legs. Lukewarm water dribbled in slowly when she turned the tap. She smiled at her reflection in the tall oval mirror. There had been a mirror somewhat like it at the rekindling

house. On the morning after her awakening, five or six
deads had come into her room to celebrate with her her
successful transition across the interface, and they had
had that big mirror with them; delicately, with great
ceremoniousness, they had drawn the coverlet down to
show herself to her in it, naked, slender, narrow-waisted,
high-breasted, the beauty of her body unchanged,
marred neither by dying nor by rekindling, indeed enhanced by it, so that she had become more youthful-
looking and even radiant in her passage across that terrible gulf.

—You're a very beautiful woman.

That was Pablo. She would learn his name and all
the other names later.

—I feel such a flood of relief. I was afraid I'd wake
up and find myself a shriveled ruin.

—That could not have happened, Pablo said.

—And never will happen, said a young woman.
Nerita, she was.

—But deads do age, don't they?

—Oh, yes, we age, just as the warms do. But not
just as.

—More slowly?

—Very much more slowly. And differently. All our
biological processes operate more slowly, except the
functions of the brain, which tend to be quicker than
they were in life.

—Quicker?

—You'll see.

—It all sounds ideal.

—We are extremely fortunate. Life has been kind
to us. Our situation is, yes, ideal. We are the new aristocracy.

—The new aristocracy—

*   *   *

Sybille slipped slowly into the tub, leaning back against the cool porcelain, wriggling a little, letting the tepid water slide up as far as her throat. She closed her eyes and drifted peacefully. All of Zanzibar was waiting for her. *Streets I never thought I should visit.* Let Zanzibar wait. Let Zanzibar wait. *Words I never thought to speak. When I left my body on a distant shore.* Time for everything, everything in its due time.

—*You're a very beautiful woman,* Pablo had told her, not meaning to flatter.

Yes. She had wanted to explain to them, that first morning, that she didn't really care all that much about the appearance of her body, that her real priorities lay elsewhere, were "higher," but there hadn't been any need to tell them that. They understood. They understood everything. Besides, she *did* care about her body. Being beautiful was less important to her than it was to those women for whom physical beauty was their only natural advantage, but her appearance mattered to her; her body pleased her and she knew it was pleasing to others, it gave her access to people, it was a means of making connections, and she had always been grateful for that. In her other existence her delight in her body had been flawed by the awareness of the inevitability of its slow steady decay, the certainty of the loss of that accidental power that beauty gave her, but now she had been granted exemption from that: she would change with time but she would not have to feel, as warms must feel, that she was gradually falling apart. Her rekindled body would not betray her by turning ugly. No.

—*We are the new aristocracy*—

After her bath she stood a few minutes by the open window, naked to the humid breeze. Sounds came to her: distant bells, the bright chatter of tropical birds, the voices of children singing in a language she could not identify. Zanzibar! Sultans and spices, Livingstone and Stanley, Tippu Tib the slaver, Sir Richard Burton spending a night in this very hotel room, perhaps. There was a dryness in her throat, a throbbing in her chest: a little excitement coming alive in her after all. She felt anticipation, even eagerness. All Zanzibar lay before her. Very well. Get moving, Sybille, put some clothes on, let's have lunch, a look at the town.

She took a light blouse and shorts from her suitcase. Just then Zacharias returned to the room, and she said, not looking up, "Kent, do you think it's all right for me to wear these shorts here? They're—" A glance at his face and her voice trailed off. "What's wrong?"

"I've just been talking to your husband."

"He's *here?*"

"He came up to me in the lobby. Knew my name. 'You're Zacharias,' he said, with a Bogarty little edge to his voice, like a deceived movie husband confronting the Other Man. 'Where is she? I have to see her.' "

"Oh, no, Kent."

"I asked him what he wanted with you. 'I'm her husband,' he said, and I told him, 'Maybe you were her husband once, but things have changed,' and then—"

"I can't imagine Jorge talking tough. He's such a *gentle* man, Kent! How did he look?"

"Schizoid," Zacharias said. "Glassy eyes, muscles bunching in his jaws, signs of terrific pressure all over him. He knows he's not supposed to do things like this, doesn't he?"

"Jorge knows exactly how he's supposed to behave. Oh, Kent, what a stupid mess! Where is he now?"

"Still downstairs. Nerita and Laurence are talking to him. You don't want to see him, do you?"

"Of course not."

"Write him a note to that effect and I'll take it down to him. Tell him to clear off."

Sybille shook her head. "I don't want to hurt him."

"Hurt him? He's followed you halfway around the world like a lovesick boy, he's tried to violate your privacy, he's·disrupted an important trip, he's refused to abide by the conventions that govern the relationships of warms and deads, and you—"

"He loves me, Kent."

"He loved you. All right, I concede that. But the person he loved doesn't exist any more. He has to be made to realize that."

Sybille closed her eyes. "I don't want to hurt him. I don't want you to hurt him either."

"I won't hurt him. Are you going to see him?"

"No," she said. She grunted in annoyance and threw her shorts and blouse into a chair. There was a fierce pounding at her temples, a sensation of being challenged, of being threatened, that she had not felt since that awful day at the Newark mounds. She strode to the window and looked out, half expecting to see Jorge arguing with Nerita and Laurence in the courtyard. But there was no one down there except a houseboy who looked up as if her bare breasts were beacons and gave her a broad dazzling smile. Sybille turned her back to him and said dully, "Go back down. Tell him that it's impossible for me to see him. Use that word. Not that I *won't* see him, not that I *don't want to* see him, not that it isn't *right* for me to see him, just that it's impossible. And then phone the airport. I want to go back to Dar on the evening plane."

"But we've only just arrived!"

"No matter. We'll come back some other time.

Jorge is very persistent; he won't accept anything but a brutal rebuff, and I can't do that to him. So we'll leave."

Klein had never seen deads at close range before. Cautiously, uneasily, he stole quick intense looks at Kent Zacharias as they sat side by side on rattan chairs among the potted palms in the lobby of the hotel. Jijibhoi had told him that it hardly showed, that you perceived it more subliminally than by any outward manifestation, and that was true; there was a certain look about the eyes, of course, the famous fixity of the deads, and there was something oddly pallid about Zacharias' skin *beneath* the florid complexion, but if Klein had not known what Zacharias was, he might not have guessed it. He tried to imagine this man, this red-haired red-faced dead archaeologist, this digger of dirt mounds, in bed with Sybille. Doing with her whatever it was that the deads did in their couplings. Even Jijibhoi wasn't sure. Something with hands, with eyes, with whispers and smiles, not at all genital—so Jijibhoi believed. *This is Sybille's lover I'm talking to. This is Sybille's lover.* How strange that it bothered him so. She had had affairs when she was living; so had he; so had everyone; it was the way of life. But he felt threatened, overwhelmed, defeated, by this walking corpse of a lover.

Klein said, "Impossible?"

"That was the word she used."

"Can't I have ten minutes with her?"

"Impossible."

"Would you let me see her for a few moments, at least? I'd just like to find out how she looks."

"Don't you find it humiliating, doing all this scratching around just for a glimpse of her?"

"Yes."

"And you still want it?"

"Yes."

Zacharias sighed. "There's nothing I can do for you. I'm sorry."

"Perhaps Sybille is tired from having done so much traveling. Do you think she might be in a more receptive mood tomorrow?"

"Maybe," Zacharias said. "Why don't you come back then?"

"You've been very kind."

"*De nada.*"

"Can I buy you a drink?"

"Thanks, no," Zacharias said. "I don't indulge any more. Not since—" He smiled.

Klein could smell whiskey on Zacharias' breath. All right, though. All right. He would go away. A driver waiting outside the hotel grounds poked his head out of his cab window and said hopefully, "Tour of the island, gentleman? See the clove plantations, see the athlete stadium?"

"I've seen them already," Klein said. He shrugged. "Take me to the beach."

He spent the afternoon watching turquoise wavelets lapping pink sand. The next morning he returned to Sybille's hotel, but they were gone, all five of them, gone on last night's flight to Dar, said the apologetic desk clerk. Klein asked if he could make a telephone call, and the clerk showed him an ancient instrument in an alcove near the bar. He phone Barwani. "What's going on?" he demanded. "You told me they'd be staying at least a week!"

"Oh, sir, things change," Barwani said softly.

Four

What portends? What will the future bring? I do not know, I have no presentiment. When a spider hurls itself down from some fixed point, consistently with its nature, it always sees before it only an empty space wherein it can find no foothold however much it sprawls. And so it is with me: always before me an empty space; what drives me forward is a consistency which lies behind me. This life is topsy-turvy and terrible, not to be endured.

Søren Kierkegaard: *Either/Or*

Jijibhoi said, "In the entire question of death who is to say what is right, dear friend? When I was a boy in Bombay it was not unusual for our Hindu neighbors to practice the rite of suttee, that is, the burning of the widow on her husband's funeral pyre, and by what presumption may we call them barbarians? Of course"—his dark eyes flashed mischievously—"we *did* call them barbarians, though never when they might hear us. Will you have more curry?"

Klein repressed a sigh. He was getting full, and the curry was fiery stuff, of an incandescence far beyond his usual level of tolerance; but Jijibhoi's hospitality, unobtrusively insistent, had a certain hieratic quality about it that made Klein feel like a blasphemer whenever he refused anything in his home. He smiled and nodded, and Jijibhoi, rising, spooned a mound of rice into Klein's plate, buried it under curried lamb, bedecked it with chutneys and sambals. Silently, unbidden, Jijibhoi's wife went to the kitchen and returned with a cold bottle of Heinekens. She gave Klein a shy grin as she set it down before him. They worked well together, these two Parsees, his hosts.

They were an elegant couple—striking, even. Jijibhoi was a tall, erect man with a forceful aquiline nose, dark Levantine skin, jet-black hair, a formidable mustache. His hands and feet were extraordinarily small; his manner was polite and reserved; he moved with a quickness of action bordering on nervousness. Klein guessed that he was in his early forties, though he suspected his estimate could easily be off by ten years in either direction. His wife—strangely, Klein had never been told her name—was younger than her husband, nearly as tall, fair of complexion—a light-olive tone—and voluptuous of figure. She dressed invariably in flowing silken saris; Jijibhoi affected western business dress, suits and ties in style twenty years out of date. Klein had never seen either of them bareheaded: she wore a kerchief of white linen, he a brocaded skullcap that might lead people to mistake him for an Oriental Jew. They were childless and self-sufficient, forming a closed dyad, a perfect unit, two segments of the same entity, conjoined and indivisible, as Klein and Sybille once had been. Their harmonious interplay of thought and gesture made them a trifle disconcerting, even intimidating, to others. As Klein and Sybille once had been.

Klein said, "Among your people—"

"Oh, very different, very different, quite unique. You know of our funeral custom?"

"Exposure of the dead, isn't it?"

Jijibhoi's wife giggled. "A very ancient recycling scheme!"

"The Towers of Silence," Jijibhoi said. He went to the dining room's vast window and stood with his back to Klein, staring out at the dazzling lights of Los Angeles. The Jijibhois' house, all redwood and glass, perched precariously on stilts near the crest of Benedict Canyon, just below Mulholland: the view took in everything from Hollywood to Santa Monica. "There are five of them in Bombay," said Jijibhoi, "on Malabar Hill, a rocky ridge overlooking the Arabian Sea. They are centuries old, each one circular, several hundred feet in circumference, surrounded by a stone wall twenty or thirty feet high. When a Parsee dies—do you know of this?"

"Not as much as I'd like to know."

"When a Parsee dies, he is carried to the Towers on an iron bier by professional corpse-bearers; the mourners follow in procession, two by two, joined hand to hand by holding a white handkerchief between them. A beautiful scene, dear Jorge. There is a doorway in the stone wall through which the corpse-bearers pass, carrying their burden. No one else may enter the Tower. Within is a circular platform paved with large stone slabs and divided into three rows of shallow, open receptacles. The outer row is used for the bodies of males, the next for those of females, the innermost one for children. The dead one is given a resting-place; vultures rise from the lofty palms in the gardens adjoining the

Towers; within an hour or two, only bones remain. Later, the bare, sun-dried skeleton is cast into a pit at the center of the Tower. Rich and poor crumble together there into dust."

"And all Parsees are—ah—buried in this way?"

"Oh, no, no, by no means," Jijibhoi said heartily. "All ancient traditions are in disrepair nowadays, do you not know? Our younger people advocate cremation or even conventional interment. Still, many of us continue to see the beauty of our way."

"—beauty?—"

Jijibhoi's wife said in a quiet voice, "To bury the dead in the ground, in a moist tropical land where diseases are highly contagious, seems not sanitary to us. And to burn a body is to waste its substance. But to give the bodies of the dead to the efficient hungry birds—quickly, cleanly, without fuss—is to us a way of celebrating the economy of nature. To have one's bones mingle in the pit with the bones of the entire community is, to us, the ultimate democracy."

"And the vultures spread no contagions themselves, feeding as they do on the bodies of—"

"Never," said Jijibhoi firmly. "Nor do they contract our ills."

"And I gather that you both intend to have your bodies returned to Bombay when you—" Aghast, Klein paused, shook his head, coughed in embarrassment, forced a weak smile. "You see what this radioactive curry of yours has done to my manners? Forgive me. Here I sit, a guest at your dinner table, quizzing you about your funeral plans!"

Jijibhoi chuckled. "Death is not frightening to us, dear friend. It is—one hardly needs say it, does one?—it is a natural event. For a time we are here, and then we

go. When our time ends, yes, she and I will give ourselves to the Towers of Silence."

His wife added sharply, "Better there than the Cold
Towns! Much better!"

Klein had never observed such vehemence in her
before.

Jijibhoi swung back from the window and glared at
her. Klein had never seen that before either. It seemed
as if the fragile web of elaborate courtesy that he and
these two had been spinning all evening was suddenly
unraveling, and that even the bonds between Jijibhoi and
his wife were undergoing strain. Agitated now, fluttery,
Jijibhoi began to collect the empty dishes, and after a
long awkward moment said, "She did not mean to give
offense."

"Why should I be offended?"

"A person you love chose to go to the Cold Towns.
You might think there was implied criticism of her in
my wife's expression of distaste for—"

Klein shrugged. "She's entitled to her feelings about
rekindling. I wonder, though—"

He halted, uneasy, fearing to probe too deeply.

"Yes?"

"It was irrelevant."

"Please," Jijibhoi said. "We are old friends."

"I was wondering," said Klein slowly, "if it doesn't
make things hard for you, spending all your time among
deads, studying them, mastering their ways, devoting
your whole career to them, when your wife evidently despises the Cold Towns and everything that goes on in
them. If the theme of your work repels her, you must
not be able to share it with her."

"Oh," Jijibhoi said, tension visibly going from him,
"if it comes to that, I have even less liking for the entire
rekindling phenomenon than she."

"You do?" This was a side of Jijibhoi that Klein had never suspected. "It repels you? Then why did you choose to make such an intensive survey of it?"

Jijibhoi looked genuinely amazed. "What? Are you saying one must have personal allegiance to the subject of one's field of scholarship?" He laughed. "You are of Jewish birth, I think, and yet your doctoral thesis was concerned, was it not, with the early phases of the Third Reich?"

Klein winced. "Touché!"

"I find the subculture of the deads irresistible, as a sociologist," Jijibhoi went on. "To have such a radical new aspect of human existence erupt during one's career is an incredible gift. There is no more fertile field for me to investigate. Yet I have no wish, none at all, ever to deliver myself up for rekindling. For me, my wife, it will be the Towers of Silence, the hot sun, the obliging vultures—and finis, the end, no more, terminus."

"I had no idea you felt this way. I suppose if I'd known more about Parsee theology, I might have realized—"

"You misunderstand. Our objections are not theological. It is that we share a wish, an idiosyncratic whim, not to continue beyond the allotted time. But also I have serious reservations about the impact of rekindling on our society. I feel a profound distress at the presence among us of these deads, I feel a purely private fear of these people and the culture they are creating, I feel even an abhorrence for—" Jijibhoi cut himself short. "Your pardon. That was perhaps too strong a word. You see how complex my attitudes are toward this subject, my mixture of fascination and repulsion? I exist in constant tension between those poles. But why do I tell you all this, which if it does not disturb you, must surely bore you? Let us hear about your journey to Zanzibar."

"What can I say? I went, I waited a couple of weeks for her to show up, I wasn't able to get near her at all, and I came home. All the way to Africa and I never even had a glimpse of her."

"What a frustration, dear Jorge!"

"She stayed in her hotel room. They wouldn't let me go upstairs to her."

"They?"

"Her entourage," Klein said. "She was traveling with four other deads, a woman and three men. Sharing her room with the archaeologist, Zacharias. He was the one who shielded her from me, and did it very cleverly, too. He acts as though he owns her. Perhaps he does. What can you tell me, Framji? Do the deads marry? Is Zacharias her new husband?"

"It is very doubtful. The terms 'wife' and 'husband' are not in use among the deads. They form relationships, yes, but pair-bonding seems to be uncommon among them, possibly altogether unknown. Instead they tend to create supportive pseudo-familial groupings of three or four or even more individuals, who—"

"Do you mean that all four of her companions in Zanzibar are her lovers?"

Jijibhoi gestured eloquently. "Who can say? If you mean in a physical sense, I doubt it, but one can never be sure. Zacharias seems to be her special companion, at any rate. Several of the others may be part of her pseudo-family also, or all, or none. I have reason to think that at certain times every dead may claim a familial relationship to all others of his kind. Who can say? We perceive the doings of these people, as they say, through a glass, darkly."

"I don't see Sybille even that well. I don't even know what she looks like now."

"She has lost none of her beauty."

"So you've told me before. But I want to see her myself. You can't really comprehend, Framji, how much I want to see her. The pain I feel, not able—"

"Would you like to see her right now?"

Klein shook in a convulsion of amazement. "What? What do you mean? Is she—"

"Hiding in the next room? No, no, nothing like that. But I do have a small surprise for you. Come into the library." Smiling expansively, Jijibhoi led the way from the dining room to the small study adjoining it, a room densely packed from floor to ceiling with books in an astonishing range of languages—not merely English, French, and German, but also Sanskrit, Hindi, Gujerati, Farsi, the tongues of Jijibhoi's polyglot upbringing among the tiny Parsee colony of Bombay, a community in which no language once cherished was ever discarded. Pushing aside a stack of dog-eared professional journals, he drew forth a glistening picture-cube, activated its inner light with a touch of his thumb, and handed it to Klein.

The sharp, dazzling holographic image showed three figures in a broad grassy plain that seemed to have no limits and was without trees, boulders, or other visual interruptions, an endlessly unrolling green carpet under a blank death-blue sky. Zacharias stood at the left, his face averted from the camera; he was looking down, tinkering with the action of an enormous rifle. At the far right stood a stocky, powerful-looking dark-haired man whose pale, harsh-featured face seemed all beard and nostrils. Klein recognized him: Anthony Gracchus, one of the deads who had accompanied Sybille to Zanzibar. Sybille stood beside him, clad in khaki slacks and a crisp white blouse. Gracchus' arm was extended; evidently he had just pointed out a target to her, and she was intently aiming a gun nearly as big as Zacharias'.

Klein shifted the cube about, studying her face from various angles, and the sight of her made his fingers grow thick and clumsy, his eyelids to quiver. Jijibhoi had spoken truly: she had lost none of her beauty. Yet she was not at all the Sybille he had known. When he had last seen her, lying in her casket, she had seemed to be a flawless marble image of herself, and she had that same surreal statuary appearance now. Her face was an expressionless mask, calm, remote, aloof; her eyes were glossy mysteries; her lips registered a faint, enigmatic, barely perceptible smile. It frightened him to behold her this way, so alien, so unfamiliar. Perhaps it was the intensity of her concentration that gave her that forbidding marmoreal look, for she seemed to be pouring her entire being into the task of taking aim. By tilting the cube more extremely, Klein was able to see what she was aiming at: a strange awkward bird moving through the grass at the lower left, a bird larger than a turkey, round as a sack, with ash-gray plumage, a whitish breast and tail, yellow-white wings, and short, comical yellow legs. Its head was immense and its black bill ended in a great snubbed hook. The creature seemed solemn, rather dignified, and faintly absurd; it showed no awareness that its doom was upon it. How odd that Sybille should be about to kill it, she who had always detested the taking of life: Sybille the huntress now, Sybille the lunar goddess, Sybille-Diana!

Shaken, Klein looked up at Jijibhoi and said, "Where was this taken? On that safari in Tanzania, I suppose."

"Yes. In February. This man is the guide, the white hunter."

"I saw him in Zanzibar. Gracchus, his name is. He was one of the deads traveling with Sybille."

"He operates a hunting preserve not far from Kilimanjaro," Jijibhoi said, "that is set aside exclusively for the use of the deads. One of the more bizarre manifestations of their subculture, actually. They hunt only those animals which—"

Klein said impatiently, "How did you get this picture?"

"It was taken by Nerita Tracy, who is one of your wife's companions."

"I met her in Zanzibar too. But how—"

"A friend of hers is an acquaintance of mine, one of my informants, in fact, a valuable connection in my researches. Some months ago I asked him if he could obtain something like this for me. I did not tell him, of course, that I meant it for you." Jijibhoi looked close. "You seem troubled, dear friend."

Klein nodded. He shut his eyes as though to protect them from the glaring surfaces of Sybille's photograph. Eventually he said in a flat, toneless voice, "I have to get to see her."

"Perhaps it would be better for you if you would abandon—"

"*No.*"

"Is there no way I can convince you that it is dangerous for you to pursue your fantasy of—"

"No," Klein said. "Don't even try. It's necessary for me to reach her. Necessary."

"How will you accomplish this, then?"

Klein said mechanically, "By going to Zion Cold Town."

"You have already done that. They would not admit you."

"This time they will. They don't turn away deads."

The Parsee's eyes widened. "You will surrender your own life? Is this your plan? What are you saying, Jorge?"

Klein, laughing, said, "That isn't what I meant at all."

"I am bewildered."

"I intend to infiltrate. I'll disguise myself as one of them. I'll slip into the Cold Town the way an infidel slips into Mecca." He seized Jijibhoi's wrist. "Can you help me? Coach me in their ways, teach me their jargon?"

"They'll find you out instantly."

"Maybe not. Maybe I'll get to Sybille before they do."

"This is insanity," Jijibhoi said quietly.

"Nevertheless. You have the knowledge. Will you help me?"

Gently Jijibhoi withdrew his arm from Klein's grasp. He crossed the room and busied himself with an untidy bookshelf for some moments, fussily arranging and rearranging. At length he said, "There is little I can do for you myself. My knowledge is broad but not deep, not deep enough. But if you insist on going through with this, Jorge, I can introduce you to someone who may be able to assist you. He is one of my informants, a dead, a man who has rejected the authority of the Guide-fathers, a person who is *of* the deads but not *with* them. Possibly he can instruct you in what you would need to know."

"Call him," Klein said.

"I must warn you he is unpredictable, turbulent, perhaps even treacherous. Ordinary human values are without meaning to him in his present state."

"Call him."

"If only I could discourage you from——"

"Call him."

Five

Quarreling brings trouble. These days lions roar a great deal. Joy follows grief. It is not good to beat children much. You had better go away now and go home. It is impossible to work today. You should go to school every day. It is not advisable to follow this path, there is water in the way. Never mind, I shall be able to pass. We had better go back quickly. These lamps use a lot of oil. There are no mosquitoes in Nairobi. There are no lions here. There are people here, looking for eggs. Is there water in the well? No, there is none. If there are only three people, work will be impossible today.

D.V. Perrott: *Teach Yourself Swahili*

Gracchus signals furiously to the porters and bellows, "*Shika njia hii hii!*" Three turn, two keep trudging along. "*Ninyi nyote!*" he calls. "*Fanga kama hivi!*" He shakes his head, spits, flicks sweat from his forehead. He adds, speaking in a lower voice and in English, taking care that they will not hear him, "Do as I say, you malevolent black bastards, or you'll be deader than I am before sunset!"

Sybille laughs nervously. "Do you always talk to them like that?"

"I try to be easy on them. But what good does it do, what good does any of it do? Come on, let's keep up with them."

It is less than an hour after dawn, but already the sun is very hot, here in the flat dry country between Kilimanjaro and Serengeti. Gracchus is leading the party northward across the high grass, following the spoor of what he thinks is a quagga, but breaking a trail in the high grass is hard work and the porters keep veering away toward a ravine that offers the tempting shade of a thicket of thorn trees, and he constantly has to harass them in order to hold them to the route he wants. Sybille has noticed that Gracchus shouts fiercely to his blacks, as if they were no more than recalcitrant beasts, and speaks of them behind their backs with a rough contempt, but it all seems done for show, all part of his white-hunter role: she has also noticed, at times when she was not supposed to notice, that privately Gracchus is in fact gentle, tender, even loving among the porters, teasing them—she supposes—with affectionate Swahili banter and playful mock-punches. The porters are role-players too: they behave in the traditional manner of their profession, alternately deferential and patronizing to the clients, alternately posing as all-knowing repositories of the lore of the bush and as simple, guileless savages fit only for carrying burdens. But the clients they serve are not quite like the sportsmen of Hemingway's time, since they are deads, and secretly the porters are terrified of the strange beings whom they serve. Sybille has seen them muttering prayers and fondling amulets whenever they accidentally touch one of the deads, and has occasionally detected an unguarded glance conveying unalloyed fear, possibly revulsion. Gracchus is no friend of theirs, however jolly he may get with them: they appear to regard him as some sort of monstrous sorcerer and the clients as fiends made manifest.

Sweating, saying little, the hunters move in single file, first the porters with the guns and supplies, then Gracchus, Zacharias, Sybille, Nerita constantly clicking her camera, and Mortimer. Patches of white cloud drift slowly across the immense arch of the sky. The grass is lush and thick, for the short rains were unusually heavy in December. Small animals scurry through it, visible only in quick flashes, squirrels and jackals and guinea-fowl. Now and then larger creatures can be seen: three haughty ostriches, a pair of snuffling hyenas, a band of Thomson gazelles flowing like a tawny river across the plain. Yesterday Sybille spied two wart hogs, some giraffes, and a serval, an elegant big-eared wildcat that slithered along like a miniature cheetah. None of these beasts may be hunted, but only those special ones that the operators of the preserve have introduced for the special needs of their clients; anything considered native African wildlife, which is to say anything that was living here before the deads leased this tract from the Masai, is protected by government decree. The Masai themselves are allowed to do some lion-hunting, since this is their reservation, but there are so few Masai left that they can do little harm. Yesterday, after the wart hogs and before the giraffes, Sybille saw her first Masai, five lean, handsome, long-bodied men, naked under skimpy red robes, drifting silently through the bush, pausing frequently to stand thoughtfully on one leg, propped against their spears. At close range they were less hand-some—toothless, fly-specked, herniated. They offered to sell their spears and their beaded collars for a few shillings, but the safarigoers had already stocked up on Masai artifacts in Nairobi's curio shops, at astonishingly higher prices.

All through the morning they stalk the quagga, Gracchus pointing out hoofprints here, fresh dung there. It is Zacharias who has asked to shoot a quagga. "How can you tell we're not following a zebra?" he asks peevishly.

Gracchus winks. "Trust me. We'll find zebras up ahead too. But you'll get your quagga. I guarantee it."

Ngiri, the head porter, turns and grins. "*Piga quagga m'uzuri, bwana,*" he says to Zacharias, and winks also, and then—Sybille sees it plainly—his jovial confident smile fades as though he has had the courage to sustain it only for an instant, and a veil of dread covers his dark glossy face.

"What did he say?" Zacharias asks.

"That you'll shoot a fine quagga," Gracchus replies.

Quaggas. The last wild one was killed about 1870, leaving only three in the world, all females, in European zoos. The Boers had hunted them to the edge of extinction in order to feed their tender meat to Hottentot slaves and to make from their striped hides sacks for Boer grain, leather *veldschoen* for Boer feet. The quagga of the London zoo died in 1872, that in Berlin in 1875, the Amsterdam quagga in 1883, and none was seen alive again until the artificial revival of the species through breedback selection and genetic manipulation in 1990, when this hunting preserve was opened to a limited and special clientele.

It is nearly noon, now, and not a shot has been fired all morning. The animals have begun heading for cover; they will not emerge until the shadows lengthen. Time to halt, pitch camp, break out the beer and sandwiches, tell tall tales of harrowing adventures with maddened buffaloes and edgy elephants. But not quite yet. The marchers come over a low hill and see, in the long sloping hollow beyond, a flock of ostriches and several hundred grazing zebras. As the humans appear, the ostriches begin slowly and warily to move off, but the zebras, altogether unafraid, continue to graze. Ngiri points and says, "*Piga quagga, bwana.*"

"Just a bunch of zebras," Zacharias says.

Gracchus shakes his head. "No. Listen. You hear the sound?"

At first no one perceives anything unusual. But then, yes, Sybille hears it: a shrill barking neigh, very strange, a sound out of lost time, the cry of some beast she has never known. It is a song of the dead. Nerita hears it too, and Mortimer, and finally Zacharias. Gracchus nods toward the far side of the hollow. There, among the zebras, are half a dozen animals that might almost be zebras, but are not—unfinished zebras, striped only on their heads and foreparts; the rest of their bodies are yellowish brown, their legs are white, their manes are dark-brown with pale stripes. Their coats sparkle like mica in the sunshine. Now and again they lift their heads, emit that weird percussive whistling snort, and bend to the grass again. Quaggas. Strays out of the past, relicts, rekindled specters. Gracchus signals and the party fans out along the peak of the hill. Ngiri hands Zacharias his colossal gun. Zacharias kneels, sights.

"No hurry," Gracchus murmurs. "We have all afternoon."

"Do I seem to be hurrying?" Zacharias asks. The zebras now block the little group of quaggas from his view, almost as if by design. He must not shoot a zebra, of course, or there will be trouble with the rangers. Minutes go by. Then the screen of zebras abruptly parts and Zacharias squeezes his trigger. There is a vast explosion; zebras bolt in ten directions, so that the eye is bombarded with dizzying stroboscopic waves of black and white; when the convulsive confusion passes, one of the quaggas is lying on its side, alone in the field, having made the transition across the interface. Sybille regards it calmly. Death once dismayed her, death of any kind, but no longer.

"*Piga m'uzuri!*" the porters cry exultantly.

"*Kufa,*" Gracchus says. "Dead. A neat shot. You have your trophy."

Ngiri is quick with the skinning-knife. That night, camping below Kilimanjaro's broad flank, they dine on roast quagga, deads and porters alike. The meat is juicy, robust, faintly tangy.

Late the following afternoon, as they pass through cooler stream-broken country thick with tall, scrubby gray-green vase-shaped trees, they come upon a monstrosity, a shaggy shambling thing twelve or fifteen feet high, standing upright on ponderous hind legs and balancing itself on an incredibly thick, heavy tail. It leans against a tree, pulling at its top branches with long forelimbs that are tipped with ferocious claws like a row of sickles; it munches voraciously on leaves and twigs. Briefly it notices them, and looks around, studying them with small stupid yellow eyes; then it returns to its meal.

"A rarity," Gracchus says. "I know hunters who have been all over this park without ever running into one. Have you ever seen anything so ugly?"

"What is it?" Sybille asks.

"Megatherium. Giant ground sloth. South American, really, but we weren't fussy about geography when we were stocking this place. We have only four of them, and it costs God knows how many thousands of dollars to shoot one. Nobody's signed up for a ground sloth yet. I doubt anyone will."

Sybille wonders where the beast might be vulnerable to a bullet: surely not in its dim peanut-sized brain. She wonders, too, what sort of sportsman would find pleasure in killing such a thing. For a while they watch as the sluggish monster tears the tree apart. Then they move on.

Gracchus shows them another prodigy at sundown: a pale dome, like some huge melon, nestling in a mound of dense grass beside a stream. "Ostrich egg?" Mortimer guesses.

"Close. Very close. It's a moa egg. World's biggest bird. From New Zealand, extinct since about the eighteenth century."

Nerita crouches and lightly taps the egg. "What an omelet we could make!"

"There's enough there to feed seventy-five of us," Gracchus says. "Two gallons of fluid, easy. But of course we mustn't meddle with it. Natural increase is very important in keeping this park stocked."

"And where's mama moa?" Sybille asks. "Should she have abandoned the egg?"

"Moas aren't very bright," Gracchus answers. "That's one good reason why they became extinct. She must have wandered off to find some dinner. And—"

"Good God," Zacharias blurts.

The moa has returned, emerging suddenly from a thicket. She stands like a feathered mountain above them, limned by the deep-blue of twilight: an ostrich, more or less, but a magnified ostrich, an ultimate ostrich, a bird a dozen feet high, with a heavy rounded body and a great thick hose of a neck and taloned legs sturdy as saplings. Surely this is Sinbad's rukh, that can fly off with elephants in its grasp! The bird peers at them, sadly contemplating the band of small beings clustered about her egg; she arches her neck as though readying for an attack, and Zacharias reaches for one of the rifles, but Gracchus checks his hand, for the moa is merely rearing back to protest. It utters a deep mournful mooing sound and does not move. "Just back slowly away," Gracchus tells them. "It won't attack. But keep away from the feet; one kick can kill you."

"I was going to apply for a license on a moa," Mortimer says.

"Killing them's a bore," Gracchus tells him. "They just stand there and let you shoot. You're better off with what you signed up for."

What Mortimer has signed up for is an aurochs, the vanished wild ox of the European forests, known to Caesar, known to Pliny, hunted by the hero Siegfried, altogether exterminated by the year 1627. The plains of East Africa are not a comfortable environment for the aurochs and the herd that has been conjured by the genetic necromancers keeps to itself in the wooded highlands, several days' journey from the haunts of quaggas and ground sloths. In this dark grove the hunters come upon troops of chattering baboons and solitary big-eared elephants and, in a place of broken sunlight and shadow, a splendid antelope, a bull bongo with a fine curving pair of horns. Gracchus leads them onward, deeper in. He seems tense: there is peril here. The porters slip through the forest like black wraiths, spreading out in arching crab-claw patterns, communicating with one another and with Gracchus by whistling. Everyone keeps weapons ready in here. Sybille half expects to see leopards draped on overhanging branches, cobras slithering through the undergrowth. But she feels no fear.

They approach a clearing.

"Aurochs," Gracchus says.

A dozen of them are cropping the shrubbery: big short-haired long-horned cattle, muscular and alert. Picking up the scent of the intruders, they lift their heavy heads, sniff, glare. Gracchus and Ngiri confer with eyebrows. Nodding, Gracchus mutters to Mortimer, "Too many of them. Wait for them to thin off." Mortimer smiles. He looks a little nervous. The aurochs has a reputation for attacking without warning. Four, five, six of the beasts slip away, and the others withdraw to the edge of the clearing, as if to plan strategy; but one big bull, sour-eyed and grim, stands his ground, glowering. Gracchus rolls on the balls of his feet. His burly body seems, to Sybille, a study in mobility, in preparedness.

"Now," he says.

In the same moment the bull aurochs charges, moving with extraordinary swiftness, head lowered, horns extended like spears. Mortimer fires. The bullet strikes with a loud whonking sound, crashing into the shoulder of the aurochs, a perfect shot, but the animal does not fall, and Mortimer shoots again, less gracefully ripping into the belly, and then Gracchus and Ngiri are firing also, not at Mortimer's aurochs but over the heads of the others, to drive them away, and the risky tactic works, for the other animals go stampeding off into the woods. The one Mortimer has shot continues toward him, staggering now, losing momentum, and falls practically at his feet, rolling over, knifing the forest floor with its hooves.

"*Kufa,*" Ngiri says. "*Piga nyati m'uzuri, bwana.*"

Mortimer grins. "*Piga,*" he says.

Gracchus salutes him. "More exciting than moa," he says.

"And these are mine," says Nerita three hours later, indicating a tree at the outer rim of the forest. Several hundred large pigeons nest in its boughs, so many of them that the tree seems to be sprouting birds rather than leaves. The females are plain—light-brown above, gray below—but the males are flamboyant, with rich, glossy blue plumage on their wings and backs, breasts of a wine-red chestnut color, iridescent spots of bronze and green on their necks, and weird, vivid eyes of a bright, fiery orange. Gracchus says, "Right. You've found your passenger pigeons."

"Where's the thrill in shooting pigeons out of a tree?" Mortimer asks.

Nerita gives him a withering look. "Where's the thrill in gunning down a charging bull?" She signals to Ngiri, who fires a shot into the air. The startled pigeons burst from their perches and fly in low circles. In the old days, a century and a half ago in the forests of North America, no one troubled to shoot passenger pigeons on the wing: the pigeons were food, not sport, and it was simpler to blast them as they sat, for that way a single hunter might kill thousands of birds in one day. Thus it took only fifty years to reduce the passenger pigeon population from uncountable sky-blackening billions to zero. Nerita is more sporting. This is a test of her skill, after all. She aims her shotgun, shoots, pumps, shoots, pumps. Stunned birds drop to the ground. She and her gun are a single entity, sharing one purpose. In moments it is all over. The porters retrieve the fallen birds and snap their necks. Nerita has the dozen pigeons her license allows: a pair to mount, the rest for tonight's dinner. The survivors have returned to their tree and stare placidly, unreproachfully, at the hunters.

"They breed so damned fast," Gracchus mutters. "If we aren't careful, they'll be getting out of the preserve and taking over all of Africa."

Sybille laughs. "Don't worry. We'll cope. We wiped them out once and we can do it again, if we have to."

Sybille's prey is a dodo. In Dar, when they were applying for their licenses, the others mocked her choice: a fat flightless bird, unable to run or fight, so feeble of wit that it fears nothing. She ignored them. She wants a dodo because to her it is the essence of extinction, the prototype of all that is dead and vanished. That there is no sport in shooting foolish dodos means little to Sybille. Hunting itself is meaningless for her.

Through this vast park she wanders as in a dream. She sees ground sloths, great auks, quaggas, moas, heath hens, Javan rhinos, giant armadillos, and many other rarities. The place is an abode of ghosts. The ingenuities of the genetic craftsmen are limitless; someday, perhaps, the preserve will offer trilobites, tyrannosaurs, mastodons, saber-toothed cats, baluchitheria, even—why not? —packs of Australopithecines, tribes of Neanderthals. For the amusement of the deads, whose games tend to be somber. Sybille wonders whether it can really be considered killing, this slaughter of laboratory-spawned novelties. Are these animals real or artificial? Living things, or cleverly animated constructs? Real, she decides. Living. They eat, they metabolize, they reproduce. They must seem real to themselves, and so they are real, realer, maybe, than dead human beings who walk again in their own cast-off bodies.

"Shotgun," Sybille says to the closest porter.

There is the bird, ugly, ridiculous, waddling laboriously through the tall grass. Sybille accepts a weapon and sights along its barrel. "Wait," Nerita says. "I'd like to get a picture of this." She moves slantwise around the group, taking exaggerated care not to frighten the dodo, but the dodo does not seem to be aware of any of them. Like an emissary from the realm of darkness, carrying good news of death to those creatures not yet extinct, it plods diligently across their path. "Fine," Nerita says. "Anthony, point at the dodo, will you, as if you've just noticed it? Kent, I'd like you to look down at your gun, study its bolt or something. Fine. And Sybille, just hold that pose—aiming—yes—"

Nerita takes the picture.

Calmly Sybille pulls the trigger.

"*Kazi imekwisha*," Gracchus says. "The work is finished."

Six

Although to be driven back upon oneself is an uneasy affair at best, rather like trying to cross a border with borrowed credentials, it seems to be now the one condition necessary to the beginnings of real self-respect. Most of our platitudes notwithstanding, self-deception remains the most difficult deception. The tricks that work on others count for nothing in that very well-lit back alley where one keeps assignations with oneself: no winning smiles will do here, no prettily drawn lists of good intentions.

Joan Didion: *On Self-Respect*

"You better believe what Jeej is trying to tell you," Dolorosa said. "Ten minutes inside the Cold Town, they'll have your number. Five minutes."

Jijibhoi's man was small, rumpled-looking, forty or fifty years old, with untidy long dark hair and wide-set smoldering eyes. His skin was sallow and his face was gaunt. Such other deads as Klein had seen at close range had about them an air of unearthly serenity, but not this one: Dolorosa was tense, fidgety, a knuckle-cracker, a lip-gnawer. Yet somehow there could be no doubt he was a dead, as much a dead as Zacharias, as Gracchus, as Mortimer.

"They'll have my what?" Klein asked.

"Your number. Your number. They'll know you aren't a dead, because it can't be faked. Jesus, don't you even speak English? Jorge, that's a foreign name. I should have known. Where are you from?"

"Argentina, as a matter of fact, but I was brought to California when I was a small boy. In 1955. Look, if they catch me, they catch me. I just want to get in there and spend half an hour talking with my wife."

"Mister, you don't have any wife any more."

"With Sybille," Klein said, exasperated. "To talk with Sybille, my—my former wife."

"All right. I'll get you inside."

"What will it cost?"

"Never mind that," Dolorosa said. "I owe Jeej here a few favors. More than a few. So I'll get you the drug—"

"Drug?"

"The drug the Treasury agents use when they infiltrate the Cold Towns. It narrows the pupils, contracts the capillaries, gives you that good old zombie look. The agents always get caught and thrown out, and so will you, but at least you'll go in there feeling that you've got a convincing disguise. Little oily capsule, one every morning before breakfast."

Klein looked at Jijibhoi. "Why do Treasury agents infiltrate the Cold Towns?"

"For the same reasons they infiltrate anywhere else," Jijibhoi said. "To spy. They are trying to compile dossiers on the financial dealings of the deads, you see, and until proper life-defining legislation is approved by Congress there is no precise way of compelling a person who is deemed legally dead to divulge—"

Dolorosa said, "Next, the background. I can get you a card of residence from Albany Cold Town in New York. You died last December, okay, and they rekindled you back east because—let's see—"

"I could have been attending the annual meeting of the American Historical Association in New York," Klein suggested. "That's what I do, you understand, professor of contemporary history at UCLA. Because of the Christmas holiday my body couldn't be shipped back to California, no room on any flight, and so they took me to Albany. How does that sound?"

Dolorosa smiled. "You really enjoy making up lies, Professor, don't you? I can dig that quality in you. Okay, Albany Cold Town, and this is your first trip out of there, your drying-off trip—that's what it's called, drying-off—you come out of the Cold Town like a new butterfly just out of its cocoon, all soft and damp, and you're on your own in a strange place. Now, there's a lot of stuff you'll need to know about how to behave, little mannerisms, social graces, that kind of crap, and I'll work on that with you tomorrow and Wednesday and Friday, three sessions; that ought to be enough. Meanwhile let me give you the basics. There are only three things you really have to remember while you're inside:

"(1) Never ask a direct question.

"(2) Never lean on anybody's arm. You know what I mean?

"(3) Keep in mind that to a dead the whole universe is plastic, nothing's real, nothing matters a hell of a lot, it's all only a joke. Only a joke, friend, only a joke."

*   *   *

Early in April he flew to Salt Lake City, rented a
car, and drove out past Moab into the high plateau
rimmed by red-rock mountains where the deads had
built Zion Cold Town. This was Klein's second visit to
the necropolis. The other had been in the late summer
of '91, a hot, parched season when the sun filled half
the sky and even the gnarled junipers looked dazed from
thirst; but now it was a frosty afternoon, with faint pale
light streaming out of the wintry western hills and occasional gusts of light snow whirling through the iron-
blue air. Jijibhoi's route instructions pulsed from the
memo screen on his dashboard. Fourteen miles from
town, yes, narrow paved lane turns off highway, yes,
discreet little sign announcing PRIVATE ROAD, NO AD-
MITTANCE, yes, a second sign a thousand yards in, ZION
COLD TOWN, MEMBERS ONLY, yes, and then just beyond
that the barrier of green light across the road, the scan-
ner system, the roadblocks sliding like scythes out of
the underground installations, a voice on an invisible
loudspeaker saying, "If you have a permit to enter Zion
Cold Town, please place it under your left-hand windshield wiper."

That other time he had had no permit, and he had
gone no farther than this, though at least he had managed a little colloquy with the unseen gatekeeper out
of which he had squeezed the information that Sybille
was indeed living in that particular Cold Town. This
time he affixed Dolorosa's forged card of residence to
his windshield, and waited tensely, and in thirty seconds
the roadblocks slid from sight. He drove on, along a
winding road that followed the natural contours of a
dense forest of scrubby conifers, and came at last to a
brick wall that curved away into the trees as though it
encircled the entire town. Probably it did. Klein had an
overpowering sense of the Cold Town as a hermetic

city, ponderous and sealed as old Egypt. There was a
metal gate in the brick wall; green electronic eyes sur-
veyed him, signaled their approval, and the wall rolled
open.

He drove slowly toward the center of town, passing
through a zone of what he supposed were utility buildings—storage depots, a power substation, the municipal waterworks, whatever, a bunch of grim windowless
one-story cinderblock affairs—and then into the resi-
dential district, which was not much lovelier. The streets
were laid out on a rectangular grid; the buildings were
squat, dreary, impersonal, homogeneous. There was
practically no automobile traffic, and in a dozen blocks
he saw no more than ten pedestrians, who did not even
glance at him. So this was the environment in which the
deads chose to spend their second lives. But why such
deliberate bleakness? "You will never understand us,"
Dolorosa had warned. Dolorosa was right. Jijibhoi had
told him that Cold Towns were something less than
charming, but Klein had not been prepared for this.
There was a glacial quality about the place, as though
it were wholly entombed in a block of clear ice: silence,
sterility, a mortuary calm. Cold Town, yes, aptly named.
Architecturally, the town looked like the worst of all
possible cheap-and-sleazy tract developments, but the
psychic texture it projected was even more depressing,
more like that of one of those ghastly retirement com-
munities, one of the innumerable Leisure Worlds or
Sun Manors, those childless joyless retreats where colo-
nies of that other kind of living dead collected to await
the last trumpet. Klein shivered.

At last, another few minutes deeper into the town,
a sign of activity, if not exactly of life: a shopping center, flat-topped brown stucco buildings around a

U-shaped courtyard, a steady flow of shoppers moving
about. All right. His first test was about to commence.
He parked his car near the mouth of the U and strolled
uneasily inward. He felt as if his forehead were a beacon,
flashing glowing betrayals at rhythmic intervals:

   FRAUD   INTRUDER   INTERLOPER   SPY

Go ahead, he thought, seize me, seize the impostor, get
it over with, throw me out, string me up, crucify me.
But no one seemed to pick up the signals. He was altogether ignored. Out of courtesy? Or just contempt?
He stole what he hoped were covert glances at the shoppers, half expecting to run across Sybille right away.
They all looked like sleepwalkers, moving in glazed silence about their errands. No smiles, no chatter: the icy
aloofness of these self-contained people heightened the
familiar suburban atmosphere of the shopping center
into surrealist intensity, Norman Rockwell with an over-
lay of Dali or De Chirico. The shopping center looked
like all other shopping centers: clothing stores, a bank, a
record shop, snack bars, a florist, a TV-stereo outlet, a
theater, a five-and-dime. One difference, though, became
apparent as Klein wandered from shop to shop: the whole
place was automated. There were no clerks anywhere,
only the ubiquitous data screens, and no doubt a battery
of hidden scanners to discourage shoplifters. (Or did
the impulse toward petty theft perish with the body's
first death?) The customers selected all the merchandise
themselves, checked it out via data screens, touched
their thumbs to charge-plates to debit their accounts. Of
course. No one was going to waste his precious rekindled existence standing behind a counter to sell ten-
nis shoes or cotton candy. Nor were the dwellers in the
Cold Towns likely to dilute their isolation by hiring a
labor force of imported warms. Somebody here had to
do a little work, obviously—how did the merchandise

get into the stores?—but, in general, Klein realized, what could not be done here by machines would not be done at all.

For ten minutes he prowled the center. Just when he was beginning to think he must be entirely invisible to these people, a short, broad-shouldered man, bald but with oddly youthful features, paused in front of him and said, "I am Pablo. I welcome you to Zion Cold Town." This unexpected puncturing of the silence so startled Klein that he had to fight to retain appropriate deadlike imperturbability. Pablo smiled warmly and touched both his hands to Klein's in friendly greeting, but his eyes were frigid, hostile, remote, a terrifying contradiction. "I've been sent to bring you to the lodging-place. Come: your car."

Other than to give directions, Pablo spoke only three times during the five-minute drive. "Here is the rekindling house," he said. A five-story building, as inviting as a hospital, with walls of dark bronze and windows black as onyx. "This is Guidefather's house," Pablo said a moment later. A modest brick building, like a rectory, at the edge of a small park. And, finally: "This is where you will stay. Enjoy your visit." Abruptly he got out of the car and walked rapidly away.

This was the house of strangers, the hotel for visiting deads, a long low cinderblock structure, functional and unglamorous, one of the least seductive buildings in this city of stark disagreeable buildings. However else it might be with the deads, they clearly had no craving for fancy architecture. A voice out of a data screen in the spartan lobby assigned him to a room: a white-walled box, square, high of ceiling. He had his own toilet, his own data screen, a narrow bed, a chest of drawers, a modest closet, a small window that gave him a view of a neighboring building just as drab as this. Nothing had been said about rental; perhaps he was a guest of the city. Nothing had been said about anything. It seemed that he had been accepted. So much for Jijibhoi's gloomy assurance that he would instantly be found out, so much for Dolorosa's insistence that they would have his number in ten minutes or less. He had been in Zion Cold Town for half an hour. Did they have his number?

"Eating isn't important among us," Dolorosa had said.

"But you do eat?"

"Of course we eat. It just isn't *important*."

It was important to Klein, though. Not *haute cuisine*, necessarily, but some sort of food, preferably three times a day. He was getting hungry now. Ring for room service? There were no servants in this city. He turned to the data screen. Dolorosa's first rule: *Never ask a direct question.* Surely that didn't apply to the data screen, only to his fellow deads. He didn't have to observe the niceties of etiquette when talking to a computer. Still, the voice behind the screen might not be that of a computer after all, so he tried to employ the oblique, elliptical conversational style that Dolorosa said the deads favored among themselves:

"Dinner?"

"Commissary."

"Where?"

"Central Four," said the screen.

Central Four? All right. He would find the way. He changed into fresh clothing and went down the long vinyl-floored hallway to the lobby. Night had come; street lamps were glowing; under cloak of darkness the city's ugliness was no longer so obtrusive, and there was even a kind of controlled beauty about the brutal regularity of its streets.

The streets were unmarked, though, and deserted. Klein walked at random for ten minutes, hoping to meet someone heading for the Central Four commissary. But when he did come upon someone, a tall and regal woman well advanced in years, he found himself incapable of approaching her. (*Never ask a direct question. Never lean on anybody's arm.*) He walked alongside her, in silence and at a distance, until she turned suddenly to enter a house. For ten minutes more he wandered alone again. This is ridiculous, he thought: dead or warm, I'm a stranger in town, I should be entitled to a little assistance. Maybe Dolorosa was just trying to complicate things. On the next corner, when Klein caught sight of a man hunched away from the wind, lighting a cigarette, he went boldly over to him. "Excuse me, but—"

The other looked up. "Klein?" he said. "Yes. Of course. Well, so you've made the crossing too!"

He was one of Sybille's Zanzibar companions, Klein realized. The quick-eyed, sharp-edged one—Mortimer. A member of her pseudo-familial grouping, whatever that might be. Klein stared sullenly at him. This had to be the moment when his imposture would be exposed, for only some six weeks had passed since he had argued with Mortimer in the gardens of Sybille's Zanzibar hotel, not nearly enough time for someone to have died and been rekindled and gone through his drying-off. But a moment passed and Mortimer said nothing. At length Klein said, "I just got here. Pablo showed me to the house of strangers and now I'm looking for the commissary."

"Central Four? I'm going there myself. How lucky for you." No sign of suspicion in Mortimer's face. Perhaps an elusive smile revealed his awareness that Klein could not be what he claimed to be. *Keep in mind that to a dead the whole universe is plastic, it's all only a joke.* "I'm waiting for Nerita," Mortimer said. "We can all eat together."

Klein said heavily, "I was rekindled in Albany Cold Town. I've just emerged."

"How nice," Mortimer said.

Nerita Tracy stepped out of a building just beyond the corner—a slim, athletic-looking woman, about forty, with short reddish-brown hair. As she swept toward them, Mortimer said, "Here's Klein, who we met in Zanzibar. Just rekindled, out of Albany."

"Sybille will be amused."

"Is she in town?" Klein blurted.

Mortimer and Nerita exchanged sly glances. Klein felt abashed. *Never ask a direct question.* Damn Dolorosa!

Nerita said, "You'll see her before long. Shall we go to dinner?"

The commissary was less austere than Klein had expected: actually quite an inviting restaurant, elaborately constructed on five or six levels divided by lustrous dark hangings into small, secluded dining areas. It had the warm, rich look of a tropical resort. But the food, which came automat-style out of revolving dispensers, was prefabricated and cheerless—another jarring contradiction. *Only a joke, friend, only a joke.* In any case he was less hungry than he had imagined at the hotel. He sat with Mortimer and Nerita, picking at his meal, while their conversation flowed past him at several times the speed of thought. They spoke in fragments and ellipses, in periphrastics and aposiopeses, in a style abundant in chiasmus, metonymy, meiosis,

oxymoron, and zeugma; their dazzling rhetorical techniques left him baffled and uncomfortable, which beyond
much doubt was their intention. Now and again they
would dart from a thicket of indirection to skewer him
with a quick corroborative stab: Isn't that so, they
would say, and he would smile and nod, nod and smile,
saying, Yes, yes, absolutely. Did they know he was a
fake, and were they merely playing with him, or had
they, somehow, impossibly, accepted him as one of
them? So subtle was their style that he could not tell.
A very new member of the society of the rekindled, he
told himself, would be nearly as much at sea here as a
warm in deadface.

Then Nerita said—no verbal games, this time—
"You still miss her terribly, don't you?"

"I do. Some things evidently never perish."

"Everything perishes," Mortimer said. "The dodo,
the aurochs, the Holy Roman Empire, the T'ang Dynasty, the walls of Byzantium, the language of Mohenjo-daro."

"But not the Great Pyramid, the Yangtze, the
coelacanth, or the skullcap of Pithecanthropus," Klein
countered. "Some things persist and endure. And some
can be regenerated. Lost languages have been deciph-
ered. I believe the dodo and the aurochs are hunted in
a certain African park in this very era."

"Replicas," Mortimer said.

"Convincing replicas. Simulations as good as the
original."

"Is that what you want?" Nerita asked.

"I want what's possible to have."

"A convincing replica of lost love?"

"I might be willing to settle for five minutes of conversation with her."

"You'll have it. Not tonight. See? There she is. But don't bother her now." Nerita nodded across the gulf in the center of the restaurant; on the far side, three levels up from where they sat, Sybille and Kent Zacharias had appeared. They stood for a brief while at the edge of their dining alcove, staring blandly and emotionlessly into the restaurant's central well. Klein felt a muscle jerking uncontrollably in his cheek, a damning revelation of undeadlike uncoolness, and pressed his hand over it, so that it twanged and throbbed against his palm. She was like a goddess up there, manifesting herself in her sanctum to her worshipers, a pale shimmering figure, more beautiful even than she had become to him through the anguished enhancements of memory, and it seemed impossible to him that that being had ever been his wife, that he had known her when her eyes were puffy and reddened from a night of study, that he had looked down at her face as they made love and had seen her lips pull back in that spasm of ecstasy that is so close to a grimace of pain, that he had known her crochety and unkind in her illness, short-tempered and impatient in health, a person of flaws and weaknesses, of odors and blemishes, in short a human being, this goddess, this unreal rekindled creature, this object of his quest, this Sybille. Serenely she turned, serenely she vanished into her cloaked alcove. "She knows you're here," Nerita told him. "You'll see her. Perhaps tomorrow." Then Mortimer said something maddeningly oblique, and Nerita replied with the same off-center mystification, and Klein once more was plunged into the river of their easy dancing wordplay, down into it, down and down and down, and as he struggled to keep from drowning, as he fought to comprehend their interchanges, he never once looked toward the place where Sybille sat, not even once, and congratulated himself on having accomplished that much at least in his masquerade.

That night, lying alone in his room at the house of strangers, he wonders what he will say to Sybille when they finally meet, and what she will say to him. Will he dare bluntly to ask her to describe to him the quality of her new existence? That is all that he wants from her, really, that knowledge, that opening of an aperture into her transfigured self; that is as much as he hopes to get from her, knowing as he does that there is scarcely a chance of regaining her, but will he dare to ask, will he dare even that? Of course his asking such things will reveal to her that he is still a warm, too dense and gross of perception to comprehend the life of a dead; but he is certain she will sense that anyway, instantly. What will he say, what will he say? He plays out an imagined script of their conversation in the theater of his mind:

—Tell me what it's like, Sybille, to be the way you are now.

—Like swimming under a sheet of glass.

—I don't follow.

—Everything is quiet where I am, Jorge. There's a peace that passeth all understanding. I used to feel sometimes that I was caught up in a great storm, that I was being buffeted by every breeze, that my life was being consumed by agitations and frenzies, but now, now, I'm at the eye of the storm, at the place where everything is always calm. I observe rather than let myself be acted upon.

—But isn't there a loss of feeling that way? Don't you feel that you're wrapped in an insulating layer? Like swimming under glass, you say—that conveys being insulated, being cut off, being almost numb.

—I suppose you might think so. The way it is, is that one no longer is affected by the unnecessary.

—It sounds to me like a limited existence.

—Less limited than the grave, Jorge.

—I never understood why you wanted rekindling. You were such a world-devourer, Sybille, you lived with such intensity, such passion. To settle for the kind of existence you have now, to be only half-alive—

—Don't be a fool, Jorge. To be half-alive is better than to be rotting in the ground. I was so young. There was so much else still to see and do.

—But to see it and do it half-alive?

—Those were your words, not mine. I'm not alive at all. I'm neither less nor more than the person you knew. I'm another kind of being altogether. Neither less nor more, only different.

—Are all your perceptions different?

—Very much so. My perspective is broader. Little things stand revealed as little things.

—Give me an example, Sybille.

—I'd rather not. How could I make anything clear to you? Die and be with us, and you'll understand.

—You know I'm not dead?

—Oh, Jorge, how funny you are!

—How nice that I can still amuse you.

—You look so hurt, so tragic. I could almost feel sorry for you. Come: ask me anything.

—Could you leave your companions and live in the world again?

—I've never considered that.

—Could you?

—I suppose I could. But why should I? This is my world now.

—This ghetto.

—Is that how it seems to you?

—You lock yourselves into a closed society of your peers, a tight subculture. Your own jargon, your own wall of etiquette and idiosyncrasy. Designed, I think, mainly to keep the outsiders off balance, to keep them feeling like outsiders. It's a defensive thing. The hippies, the blacks, the gays, the deads—same mechanism, same process.

The Jews, too. Don't forget the Jews.

—All right, Sybille, the Jews. With their little tribal jokes, their special holidays, their own mysterious language, yes, a good case in point.

—So I've joined a new tribe. What's wrong with that?

—Did you need to be part of a tribe?

—What did I have before? The tribe of Californians? The tribe of academics?

—The tribe of Jorge and Sybille Klein.

—Too narrow. Anyway, I've been expelled from that tribe. I needed to join another one.

—Expelled?

—By death. After that there's no going back.

—You could go back. Any time.

—Oh, no, no, no, Jorge, I can't, I can't, I'm not Sybille Klein any more, I never will be again. How can I explain it to you? There's no way. Death brings on changes. Die and see, Jorge. Die and see.

Nerita said, "She's waiting for you in the lounge."

It was a big, coldly furnished room at the far end of the other wing of the house of strangers. Sybille stood by a window through which pale, chilly morning light was streaming. Mortimer was with her, and also Kent Zacharias. The two men favored Klein with mysterious oblique smiles—courteous or derisive, he could not tell which. "Do you like our town?" Zacharias asked. "Have you been seeing the sights?" Klein chose not to reply. He acknowledged the question with a faint nod and turned to Sybille. Strangely, he felt altogether calm at this moment of attaining a years-old desire: he felt nothing at all in her presence, no panic, no yearning, no dismay, no nostalgia, nothing, nothing. As though he were truly a dead. He knew it was the tranquility of utter terror.

"We'll leave you two alone," Zacharias said. "You must have so much to tell each other." He went out, with Nerita and Mortimer. Klein's eyes met Sybille's and lingered there. She was looking at him coolly, in a kind of impersonal appraisal. That damnable smile of hers, Klein thought: dying turns them all into Mona Lisas.

She said, "Do you plan to stay here long?"

"Probably not. A few days, maybe a week." He moistened his lips. "How have you been, Sybille? How has it been going?"

"It's all been about as I expected."

What do you mean by that? Can you give me some details? Are you at all disappointed? Have there been any surprises? What has it been like for you, Sybille? Oh, Jesus—

—Never ask a direct question—

He said, "I wish you had let me visit with you in Zanzibar."

"That wasn't possible. Let's not talk about it now." She dismissed the episode with a casual wave. After a moment she said, "Would you like to hear a fascinating story I've uncovered about the early days of Omani influence in Zanzibar?"

The impersonality of the question startled him. How could she display such absolute lack of curiosity about his presence in Zion Cold Town, his claim to be a dead, his reasons for wanting to see her? How could she plunge so quickly, so coldly, into a discussion of archaic political events in Zanzibar?

"I suppose so," he said weakly.

"It's a sort of Arabian Nights story, really. It's the story of how Ahmad the Sly overthrew Abdullah ibn Muhammad Alawi."

The names were strange to him. He had indeed taken some small part in her historical researches, but it was years since he had worked with her, and everything had drifted about in his mind, leaving a jumbled residue of Ahmads and Hasans and Abdullahs. "I'm sorry," he said. "I don't recall who they were.".

Unperturbed, Sybille said, "Certainly you remember that in the eighteenth and early nineteenth centuries the chief power in the Indian Ocean was the Arab state of Oman, ruled from Muscat on the Persian Gulf. Under the Busaidi dynasty, founded in 1744 by Ahmad ibn Said al-Busaidi, the Omani extended their power to East Africa. The logical capital for their African empire was the port of Mombasa, but they were unable to evict a rival dynasty reigning there, so the Busaidi looked toward nearby Zanzibar—a cosmopolitan island of mixed Arab, Indian, and African population. Zanzibar's strategic placement on the coast and its spacious and well-protected harbor made it an ideal base for the East African slave trade that the Busaidi of Oman intended to dominate."

"It comes back to me now, I think."

"Very well. The founder of the Omani Sultanate of Zanzibar was Ahmad ibn Majid the Sly, who came to the throne of Oman in 1811—do you remember?—upon the death of his uncle Abd-er-Rahman al-Busaidi."

"The names sound familiar," Klein said doubt-
fully.

"Seven years later," Sybille continued, "seeking to
conquer Zanzibar without the use of force, Ahmad the
Sly shaved his beard and mustache and visited the island
disguised as a soothsayer, wearing yellow robes and a
costly emerald in his turban. At that time most of Zanzibar was governed by a native ruler of mixed Arab and
African blood, Abdullah ibn Muhammad Alawi, whose
hereditary title was Mwenyi Mkuu. The Mwenyi
Mkuu's subjects were mainly Africans, members of a
tribe called the Hadimu. Sultan Ahmad, arriving in
Zanzibar Town, gave a demonstration of his soothsay-
ing skills on the waterfront and attracted so much attention that he speedily gained an audience at the court
of the Mwenyi Mkuu. Ahmad predicted a glowing future for Abdullah, declaring that a powerful prince
famed throughout the world would come to Zanzibar,
make the Mwenyi Mkuu his high lieutenant, and con-
firm him and his descendants as lords of Zanzibar forever.

" 'How do you know these things?' asked the
Mwenyi Mkuu.

" 'There is a potion I drink,' Sultan Ahmad replied, 'that enables me to see what is to come. Do you
wish to taste of it?'

" 'Most surely I do,' Abdullah said, and Ahmad
thereupon gave him a drug that sent him into raptur-
ous transports and showed him visions of paradise.
Looking down from his place near the footstool of Al-
lah, the Mwenyi Mkuu saw a rich and happy Zanzibar
governed by his children's children's children. For hours
he wandered in fantasies of almighty power.

"Ahmad then departed, and let his beard and

mustache grow again, and returned to Zanzibar ten weeks later in his full regalia as Sultan of Oman, at the head of an imposing and powerful armada. He went at once to the court of the Mwenyi Mkuu and proposed, just as the soothsayer had prophesied, that Oman and Zanzibar enter into a treaty of alliance under which Oman would assume responsibility for much of Zanzibar's external relations—including the slave trade— while guaranteeing the authority of the Mwenyi Mkuu over domestic affairs. In return for his partial abdication of authority, the Mwenyi Mkuu would receive financial compensation from Oman. Remembering the vision the soothsayer had revealed to him, Abdullah at once signed the treaty, thereby legitimizing what was, in effect, the Omani conquest of Zanzibar. A great feast was held to celebrate the treaty, and, as a mark of honor, the Mwenyi Mkuu offered Sultan Ahmad a rare drug used locally, known as *borqash,* or 'the flower of truth.' Ahmad only pretended to put the pipe to his lips, for he loathed all mind-altering drugs, but Abdullah, as the flower of truth possessed him, looked at Ahmad and recognized the outlines of the soothsayer's face behind the Sultan's new beard. Realizing that he had been deceived, the Mwenyi Mkuu thrust his dagger, the tip of which was poisoned, deep into the Sultan's side and fled the banquet hall, taking up residence on the neighboring island of Pemba. Ahmad ibn Majid survived, but the poison consumed his vital organs and the remaining ten years of his life were spent in constant agony. As for the Mwenyi Mkuu, the Sultan's men hunted him down and put him to death along with ninety members of his family, and native rule in Zanzibar was therewith extinguished."

Sybille paused. "Is that not a gaudy and wonderful story?" she asked at last.

"Fascinating," Klein said. "Where did you find it?"

"Unpublished memoirs of Claude Richburn of the East India Company. Buried deep in the London archives. Strange that no historian ever came upon it before, isn't it? The standard texts simply say that Ahmad used his navy to bully Abdullah into signing the treaty, and then had the Mwenyi Mkuu assassinated at the first convenient moment."

"Very strange," Klein agreed. But he had not come here to listen to romantic tales of visionary potions and royal treacheries. He groped for some way to bring the conversation to a more personal level. Fragments of his imaginary dialogue with Sybille floated through his mind. *Everything is quiet where I am, Jorge. There's a peace that passeth all understanding. Like swimming under a sheet of glass. The way it is, is that one no longer is affected by the unnecessary. Little things stand revealed as little things. Die and be with us, and you'll understand.* Yes. Perhaps. But did she really believe any of that? He had put all the words in her mouth; everything he had imagined her to say was his own construct, worthless as a key to the true Sybille. Where would he find the key, though?

She gave him no chance. "I will be going back to Zanzibar soon," she said. "There's much I want to learn about this incident from the people in the back country—old legends about the last days of the Mwenyi Mkuu, perhaps variants on the basic story—"

"May I accompany you?"

"Don't you have your own research to resume, Jorge?" she asked, and did not wait for an answer. She walked briskly toward the door of the lounge and went out, and he was alone.

Seven

I mean what they and their hired psychiatrists call "delusional systems." Needless to say, "delusions" are always officially defined. We don't have to worry about questions of real or unreal. They only talk out of expediency. It's the *system* that matters. How the data arrange themselves inside it. Some are consistent, others fall apart.

Thomas Pynchon: *Gravity's Rainbow*

Once more the deads, this time only three of them, coming over on the morning flight from Dar. Three was better than five, Daud Mahmoud Barwani supposed, but three was still more than a sufficiency. Not that those others, two months back, had caused any trouble, staying just the one day and flitting off to the mainland again, but it made him uncomfortable to think of such creatures on the same small island as himself. With all the world to choose, why did they keep coming to Zanzibar?

"The plane is here," said the flight controller.

Thirteen passengers. The health officer let the local people through the gate first—two newspapermen and four legislators coming back from the Pan-African Conference in Capetown—and then processed a party of four Japanese tourists, unsmiling owlish men festooned with cameras. And then the deads: and Barwani was surprised to discover that they were the same ones as before, the red-haired man, the brown-haired man without the beard, the black-haired woman. Did deads have so much money that they could fly from America to Zanzibar every few months? Barwani had heard a tale to the effect that each new dead, when he rose from his coffin, was presented with bars of gold equal to his own weight, and now he thought he believed it. No good will come of having such beings loose in the world, he told himself, and certainly none from letting them into Zanzibar. Yet he had no choice. "Welcome once again to the isle of cloves," he said unctuously, and smiled a bureaucratic smile, and wondered, not for the first time, what would become of Daud Mahmoud Barwani once his days on earth had reached their end.

"—Ahmad the Sly versus Abdullah Something," Klein said. "That's all she would talk about. The history of Zanzibar." He was in Jijibhoi's study. The night was warm and a late-season rain was falling, blurring the million sparkling lights of the Los Angeles basin. "It would have been, you know, gauche to ask her any direct questions. Gauche. I haven't felt so gauche since I was fourteen. I was helpless among them, a foreigner, a child."

"Do you think they saw through your disguise?" Jijibhoi asked.

"I can't tell. They seemed to be toying with me, to

be having sport with me, but that may just have been their general style with any newcomer. Nobody challenged me. Nobody hinted I might be an impostor. Nobody seemed to care very much about me or what I was doing there or how I had happened to become a dead. Sybille and I stood face to face, and I wanted to reach out to her, I wanted her to reach out to me, and there was no contact, none, none at all, it was as though we had just met at some academic cocktail party and the only thing on her mind was the new nugget of obscure history she had just unearthed, and so she told me all about how Sultan Ahmad outfoxed Abdullah and Abdullah stabbed the Sultan." Klein caught sight of a set of familiar books on Jijibhoi's crowded shelves—Oliver and Mathew, *History of East Africa,* books that had traveled everywhere with Sybille in the years of their marriage. He pulled forth Volume I, saying, "She claimed that the standard histories give a sketchy and inaccurate description of the incident and that she's only now discovered the true story. For all I know, she was just playing a game with me, telling me a piece of established history as though it were something nobody knew till last week. Let me see—Ahmad, Ahmad, Ahmad—"

He examined the index. Five Ahmads were listed, but there was no entry for a Sultan Ahmad ibn Majid the Sly. Indeed, an Ahmad ibn Majid was cited, but he was mentioned only in a footnote and appeared to be an Arab chronicler. Klein found three Abdullahs, none of them a man of Zanzibar. "Something's wrong," he murmured.

"It does not matter, dear Jorge," Jijibhoi said mildly.

"It does. Wait a minute." He prowled the listings. Under *Zanzibar, Rulers,* he found no Ahmads, no Abdullahs; he did discover a Majid ibn Said, but when he checked the reference he found that he had reigned somewhere in the second half of the nineteenth century. Desperately Klein flipped pages, skimming, turning back, searching. Eventually he looked up and said, "It's all wrong!"

"The Oxford *History of East Africa?*"

"The details of Sybille's story. Look, she said this Ahmad the Sly gained the throne of Oman in 1811, and seized Zanzibar seven years later. But the book says that a certain Seyyid Said al-Busaidi became Sultan of Oman in 1806, and ruled for *fifty years*. He was the one, not this nonexistent Ahmad the Sly, who grabbed Zanzibar, but he did it in 1828, and the ruler he compelled to sign a treaty with him, the Mwenyi Mkuu, was named Hasan ibn Ahmad Alawi, and—" Klein shook his head. "It's an altogether different cast of characters. No stabbings, no assassinations, the dates are entirely different, the whole thing—"

Jijibhoi smiled sadly. "The deads are often mischievous."

"But why would she invent a complete fantasy and palm it off as a sensational new discovery? Sybille was the most scrupulous scholar I ever knew! She would never—"

"That was the Sybille you knew, dear friend. I keep urging you to realize that this is another person, a new person, within her body."

"A person who would lie about history?"

"A person who would tease," Jijibhoi said.

— "Yes," Klein muttered. "Who would tease." *Keep in mind that to a dead the whole universe is plastic, nothing's real, nothing matters a hell of a lot.* "Who would tease a stupid, boring, annoyingly persistent ex-husband who has shown up in her Cold Town, wearing a transparent disguise and pretending to be a dead. Who

would invent not only an anecdote but even its princi-
pals, as a joke, a game, a *jeu d'esprit*. Oh, God. Oh,
God, how cruel she is, how foolish I was! It was her
way of telling me she knew I was a phony dead. Quid
pro quo, fraud for fraud!"

"What will you do?"

"I don't know," Klein said.

What he did, against Jijibhoi's strong advice and
his own better judgment, was to get more pills from
Dolorosa and return to Zion Cold Town. There would be
a fitful joy, like that of probing the socket of a missing
tooth, in confronting Sybille with the evidence of her
fictional Ahmad, her imaginary Abdullah. Let there be
no more games between us, he would say. Tell me what
I need to know, Sybille, and then let me go away; but tell
me only truth. All the way to Utah he rehearsed his
speech, polishing and embellishing. There was no need
for it, though, since this time the gate of Zion Cold
Town would not open for him. The scanners scanned his
forged Albany card and the loudspeaker said, "Your
credentials are invalid."

Which could have ended it. He might have returned
to Los Angeles and picked up the pieces of his life. All
this semester he had been on sabbatical leave, but the
summer term was coming and there was work to do. He
did return to Los Angeles, but only long enough to pack
a somewhat larger suitcase, find his passport, and drive
to the airport. On a sweet May evening a BOAC jet took
him over the Pole to London, where, barely pausing for
coffee and buns at an airport shop, he boarded another
plane that carried him southeast toward Africa. More
asleep than awake, he watched the dreamy landmarks
drifting past: the Mediterranean, coming and going with
surprising rapidity, and the tawny carpet of the Libyan

Desert, and the mighty Nile, reduced to a brown thread's thickness when viewed from a height of ten miles. Suddenly Kilimanjaro, mist-wrapped, snow-bound, loomed like a giant double-headed blister to his right, far below, and he thought he could make out to his left the distant glare of the sun on the Indian Ocean. Then the big needle-nosed plane began its abrupt swooping descent, and he found himself, soon after, stepping out into the warm humid air and dazzling sunlight of Dar es Salaam.

Too soon, too soon. He felt unready to go on to Zanzibar. A day or two of rest, perhaps: he picked a Dar hotel at random, the Agip, liking the strange sound of its name, and hired a taxi. The hotel was sleek and clean, a streamlined affair in the glossy 1960's style, much cheaper than the Kilimanjaro, where he had stayed briefly on the other trip, and located in a pleasant leafy quarter of the city, near the ocean. He strolled about for a short while, discovered that he was altogether exhausted, returned to his room for a nap that stretched on for nearly five hours, and awakening groggy, showered and dressed for dinner. The hotel's dining room was full of beefy red-faced fair-haired men, jacketless and wearing open-throated white shirts, all of whom reminded him disturbingly of Kent Zacharias; but these were warms, Britishers from their accents, engineers, he suspected, from their conversation. They were building a damn and a power plant somewhere up the coast, it seemed, or perhaps a power plant without a dam; it was hard to follow what they said. They drank a good deal of gin and spoke in hearty booming shouts. There were also a good many Japanese businessmen, of course, looking trim and restrained in dark-blue suits and narrow ties, and at the table next to Klein's were five tanned curly-haired men talking in rapid Hebrew—Israelis, surely.

The only Africans in sight were waiters and bartenders. Klein ordered Mombasa oysters, steak, and a carafe of red wine, and found the food unexpectedly good, but left most of it on his plate. It was late evening in Tanzania, but for him it was ten o'clock in the morning, and his body was confused. He tumbled into bed, meditated vaguely on the probable presence of Sybille just a few air-minutes away in Zanzibar, and dropped into a sound sleep from which he awakened, what seemed like many hours later, to discover that it was still well before dawn.

He dawdled away the morning sightseeing in the old native quarter, hot and dusty, with unpaved streets and rows of tin shacks, and at midday returned to his hotel for a shower and lunch. Much the same national distribution in the restaurant—British, Japanese, Israeli —though the faces seemed different. He was on his second beer when Anthony Gracchus came in. The white hunter, broad-shouldered, pale, densely bearded, clad in khaki shorts, khaki shirt, seemed almost to have stepped out of the picture-cube Jijibhoi had once shown him. Instinctively Klein shrank back, turning toward the window, but too late: Gracchus had seen him. All chatter came to a halt in the restaurant as the dead man strode to Klein's table, pulled out a chair unasked, and seated himself; then, as though a motion-picture projector had been halted and started again, the British engineers resumed their shouting, sounding somewhat strained now. "Small world," Gracchus said. "Crowded one, anyway. On your way to Zanzibar, are you, Klein?"

"In a day or so. Did you know I was here?"

"Of course not." Gracchus' harsh eyes twinkled slyly. "Sheer coincidence is what this is. She's there already."

"She is?"

"She and Zacharias and Mortimer. I hear you wiggled your way into Zion."

"Briefly," Klein said. "I saw Sybille. Briefly."

"Unsatisfactorily. So once again you've followed her here. Give it up, man. Give it up."

"I can't."

"*Can't!*" Gracchus scowled. "A neurotic's word, *can't*. What you mean is *won't*. A mature man can do anything he wants to that isn't a physical impossibility. Forget her. You're only annoying her, this way, interfering with her work, interfering with her——" Gracchus smiled. "With her life. She's been dead almost three years, hasn't she? Forget her. The world's full of other women. You're still young, you have money, you aren't ugly, you have professional standing——"

"Is this what you were sent here to tell me?"

"I wasn't sent here to tell you anything, friend. I'm only trying to save you from yourself. Don't go to Zanzibar. Go home and start your life again."

"When I saw her at Zion," Klein said, "she treated me with contempt. She amused herself at my expense. I want to ask her why she did that."

"Because you're a warm and she's a dead. To her you're a clown. To all of us you're a clown. It's nothing personal, Klein. There's simply a gulf in attitudes, a gulf too wide for you to cross. You went to Zion drugged up like a Treasury man, didn't you? Pale face, bulgy eyes? You didn't fool anyone. You certainly didn't fool *her*. The game she played with you was her way of telling you that. Don't you know that?"

"I know it, yes."

"What more do you want, then? More humiliation?"

Klein shook his head wearily and stared at the

tablecloth. After a moment he looked up, and his eyes met those of Gracchus, and he was astounded to realize that he trusted the hunter, that for the first time in his dealings with the deads he felt he was being met with sincerity. He said in a low voice, "We were very close, Sybille and I, and then she died, and now I'm nothing to her. I haven't been able to come to terms with that. I need her, still. I want to share my life with her, even now."

"But you can't."

"I know that. And still I can't help doing what I've been doing."

"There's only one thing you *can* share with her," Gracchus said. "That's your death. She won't descend to your level: you have to climb to hers."

"Don't be asburd."

"Who's absurd, me or you? Listen to me, Klein. I think you're a fool, I think you're a weakling, but I don't dislike you, I don't hold you to blame for your own foolishness. And so I'll help you, if you'll allow me." He reached into his breast pocket and withdrew a tiny metal tube with a safety catch at one end. "Do you know what this is?" Gracchus asked. "It's a self-defense dart, the kind all the women in New York carry. A good many deads carry them, too, because we never know when the reaction will start, when the mobs will turn against us. Only we don't use anesthetic drugs in ours. Listen, we can walk into any tavern in the native quarter and have a decent brawl going in five minutes, and in the confusion I'll put one of these darts into you, and we'll have you in Dar General Hospital fifteen minutes after that, crammed into a deep-freeze unit, and for a few thousand dollars we can ship you unthawed to California, and this time Friday night you'll be undergoing rekindling in, say, San Diego Cold Town. And when you come out of it you and Sybille will be on the same side of the gulf, do you see? If you're destined to get back together with her, ever, that's the only way. That way you have a chance. This way you have none."

"It's unthinkable," Klein said.

"Unacceptable, maybe. But not unthinkable. Nothing's unthinkable once somebody's thought it. You think it some more. Will you promise me that? Think about it before you get aboard that plane for Zanzibar. I'll be staying here tonight and tomorrow, and then I'm going out to Arusha to meet some deads coming in for the hunting, and any time before then I'll do it for you if you say the word. Think about it. Will you think about it? Promise me that you'll think about it."

"I'll think about it," Klein said.

"Good. Good. Thank you. Now let's have lunch and change the subject. Do you like eating here?"

"One thing puzzles me. Why does this place have a clientele that's exclusively non-African? Does it dare to discriminate against blacks in a black republic?"

Gracchus laughed. "It's the blacks who discriminate, friend. This is considered a second-class hotel. All the blacks are at the Kilimanjaro or the Nyerere. Still, it's not such a bad place. I recommend the fish dishes, if you haven't tried them, and there's a decent white wine from Israel that—"

Eight

O Lord, methought what pain it was to drown!
What dreadful noise of water in mine ears!
What sights of ugly death within mine eyes!
Methoughts I saw a thousand fearful wracks;
A thousand men that fishes gnawed upon;
Wedges of gold, great anchors, heaps of pearl,
Inestimable stones, unvalued jewels,
All scatt'red in the bottom of the sea.
Some lay in dead men's skulls, and in the holes
Where eyes did once inhabit there were crept,
As 'twere in scorn of eyes, reflecting gems
That wooed the slimy bottom of the deep
And mocked the dead bones that lay scatt'red by.

Shakespeare: *Richard III*

"—Israeli wine," Mick Dongan was saying. "Well, I'll try anything once, especially if there's some neat little irony attached to it. I mean, there we were in Egypt, in *Egypt,* at this fabulous dinner party in the hills at Luxor, and our host is a Saudi prince, no less, in full tribal costume right down to the sunglasses, and when they bring out the roast lamb he grins devilishly and says, 'Of course we could always drink Mouton-Rothschild, but I do happen to have a small stock of select Israeli wines in my cellar, and because I think you are, like myself, a connoisseur of small incongruities, I've asked my steward to open a bottle or two of'—Klein, do you see that girl who just came in?" It is January, 1981, early afternoon, a fine drizzle in the air. Klein is lunching with six colleagues from the history department at the Hanging Gardens atop the Westwood Plaza. The hotel is a huge ziggurat on stilts; the Hanging Gardens is a rooftop restaurant, ninety stories up, in freaky neo-Babylonian décor, all winged bulls and snorting dragons of blue and yellow tile, waiters with long curly beards and scimitars at their hips—gaudy nightclub by dark, campy faculty hangout by day. Klein looks to his left. Yes, a handsome woman, mid-twenties, coolly beautiful, serious-looking, taking a seat by herself, putting a stack of books and cassettes down on the table before her. Klein does not pick up strange girls: a matter of moral policy, and also a matter of innate shyness. Dongan teases him. "Go on over, will you? She's your type, I swear. Her eyes are the right color for you, aren't they?"

Klein has been complaining, lately, that there are too many blue-eyed girls in southern California. Blue eyes are disturbing to him, somehow, even menacing. His own eyes are brown. So are hers: dark, warm, sparkling. He thinks he has seen her occasionally in the library. Perhaps they have even exchanged brief glances. "Go on," Dongan says. "Go *on,* Jorge. Go." Klein glares at him. He will not go. How can he intrude on this woman's privacy? To force himself on her—it would almost be like rape. Dongan smiles complacently; his bland grin is a merciless prod. Klein refuses to be stampeded. But then, as he hesitates, the girl smiles too, a quick shy smile, gone so soon he is not altogether sure it happened at all, but he is sure enough, and he finds himself rising, crossing the alabaster floor, hovering awkwardly over her, searching for some inspired words with which to make contact, and no words come, but still they make contact the old-fashioned way, eye to eye, and he is stunned by the intensity of what passes between them in that first implausible moment.

"Are you waiting for someone?" he mutters, shaken.

"No." The smile again, far less tentative. "Would you like to join me?"

She is a graduate student, he discovers quickly. Just got her master's, beginning now on her doctorate—the nineteenth-century East African slave trade, particular emphasis on Zanzibar. "How romantic," he says. "Zanzibar! Have you been there?"

"Never. I hope to go some day. Have you?"

"Not ever. But it always interested me, ever since I was a small boy collecting stamps. It was the last country in my album."

"Not in mine," she says. "Zululand was."

She knows him by name, it turns out. She had even been thinking of enrolling in his course on Nazism and Its Offspring. "Are you South American?" she asks.

"Born there. Raised here. My grandparents escaped to Buenos Aires in '37."

"Why Argentina? I thought that was a hotbed of Nazis."

"Was. Also full of German-speaking refugees, though. All their friends went there. But it was too unstable. My parents got out in '55, just before one of the big revolutions, and came to California. What about you?"

"British family. I was born in Seattle. My father's in the consular service. He—"

A waiter looms. They order sandwiches offhandedly. Lunch seems very unimportant now. The contact still holds. He sees Conrad's *Nostromo* in her stack of books; she is halfway through it, and he has just finished it, and the coincidence amuses them. Conrad is one of her favorites, she says. One of his, too. What about Faulkner? Yes, and Mann, and Virginia Woolf, and they share even a fondness for Hermann Broch, and a dislike for Hesse. How odd. Operas? *Freischütz, Holländer, Fidelio*, yes. "We have very Teutonic tastes," she observes.

"We have very similar tastes," he adds. He finds himself holding her hand.

"Amazingly similar," she says.

Mick Dongan leers at him from the far side of the room; Klein gives him a terrible scowl. Dongan winks. "Let's get out of here," Klein says, just as she starts to say the same thing.

They talk half the night and make love until dawn. "You ought to know," he tells her solemnly over breakfast, "that I decided long ago never to get married and certainly never to have a child."

"So did I," she says. "When I was fifteen."

They were married four months later. Mick Dongan was his best man.

Gracchus said, as they left the restaurant, "You will think things over, won't you?"

"I will," Klein said. "I promised you that."

He went to his room, packed his suitcase, checked out, and took a cab to the airport, arriving in plenty of time for the afternoon flight to Zanzibar. The same melancholy little man was on duty as health officer when he landed, Barwani. "Sir, you have come back," Barwani said. "I thought you might. The other people have been here several days already."

"The other people?"

"When you were here last, sir, you kindly offered me a retainer in order that you might be informed when a certain person reached this island." Barwani's eyes gleamed. "That person, with two of her former companions, is here now."

Klein carefully placed a twenty-shilling note on the health officer's desk.

"At which hotel?"

Barwani's lips quirked. Evidently twenty shillings fell short of expectations. But Klein did not take out another banknote, and after a moment Barwani said, "As before. The Zanzibar House. And you, sir?"

"As before," Klein said. "I'll be staying at the Shirazi."

Sybille was in the garden of the hotel, going over that day's research notes, when the telephone call came from Barwani. "Don't let my papers blow away," she said to Zacharias, and went inside.

When she returned, looking bothered, Zacharias said, "Is there trouble?"

She sighed. "Jorge. He's on his way to his hotel now."

"What a bore," Mortimer murmured. "I thought Gracchus might have brought him to his senses."

"Evidently not," Sybille said. "What are we going to do?"

"What would you like to do?" Zacharias asked.

She shook her head. "We can't allow this to go on, can we?"

The evening air was humid and fragrant. The long rains had come and gone, and the island was in the grip of the new season's lunatic fertility: outside the window of Klein's hotel room some vast twining vine was putting forth monstrous trumpet-shaped yellow flowers, and all about the hotel grounds everything was in blossom, everything was in a frenzy of moist young leaves. Klein's sensibility reverberated to that feeling of universal vigorous thrusting newness; he paced the room, full of energy, trying to devise some feasible stratagem. Go immediately to see Sybille? Force his way in, if necessary, with shouts and alarums, and demand to know why she had told him that fantastic tale of imaginary sultans? No. No. He would do no more confronting, no more lamenting; now that he was here, now that he was close by her, he would seek her out calmly, he would talk quietly, he would invoke memories of their old love, he would speak of Rilke and Woolf and Broch, of afternoons in Puerto Vallarta and nights in Santa Fe, of music heard and caresses shared, he would rekindle not their marriage, for that was impossible, but merely the remembrance of the bond that once had existed, he would win from her some acknowledgment of what had been, and then he would soberly and quietly exorcise that bond, he and she together, they would work to free him by speaking softly of the change that had come over their lives, until, after three hours or four or five, he had brought himself with her help to an acceptance of the unacceptable. That was all. He would demand nothing, he would beg for nothing, except only that she assist him for one evening in ridding his soul of this useless, destructive obsession. Even a dead, even a capricious, wayward, volatile, whimsical, wanton dead, would surely see the desirability of that, and would freely give him her cooperation. Surely. And then home, and then new beginnings, too long postponed.

He made ready to go out.

There was a soft knock at the door. "Sir? Sir? You have visitors downstairs."

"Who?" Klein asked, though he knew the answer.

"A lady and two gentlemen," the bellhop replied. "The taxi has brought them from the Zanzibar House. They wait for you in the bar."

"Tell them I'll be down in a moment."

He went to the iced pitcher on the dresser, drank a glass of cold water mechanically, unthinkingly, poured himself a second, drained that too. This visit was unexpected; and why had she brought her entourage along? He had to struggle to regain that centeredness, that sense of purpose understood, which he thought he had attained before the knock. Eventually he left the room.

They were dressed crisply and impeccably this damp night, Zacharias in a tawny frock coat and pale-green trousers, Mortimer in a belted white caftan trimmed with intricate brocade, Sybille in a simple lavender tunic. Their pale faces were unmarred by perspiration; they seemed perfectly composed, models of poise. No one sat near them in the bar. As Klein entered, they stood to greet him, but their smiles appeared sinister, having nothing of friendliness in them. Klein clung tight to his intended calmness. He said quietly, "It was kind of you to come. May I buy drinks for you?"

"We have ours already," Zacharias pointed out. "Let us be your hosts. What will you have?"

"Pimm's Number Six," Klein said. He tried to match their frosty smiles. "I admire your tunic, Sybille. You all look so debonair tonight that I feel shamed."

"You never were famous for your clothes," she said.

Zacharias returned from the counter with Klein's drink. He took it and toasted them gravely.

After a short while Klein said, "Do you think I could talk privately with you, Sybille?"

"There's nothing we have to say to one another that can't be said in front of Kent and Laurence."

"Nevertheless."

"I prefer not to, Jorge."

"As you wish." Klein peered straight into her eyes and saw nothing there, nothing, and flinched. All that he had meant to say fled his mind. Only churning fragments danced there: Rilke, Broch, Puerto Vallarta. He gulped at his drink.

Zacharias said, "We have a problem to discuss, Klein."

"Go on."

"The problem is you. You're causing great distress to Sybille. This is the second time, now, that you've followed her to Zanzibar, to the literal end of the earth, Klein, and you've made several attempts besides to enter a closed sanctuary in Utah under false pretenses, and this is interfering with Sybille's freedom, Klein, it's an impossible, intolerable interference."

"The deads are dead," Mortimer said. "We understand the depths of your feelings for your late wife, but this compulsive pursuit of her must be brought to an end."

"It will be," Klein said, staring at a point on the stucco wall midway between Zacharias and Sybille. "I want only an hour or two of private conversation with my—with Sybille, and then I promise you that there will be no further—"

"Just as you promised Anthony Gracchus," Mortimer said, "not to go to Zanzibar."

"I wanted—"

"We have our rights," said Zacharias. "We've gone

through hell, literally through hell, to get where we are. You've infringed on our right to be left alone. You bother us. You bore us. You annoy us. We hate to be annoyed." He looked toward Sybille. She nodded. Zacharias' hand vanished into the breast pocket of his coat. Mortimer seized Klein's wrist with astonishing suddenness and jerked his arm forward. A minute metal tube glistened in Zacharias' huge fist. Klein had seen such a tube in the hand of Anthony Gracchus only the day before.

"No," Klein gasped. "I don't believe—*no!*"

Zacharias plunged the cold tip of the tube quickly into Klein's forearm.

"The freezer unit is coming," Mortimer said. "It'll be here in five minutes or less."

"What if it's late?" Sybille asked anxiously. "What if something irreversible happens to his brain before it gets here?"

"He's not even entirely dead yet," Zacharias reminded her. "There's time. There's ample time. I spoke to the doctor myself, a very intelligent Chinese, flawless command of English. He was most sympathetic. They'll have him frozen within a couple minutes of death. We'll book cargo passage aboard the morning plane for Dar. He'll be in the United States within twenty-four hours, I guarantee that. San Diego will be notified. Everything will be all right, Sybille!"

Jorge Klein lay slumped across the table. The bar had emptied the moment he had cried out and lurched forward: the half-dozen customers had fled, not caring to mar their holidays by sharing an evening with the presence of death, and the waiters and bartenders, big-eyed, terrified, lurked in the hallway. A heart attack,

Zacharias had announced, some kind of sudden attack, maybe a stroke, where's the telephone? No one had seen the tiny tube do its work.

Sybille trembled. "If anything goes wrong—"

"I hear the sirens now," Zacharias said.

From his desk at the airport Daud Mahmoud Barwani watched the bulky refrigerated coffin being loaded by grunting porters aboard the morning plane for Dar. And then, and then, and then? They would ship the dead man to the far side of the world, to America, and breathe new life into him, and he would go once more among men. Barwani shook his head. These people! The man who was alive is now dead, and these dead ones, who knows what they are? Who knows? Best that the dead remain dead, as was intended in the time of first things. Who could have foreseen a day when the dead returned from the grave? Not I. And who can foresee what we will all become, a hundred years from now? Not I. Not I. A hundred years from now I will sleep, Barwani thought. I will sleep, and it will not matter to me at all what sort of creatures walk the earth.

Nine

We die with the dying:
See, they depart, and we go with them.
We are born with the dead:
See, they return, and bring us with them.

T.S. Eliot: *Little Gidding*

On the day of his awakening he saw no one except the
attendants at the rekindling house, who bathed him and
fed him and helped him to walk slowly around his room.
They said nothing to him, nor he to them; words seemed
irrelevant. He felt strange in his skin, too snugly contained, as though all his life he had worn ill-fitting clothes
and now had for the first time encountered a competent
tailor. The images that his eyes brought him were sharp,
unnaturally clear, and faintly haloed by prismatic colors,
an effect that imperceptibly vanished as the day passed.
On the second day he was visited by the San Diego
Guidefather, not at all the formidable patriarch he had
imagined, but rather a cool, efficient executive, about

fifty years old, who greeted him cordially and told him
briefly of the disciplines and routines he must master
before he could leave the Cold Town. "What month is
this?" Klein asked, and Guidefather told him it was June,
the seventeenth of June, 1993. He had slept four weeks.

Now it is the morning of the third day after his
awakening, and he has guests: Sybille, Nerita, Zacharias,
Mortimer, Gracchus. They file into his room and stand
in an arc at the foot of his bed, radiant in the glow of
light that pierces the narrow windows. Like demigods,
like angels, glittering with a dazzling inward brilliance,
and now he is of their company. Formally they embrace
him, first Gracchus, then Nerita, then Mortimer. Zacharias advances next to his bedside, Zacharias who sent
him into death, and he smiles at Klein and Klein returns
the smile, and they embrace. Then it is Sybille's turn:
she slips her hand between his, he draws her close, her
lips brush his cheek, his touch hers, his arm encircles
her shoulders.

"Hello," she whispers.

"Hello," he says.

They ask him how he feels, how quickly his
strength is returning, whether he has been out of bed
yet, how soon he will commence his drying-off. The style
of their conversation is the oblique, elliptical style
favored by the deads, but not nearly so clipped and cryp-
tic as the way of speech they normally would use among
themselves; they are favoring him, leading him inch by
inch into their customs. Within five minutes he thinks he
is getting the knack.

He says, using their verbal shorthand, "I must have
been a great burden to you."

"You were, you were," Zacharias agrees. "But all
that is done with now."

"We forgive you," Mortimer says.

"We welcome you among us," declares Sybille.

They talk about their plans for the months ahead. Sybille is nearly finished with her work on Zanzibar; she will retreat to Zion Cold Town for the summer months to write her thesis. Mortimer and Nerita are off to Mexico to tour the ancient temples and pyramids; Zacharias is going to Ohio, to his beloved mounds. In the autumn they will reassemble at Zion and plan the winter's amusement: a tour of Egypt, perhaps, or Peru, the heights of Machu Picchu. Ruins, archaeological sites, delight them; in the places where death has been busiest, their joy is most intense. They are flushed, excited, verbose—virtually chattering, now. Away we will go, to Zimbabwe, to Palenque, to Angkor, to Knossos, to Uxmal, to Nineveh, to Mohenjo-daro. And as they go on and on, talking with hands and eyes and smiles and even words, even words, torrents of words, they blur and become unreal to him, they are mere dancing puppets jerking about a badly painted stage, they are droning insects, wasps or bees or mosquitoes, with all their talk of travels and festivals, of Boghazköy and Babylon, of Megiddo and Masada, and he ceases to hear them, he tunes them out, he lies there smiling, eyes glazed, mind adrift. It perplexes him that he has so little interest in them. But then he realizes that it is a mark of his liberation. He is freed of old chains now. Will he join their set? Why should he? Perhaps he will travel with them, perhaps not, as the whim takes him. More likely not. Almost certainly not. He does not need their company. He has his own interests. He will follow Sybille about no longer. He does not need, he does not want, he will not seek. Why should he become one of them, rootless, an amoral wanderer, a ghost made flesh? Why should he embrace the values and customs of these people who had given him to death as dispassionately as they might swat an insect, only because he had bored them, because he had annoyed them? He does not hate them for what they did to him, he feels no resentment that he can identify, he merely chooses to detach himself from them. Let them float on from ruin to ruin, let them pursue death from continent to continent; he will go his own way. Now that he has crossed the interface, he finds that Sybille no longer matters to him.

—*Oh, sir, things change*—

"We'll go now," Sybille says softly.

He nods. He makes no other reply.

"We'll see you after your drying-off," Zacharias tells him, and touches him lightly with his knuckles, a farewell gesture used only by the deads.

"See you," Mortimer says.

"See you," says Gracchus.

"Soon," Nerita says.

Never, Klein says, saying it without words, but so they will understand. Never. Never. Never. I will never see any of you. I will never see you, Sybille. The syllables echo through his brain, and the word, *never, never, never*, rolls over him like the breaking surf, cleansing him, purifying him, healing him. He is free. He is alone.

"Goodbye," Sybille calls from the hallway.

"Goodbye," he says.

It was years before he saw her again. But they spent the last days of '99 together, shooting dodos under the shadow of mighty Kilimanjaro.

Thomas
the Proclaimer

One

Moonlight, Starlight, Torchlight

How long will this night last? The blackness, though moon-pierced, star-pierced, torch-pierced, is dense and tangible. They are singing and chanting in the valley. Bitter smoke from their firebrands rises to the hilltop where Thomas stands, flanked by his closest followers. Fragments of old hymns dance through the trees. "Rock of Ages, Cleft for Me." "O God, Our Help in Ages Past." "Jesus, Lover of My Soul, Let Me to Thy Bosom Fly." Thomas is the center of all attention. A kind of invisible aura surrounds his blocky, powerful figure, an unseen crackling electrical radiance. Saul Kraft, at his side, seems eclipsed and obscured, a small, fragile-looking man, overshadowed now but far from unimportant in the events of this night. "Nearer, My God, to Thee." Thomas begins to hum the tune, then to sing. His voice, though deep and magical, the true charismatic voice, tumbles randomly from key to key: the prophet has no ear for music. Kraft smiles sourly at Thomas' dismal sounds.

> *"Watchman, tell us of the night,*
> *What its signs of promise are.*
> *Traveler, o'er yon mountain's height,*
> *See that glory-beaming star!"*

Ragged shouts from below. Occasional sobs and loud coughs. What is the hour? The hour is late. Thomas runs his hands through his long, tangled hair, tugging, smoothing, pulling the strands down toward his thick shoulders. The familiar gesture, beloved by the multitudes. He wonders if he should make an appearance. They are calling his name; he hears the rhythmic cries punching through the snarl of clashing hymns. *Tho-mas! Tho-mas! Tho-mas!* Hysteria in their voices. They want him to come forth and stretch out his arms and make the heavens move again, just as he caused them to stop. But Thomas resists that grand but hollow gesture. How easy it is to play the prophet's part! He did not cause the heavens to stop, though, and he knows that he cannot make them move again. Not of his own will alone, at any rate.

"What time is it?" he asks.

"Quarter to ten," Kraft tells him. Adding, after an instant's thought: "P.M."

So the twenty-four hours are nearly up. And still the sky hangs frozen. Well, Thomas? It this not what you asked for? Go down on your knees, you cried, and beg Him for a Sign, so that we may know He is still with us, in this our time of need. And render up to Him a great shout. And the people knelt throughout all the lands. And begged. And shouted. And the Sign was given. Why, then, this sense of foreboding? Why these fears? Surely this night will pass. Look at Kraft. Smiling serenely. Kraft has never known any doubts. Those cold eyes, those thin wide lips, the fixed expression of tranquillity.

"You ought to speak to them," Kraft says.

"I have nothing to say."

"A few words of comfort for them."

"Let's see what happens, first. What can I tell them now?"

"Empty of words, Thomas? You, who have had so much to proclaim?"

Thomas shrugs. There are times when Kraft infuriates him: the little man needling him, goading, scheming, never letting up, always pushing this Crusade toward some appointed goal grasped by Kraft alone. The intensity of Kraft's faith exhausts Thomas. Annoyed, the prophet turns away from him. Thomas sees scattered fires leaping on the horizon. Prayer meetings? Or are they riots? Peering at those distant blazes, Thomas jabs idly at the tuner of the radio before him.

". . . rounding out the unprecedented span of twenty-four hours of continuous daylight in much of the Eastern Hemisphere, an endless daybreak over the Near East and an endless noon over Siberia, eastern China, the Philippines, and Indonesia. Meanwhile western Europe and the Americas remain locked in endless night . . ."

". . . then spake Joshua to the Lord in the day when the Lord delivered up the Amorites before the children of Israel, and he said in the sight of Israel, Sun, stand thou still upon Gibeon; and thou, Moon, in the valley of Ajalon. And the sun stood still, and the moon stayed, until the people had avenged themselves upon their enemies. Is this not written in the book of Jasher? So the sun stood still in the midst of heaven, and hasted not to go down about a whole day . . ."

". . . an astonishing culmination, apparently, to the campaign led by Thomas Davidson of Reno, Nevada, known popularly as Thomas the Proclaimer. The shaggy-bearded, long-haired, self-designated Apostle of Peace brought his Crusade of Faith to a climax yesterday with the world-wide program of simultaneous prayer that appears to have been the cause of . . ."

> *"Watchman, does its beauteous ray*
> *Aught of joy or hope foretell?*
> *Traveler, yes; it brings the day,*
> *Promised day of Israel."*

Kraft says sharply, "Do you hear what they're singing, Thomas? You've got to speak to them. You got them into this; now they want you to tell them you'll get them out of it."

"Not yet, Saul."

"You mustn't let your moment slip by. Show them that God still speaks through you!"

"When God is ready to speak again," Thomas says frostily, "I'll let His words come forth. Not before." He glares at Kraft and punches for another change of station.

". . . continued meetings in Washington, but no communiqué as yet. Meanwhile, at the United Nations . . ."

". . . Behold, He cometh with clouds; and every eye shall see Him, and they also which pierced Him: and all kindreds of the Earth shall wail because of Him. Even so, Amen . . ."

". . . outbreaks of looting in Caracas, Mexico City, Oakland, and Vancouver. But in the daylight half of the world, violence and other disruption has been slight, though an unconfirmed report from Moscow . . ."

". . . and when, brethren, when did the sun cease in its course? At six in the morning, brethren, six in the morning, Jerusalem time! And on what day, brethren? Why, the sixth of June, the sixth day of the sixth month! *Six—six—six!* And what does Holy Writ tell us, my dearly beloved ones, in the thirteenth chapter of Revelations? That a beast shall rise up out of the sea, having seven heads and ten horns, and upon his horns ten crowns, and upon his heads the name of blasphemy. And the Holy Book tells us the number of the beast, beloved, and the number is six hundred three score and six, wherein we see again the significant digits, *six—six—six!* Who then can deny that these are the last days, and that the Apocalypse must be upon us? Thus in this time of woe and fire as we sit upon this stilled planet awaiting His judgment, we must . . ."

". . . latest observatory report confirms that no appreciable momentum effects could be detected as the Earth shifted to its present period of rotation. Scientists agree that the world's abrupt slowing on its axis should have produced a global catastrophe leading, perhaps, to the destruction of all life. However, nothing but minor tidal disturbances have been recorded so far. Two hours ago, we interviewed Presidential Science Adviser Raymond Bartell, who made this statement:

" 'Calculations now show that the Earth's period of rotation and its period of revolution have suddenly become equal; that is, the day and the year now have the same length. This locks the Earth into its present position relative to the sun, so that the side of the Earth now enjoying daylight will continue indefinitely to do so, while the other side will remain permanently in night. Other effects of the slowdown that might have been expected include the flooding of coastal areas, the collapse of most buildings, and a series of earthquakes and volcanic eruptions, but none of these things seem to have happened. For the moment we have no rational explanation of all this, and I must admit it's a great temptation to say that Thomas the Proclaimer must have managed to get his miracle, because there isn't any other apparent way of . . .' "

"... I am Alpha and Omega, the beginning and the ending, saith the Lord, which is, and which was, and which is to come, the Almighty ..."

With a fierce fingerthrust Thomas silences all the radio's clamoring voices. Alpha and Omega! Apocalyptist garbage! The drivel of hysterical preachers pouring from a thousand transmitters, poisoning the air! Thomas despises all these criers of doom. None of them knows anything. No one understands. His throat fills with a turbulence of angry incoherent words, almost choking him. A coppery taste of denunciations. Kraft again urges him to speak. Thomas glowers. Why doesn't Kraft do the speaking himself, for once? He's a truer believer than I am. He's the real prophet. But of course the idea is ridiculous. Kraft has no eloquence, no fire. Only ideas and visions. He'd bore everybody to splinters. Thomas succumbs. He beckons with his fingertips. "The microphone," he mutters. "Let me have the microphone."

Among his entourage there is fluttery excitement. "He wants the mike!" they murmur. "Give him the mike!" Much activity on the part of the technicians.

Kraft presses a plaque of cold metal into the Proclaimer's hand. Grins, winks. "Make their hearts soar," Kraft whispers. "Send them on a trip!" Everyone waits. In the valley the torches bob and weave; have they begun dancing down there? Overhead the pocked moon holds its corner of the sky in frosty grasp. The stars are chained to their places. Thomas draws a deep breath and lets the air travel inward, upward, surging to the recesses of his skull. He waits for the good lightheadedness to come upon him, the buoyancy that liberates his tongue. He thinks he is ready to speak. He hears the desperate chanting: *Tho-mas! Tho-mas! Tho-mas!*" It is more than half a day since his last public statement. He is tense and hollow; he has fasted throughout this Day of the Sign, and of course he has not slept. No one has slept.

"Friends," he begins. "Friends, this is Thomas."

The amplifiers hurl his voice outward. A thousand loudspeakers drifting in the air pick up his words and they bounce across the valley, returning as jagged echoes. He hears cries, eerie shrieks; his own name ascends to him in blurry distortions. *Too-mis! Too-mis! Too-mis!*

"Nearly a full day has passed," he says, "since the Lord gave us the Sign for which we asked. For us it has been a long day of darkness, and for others it has been a day of strange light, and for all of us there has been fear. But this I say to you now: BE . . . NOT . . . AFRAID. For the Lord is good and we are the Lord's."

Now he pauses. Not only for effect; his throat is raging. He signals furiously and Kraft, scowling, hands him a flask. Thomas takes a deep gulp of the good red wine, cool, strong. Ah. He glances at the screen beside him: the video pickup relayed from the valley. What lunacy down there! Wild-eyed, sweaty madmen, half-naked and worse, jumping up and down! Crying out his name, invoking him as though he were devine. *Too-mis! Too-mis!*

"There are those who tell you now," Thomas goes on, "that the end of days is at hand, that judgment is come. They talk of apocalypses and the wrath of God. And what do I say to that? I say: BE . . . NOT . . . AFRAID. The Lord God is a God of mercy. We asked Him for a Sign, and a Sign was given. Should we not therefore rejoice? Now we may be certain of His presence and His guidance. Ignore the doom-sayers. Put away your fears. We live now in God's love!"

Thomas halts again. For the first time in his memory he has no sense of being in command of his audience. Is he reaching them at all? Is he touching the right chords? Or has he begun already to lose them? Maybe it was a mistake to let Kraft nag him into speaking so soon. He thought he was ready; maybe not. Now he sees Kraft staring at him, aghast, pantomiming the gestures of speech, silently telling him, *Get with it, you've got to keep talking now!* Thomas' self-assurance momentarily wavers, and terror floods his soul, for he knows that if he falters at this point he may well be destroyed by the forces he has set loose. Teetering at the brink of an abyss, he searches frantically for his customary confidence. Where is that steely column of words that ordinarily rises unbidden from the depths of him? Another gulp of wine, fast. Good. Kraft, nervously rubbing hands together, essays a smile of encouragement. Thomas tugs at his hair. He pushes back his shoulders, thrusts out his chest. Be not afraid! He feels control returning after the frightening lapse. They are his, all those who listen. They have always been his. What are they shouting in the valley now? No longer his name, but some new cry. He strains to hear. Two words. What are they? *De-dum! De-dum! De-dum!* What? *De-dum! De-dum! De-dum, too-mis, de-dum!* What? What? "The sun," Kraft says. The sun? Yes. They want the sun. "The sun! The sun! The sun!"

"The sun," Thomas says. "Yes. This day the sun stands still, as our Sign from Him. BE NOT AFRAID! A long dawn over Jerusalem has He decreed, and a long night for us, but not so very long, and soon sped." Thomas feels the power surging at last. Kraft nods to him, and Thomas nods back and spits a stream of wine at Kraft's feet. He is aware of that consciousness of risk in which the joy of prophecy lies: I will bring forth what I see, and trust to God to make it real. That feeling of risk accepted, of triumph over doubt. Calmly he says,

"The Day of the Sign will end in a few minutes. Once more the world will turn, and moon and stars will move across the sky. So put down your torches, and go to your homes, and offer up joyful prayers of thanksgiving to Him, for this night will pass, and dawn will come at the appointed hour."

How do you know, Thomas? Why are you so sure?

He hands the microphone to Saul Kraft and calls for more wine. Around him are tense faces, rigid eyes, clamped jaws. Thomas smiles. He goes among them, slapping backs, punching shoulders, laughing, embracing, winking ribaldly, poking his fingers playfully into their ribs. Be of good cheer, ye who follow my way! Share ye not my faith in Him? He asks Kraft how he came across. Fine, Kraft says, except for that uneasy moment in the middle. Thomas slaps Kraft's back hard enough to loosen teeth. Good old Saul. My inspiration, my counselor, my beacon. Thomas pushes his flask toward Kraft's face. Kraft shakes his head. He is fastidious about drinking, about decorum in general, as fastidious as Thomas is disreputable. You disapprove of me, don't you, Saul? But you need my charisma. You need my energy and my big loud voice. Too bad, Saul, that prophets aren't as neat and housebroken as you'd like them to be. "Ten o'clock," someone says. "It's now been going on for twenty-four hours."

A woman says, "The moon! Look! Didn't the moon just start to move again?"

From Kraft: "You wouldn't be able to see it with the naked eye. Not possibly. No way."

"Ask Thomas! Ask him!"

One of the technicians cries, "I can feel it! The Earth is turning!"

"Look, the stars!"

"Thomas! Thomas!"

They rush to him. Thomas, benign, serene, stretching forth his huge hands to reassure them, tells them that he has felt it too. Yes. There is motion in the universe again. Perhaps the turnings of the heavenly bodies are too subtle to be detected in a single glance, perhaps an hour or more will be needed for verification, and yet he knows, he is sure, he is absolutely sure. The Lord has withdrawn His Sign. The Earth turns. "Let us sleep now," Thomas says joyfully, "and greet the dawn in happiness."

Two

The Dance of the Apocalyptists

In late afternoon every day a band of Apocalyptists gathers by the stinking shore of Lake Erie to dance the sunset in. Their faces are painted with grotesque nightmare stripes; their expressions are wild; they fling themselves about in jerky, lurching steps, awkward and convulsive, the classic death-dance. Two immense golden loudspeakers, mounted like idols atop metal spikes rammed into the soggy soil, bellow abstract rhythms at them from either side. The leader of the group stands thigh-deep in the fouled waters, chanting, beckoning, directing them with short blurted cries: "People . . . holy people . . . chosen people . . . blessed people . . . persecuted people . . . Dance! . . . Dance! . . . The end . . . is near . . ." And they dance. Fingers shooting electrically into the air, elbows ramming empty space, knees rising high, they scramble toward the lake, withdraw, advance, withdraw, advance, three steps forward and two steps back, a will-you-won't-you-will-you-won't-you approach to salvation.

They have been doing this seven times a week since the beginning of the year, this fateful, terminal year, but only in the week since the Day of the Sign have they drawn much of an audience. At the outset, in frozen January, no one would bother to come to watch a dozen madmen capering on the windswept ice. Then the cult began getting sporadic television coverage, and that brought a few curiosity seekers. On the milder nights of April perhaps thirty dancers and twenty onlookers could be found at the lake. But now it is June, apocalyptic June, when the Lord in all His Majesty has revealed Himself, and the nightly dances are an event that brings thousands out of Cleveland's suburbs. Police lines hold the mob at a safe distance from the performers. A closed-circuit video loop relays the action to those on the outskirts of the crowd, too far away for a direct view. Network copters hover, cameras ready in case something unusual happens—the death of a dancer, the bursting loose of the mob, mass conversions, another miracle, anything. The air is cool tonight. The sun, delicately blurred and purpled by the smoky haze that perpetually thickens this region's sky, drops toward the breast of the lake. The dancers move in frenzied patterns, those in the front rank approaching the water, dipping their toes, retreating. Their leader, slapping the lake, throwing up fountaining spumes, continues to exhort them in a high, strained voice.

"People . . . holy people . . . chosen people . . ."

"Hallelujah! Hallelujah!"

"Come and be sealed! Blessed people . . . persecuted people . . . Come! Be! Sealed! Unto! The! Lord!"

"Hallelujah!"

The spectators shift uneasily. Some nudge and snigger. Some, staring fixedly, lock their arms and glower. Some move their lips in silent prayer or silent curses. Some look tempted to lurch forward and join the dance. Some will. Each night, there are a few who go forward.

Each night, also, there are some who attempt to burst the police lines and attack the dancers. In June alone seven spectators have suffered heart seizures at the nightly festival: five fatalities.

"Servants of God!" cries the man in the water.

"Hallelujah!" reply the dancers.

"The year is speeding! The time is coming!"

"Hallelujah!"

"The trumpet shall sound! And we shall be saved!"

"Yes! Yes! Yes! Yes!"

Oh, the fervor of the dance! The wildness of the faces! The painted stripes swirl and run as sweat invades the thick greasy pigments. One could strew hot coals on the shore, now, and the dancers would advance all the same, oblivious, blissful. The choreography of their faith absorbs them wholly at this moment and they admit of no distractions. There is so little time left, after all, and such a great output of holy exertion is required of them before the end! June is almost half-spent. The year itself is almost half-spent. January approaches: the dawning of the new millennium, the day of the final trump, the moment of apocalypse. January 1, 2000: six and a half months away. And already He has given the Sign that the end of days is at hand. They dance. Through ecstatic movement comes salvation.

"Fear God, and give glory to Him; for the hour of His Judgment is come!"

"Hallelujah! Amen!"

"And worship Him that made heaven, and earth, and the sea, and the fountains of waters!"

"Hallelujah! Amen!"

They dance. The music grows more intense: prickly blurts of harsh tone flickering through the air. Spectators begin to clap hands and sway. Here comes the first convert of the night, now, a woman, middle-aged, plump, beseeching her way through the police cordon. An electronic device checks her for concealed weapons and explosive devices; she is found to be harmless; she passes the line and runs, stumbling, to join the dance.

"For the great day of His wrath is come; and who shall be able to stand?"

"Amen!"

"Servants of God! Be sealed unto Him, and be saved!"

"Sealed . . . sealed . . . We shall be sealed . . . We shall be saved . . ."

"And I saw four angels standing on the four corners of the Earth, holding the four winds of the Earth, that the wind should not blow on the Earth, nor on the sea, nor on any tree," roars the man in the water. "And I saw another angel ascending from the east, having the seal of the living God: and he cried with a loud voice to the four angels, to whom it was given to hurt the Earth and the sea, saying, Hurt not the Earth, neither the sea, nor the trees, till we have sealed the servants of our God in their foreheads."

"Sealed! Hallelujah! Amen!"

"And I heard the number of them which were sealed: and there were sealed an hundred and forty and four thousand of all the tribes of the children of Israel."

"Sealed! Sealed!"

"Come to me and be sealed! Dance and be sealed!"

The sun drops into the lake. The purple stain of sunset spreads across the horizon. The dancers shriek ecstatically and rush toward the water. They splash one another; they offer frantic baptisms in the murky lake; they drink, they spew forth what they have drunk, they drink again. Surrounding their leader. Seeking his blessing. An angry thick mutter from the onlookers. They are disgusted by this hectic show of faith. A menagerie, they say. A circus sideshow. These freaks. These godly freaks. Whom we have come to watch, so that we may despise them.

And if they are right? And if the world *does* end next January 1, and we go to hellfire, while *they* are saved? Impossible. Preposterous. Absurd. But yet, who's to say? Only last week the Earth stood still a whole day. We live under His hand now. We always have, but now we have no liberty to doubt it. We can no longer deny that He's up there, watching us, listening to us, thinking about us. And if the end is really coming, as the crazy dancers think, what should I do to prepare for it? Should I join the dance? God help me. God help us all. Now the darkness falls. Look at the lunatics wallowing in the lake.

"Hallelujah! Amen!"

Three

The Sleep of Reason Produces Monsters

When I was about seven years old, which is to say somewhere in the late 1960's, I was playing out in front of the house on a Sunday morning, perhaps stalking some ladybirds for my insect collection, when three freckle-faced Irish kids who lived on the next block came wandering by. They were on their way home from church. The youngest one was my age, and the other two must have been eight or nine. To me they were Big Boys: ragged, strong, swaggering, alien. My father was a college professor and theirs was probably a bus conductor or a coal miner, and so they were as strange to me as a trio of tourists from Patagonia would have been. They stopped and watched me for a minute, and then the biggest one called me out into the street, and he asked me how it was that they never saw me in church on Sundays.

The simplest and most tactful thing for me to tell them would have been that I didn't happen to be Roman Catholic. That was true. I think that all they wanted to find out was what church I *did* go to, since I obviously didn't go to theirs. Was I Jewish, Moslem, Presbyterian, Baptist, what? But I was a smug little snot then, and instead of handling the situation diplomatically, I cheerfully told them that I didn't go to church because I didn't believe in God.

They looked at me as though I had just blown my nose on the American flag.

"Say that again?" the biggest one demanded.

"I don't believe in God," I said. "Religion's just a big fake. My father says so, and I think he's right."

They frowned and backed off a few paces and conferred in low, earnest voices, with many glances in my direction. Evidently I was their first atheist. I assumed we would now have a debate on the existence of the Deity: they would explain to me the motives that led them to use up so many valuable hours on their knees inside the Church of Our Lady of the Sorrows, and then I would try to show them how silly it was to worry so much about an invisible old man in the sky. But a theological disputation wasn't their style. They came out of their huddle and strolled toward me, and I suddenly detected menace in their eyes, and just as the two smaller ones lunged at me I slipped past them and started to run. They had longer legs, but I was more agile; besides, I was on my home block and knew the turf better. I sprinted halfway down the street, darted into an alley, slipped through the open place in the back of the Allertons' garage, doubled back up the street via the rear lane, and made it safely into our house by way of the kitchen door. For the next couple of days I stayed close to home after school and kept a wary watch, but the pious Irish lads never came around again to punish the blasphemer. After that I learned to be more careful about expressing my opinions on religious matters.

But I never became a believer. I had a natural predisposition toward skepticism. *If you can't measure it, it isn't there.* That included not only Old Whiskers and His Only Begotten Son, but all the other mystic baggage that people liked to carry around in those tense credulous years: the flying saucers, Zen Buddhism, the Atlantis cult, Hare Krishna, macrobiotics, telepathy and other species of extrasensory perception, theosophy, entropy-worship, astrology, and such. I was willing to accept neutrinos, quasars, the theory of continental drift, and the various species of quarks, because I respected the evidence for their existence; I couldn't buy the other stuff, the irrational stuff, the assorted opiates of the masses. When the Moon is in the seventh house, etc., etc.—sorry, no. I clung to the path of reason as I made my uneasy journey toward maturity, and hardheaded littly Billy Gifford, smartypants bug collector, remained unchurched as he ripened into Professor William F. Gifford, Ph.D., of the Department of Physics, Harvard. I wasn't *hostile* to organized religion, I just ignored it, as I might ignore a newspaper account of a jai-alai tournament in Afghanistan.

I envied the faithful their faith, oh, yes. When the dark times got darker, how sweet it must have been to be able to rush to Our Lady of the Sorrows for comfort! *They* could pray, *they* had the illusion that a divine plan governed this best of all possible worlds, while I was left in bleak, stormy limbo, dismally aware that the universe makes no sense and that the only universal truth there is, is that Entropy Eventually Wins.

There were times when I wanted genuinely to be able to pray, when I was weary of operating solely on my own existential capital, when I wanted to grovel and cry out, *Okay, Lord, I give up, You take it from here.* I had favors to ask of Him. God, let my little girl's fever go down. Let my plane not crash. Let them not shoot *this* President too. Let the races learn how to live in peace before the blacks get around to burning down my street. Let the peace-loving enlightened students not bomb the computer center this semester. Let the next kindergarten drug scandal not erupt in my boy's school. Let the lion lie down with the lamb. As we zoomed along on the Chaos Express, I was sometimes tempted toward godliness the way the godly are tempted toward sin. But my love of divine reason left me no way to opt for the irrational. Call it stiffneckedness, call it rampant egomania: no matter how bad things got, Bill Gifford wasn't going to submit to the tyranny of a hobgoblin. Even a benevolent one. Even if I had favors to ask of Him. So much to ask; so little faith. Intellectual honesty *über alles,* Gifford! While every year things were a little worse than the last.

When I was growing up, in the 1970's, it was fashionable for educated and serious-minded people to get together and tell each other that western civilization was collapsing. The Germans had a word for it, *Schadenfreude,* the pleasure one gets from talking about catastrophes. And the 1970's were shadowed by catastrophes, real or expected: the pollution escalation, the population explosion, Vietnam and all the little Vietnams, the supersonic transport, black separatism, white backlash, student unrest, extremist women's lib, the neofascism of the New Left, the neonihilism of the New Right, a hundred other varieties of dynamic irrationality going full blast, yes, ample fuel for the *Schadenfreude* syndrome. Yes, my parents and their civilized friends said solemnly, sadly, gleefully, it's all blowing up, it's all going smash, it's all whooshing down the drain. Through the fumes of the Saturday-night pot came the inevitable portentous quotes from Yeats: *Things fall apart; the center cannot hold; mere anarchy is loosed upon the world.* Well, what shall we do about it? Perhaps it's really beyond our control now. Brethren, shall we pray? Lift up your voices

unto Him! But I can't. I'd feel like a damned fool.
Forgive me, God, but I must deny You! *The best lack
all conviction, while the worst are full of passionate intensity.*

And of course everything got much more awful
than the doomsayers of the 1970's really expected. Even
those who most dearly relished enumerating the calami-
ties to come still thought, beneath their grim joy, that
somehow reason ultimately would triumph. The most
gloomy Jeremiah entertained secret hopes that the noble
ecological resolutions would eventually be translated
into meaningful environmental action, that the crazy
birth spiral would be checked in time, that the strident
rhetoric of the innumerable protest groups would be
tempered and modulated as time brought them the beginning of a fulfillment of their revolutionary goals—but
no. Came the 1980's, the decade of my young manhood,
and all the hysteria jumped to the next-highest energy
level. That was when we began having the Gas Mask
Days. The programmed electrical shutdowns. The ele-
gantly orchestrated international chaos of the Third
World People's Prosperity Group. The airport riots. The
black rains. The Computer Purge. The Brazilian Pacification Program. The Claude Harkins Book List with its
accompanying library-burnings. The Ecological Police
Action. The Genetic Purity League and its even more
frightening black counterpart. The Children's Crusade
for Sanity. The Nine Weeks' War. The Night of the
Lasers. The center had long ago ceased to hold; now we
were strapped to a runaway wheel. Amidst the furies I
studied, married, brought forth young, built a career,
fought off daily terror, and like everyone else, waited for
the inevitable final calamity.

Who could doubt that it would come? Not you, not
I. And not the strange wild-eyed folk who emerged

among us like dark growths pushing out of rotting logs,
the Apocalyptists, who raised *Schadenfreude* to the sacramental level and organized an ecstatic religion of
doom. The end of the world, they told us, was scheduled
for January 1, A.D. 2000, and upon that date, 144,000
elite souls, who had "sealed" themselves unto God by
devotion and good works, would be saved; the rest of us
poor sinners would be hauled before the Judge. I could
see their point. Although I rejected their talk of the Second Coming, having long ago rejected the First, and although I shared neither their confidence in the exact
date of the apocalypse nor their notions of how the survivors would be chosen, I agreed with them that the end
was close at hand. The fact that for a quarter of a century we had been milking giddy cocktail-party chatter
out of the impending collapse of western civilization
didn't of itself guarantee that western civilization wasn't
going to collapse; *some* of the things people like to say
at cocktail parties can hit the target. As a physicist with
a decent understanding of the entropic process, I found
all the signs of advanced societal decay easy to identify:
for a century we had been increasing the complexity of
society's functions so that an ever-higher level of organization was required in order to make things run, and for
much of that time we had simultaneously been trending
toward total universal democracy, toward a world consisting of several billion self-governing republics with a
maximum of three citizens each. Any closed system
which experiences simultaneous sharp increases in mechanical complexity and in entropic diffusion is going to
go to pieces long before the maximum distribution of energy is reached. The pattern of consents and contracts
on which civilization is based is destroyed; every social
interaction, from parking your car to settling an international boundary dispute, becomes a problem that can be

handled only by means of force, since all "civilized" techniques of reconciling disagreement have been suspended as irrelevant; when the delivery of mail is a matter of private negotiation between the citizen and his postman, what hope is there for the rule of reason? Somewhere, somehow, we had passed a point of no return—in 1984, 1972, maybe even that ghastly day in November of 1963—and nothing now could save us from plunging over the brink.

Nothing?

Out of Nevada came Thomas, shaggy Thomas, Thomas the Proclaimer, rising above the slot machines and the roulette wheels to cry, If ye have faith, ye shall be saved! An anti-Apocalyptist prophet, no less, whose message was that civilization still might be preserved, that it was not yet too late. The voice of hope, the enemy of entropy, the new Apostle of Peace. Though to people like me he looked just as wild-eyed and hairy and dangerous and terrifyingly psychotic as the worshipers of the holocaust, for he, like the Apocalyptists, dealt in forces operating outside the realm of sanity. By rights he should have come out of the backwoods of Arkansas or the crazier corners of California, but he didn't, he was a desert rat, a Nevadan, a sand-eating latter-day John the Baptist. A true prophet for our times, too, seedy, disreputable, a wine-swiller, a cynic. Capable of beginning a global telecast sermon with a belch. An ex-soldier who had happily napalmed whole provinces during the Brazilian Pacification Program. A part-time dealer in bootlegged hallucinogens. An expert at pocket-picking and computer-jamming. He had gone into the evangelism business because he thought he could make an easy buck that way, peddling the Gospels and appropriating the collection box, but a funny thing had happened to him, he claimed: he had seen the Lord, he had discovered the error of his ways, he had become inflamed with righteousness. Hiding not his grimy past, he now offered himself as a walking personification of redemption: *Look ye, if I can be saved from sin, there's hope for everyone!* The media picked him up. That magnificent voice of his, that great mop of hair, those eyes, that hypnotic self-confidence—perfect. He walked from California to Florida to proclaim the coming millennium. And gathered followers, thousands, millions, all those who weren't yet ready to let Armageddon begin, and he made them pray and pray and pray, he held revival meetings that were beamed to Karachi and Katmandu and Addis Ababa and Shanghai, he preached no particular theology and no particular scripture, but only a smooth ecumenical theism that practically anybody could swallow, whether he be Confucianist or Moslem or Hindu. Listen, Thomas said, there *is* a God, some kind of all-powerful being out there whose divine plan guides the universe, and He watches over us, and don't you believe otherwise! And He is good and will not let us come to harm if we hew to His path. And He has tested us with all these troubles, in order to measure the depth of our faith in Him. So let's show Him, brethren! Let's all pray together and send up a great shout unto Him! For He would certainly give a Sign, and the unbelievers would at last be converted, and the epoch of purity would commence. People said, Why not give it a try? We've got a lot to gain and nothing to lose. A vulgar version of the old Pascal wager: if He's really there, He may help us, and if He's not, we've only wasted a little time. So the hour of beseeching was set.

In faculty circles we had a good deal of fun with the whole idea, we brittle worldly rational types, but sometimes there was a nervous edge to our jokes and a forced heartiness to our laughter, as if some of us suspected that

Pascal might have been offering pretty good odds, or that Thomas might just have hit on something. Naturally I was among the skeptics, though as usual I kept my doubts to myself. (The lesson learned so long ago, the narrow escape from the Irish lads.) I hadn't really paid much attention to Thomas and his message, any more than I did to football scores or children's video programs: not my sphere, not my concern. But as the day of prayer drew near, the old temptation beset me. *Give in at last, Gifford. Bow your head and offer homage. Even if He's the myth you've always known He is, do it. Do it!* I argued with myself. I told myself not to be an idiot, not to yield to the age-old claims of superstition. I reminded myself of the holy wars, the Inquisition, the lascivious Renaissance popes, all the crimes of the pious. *So what, Gifford? Can't you be an ordinary humble God-fearing human being for once in your life. Down on your knees beside your brethren? Read your Pascal. Suppose He exists and is listening, and suppose your refusal is the one that tips the scales against mankind? We're not asking so very much.* Still I fought the sly inner voice. To believe is absurd, I cried. I must not let despair stampede me into the renunciation of reason, even in this apocalyptic moment. Thomas is a cunning ruffian and his followers are hysterical grubby fools. *And you're an arrogant elitist, Gifford. Who may live long enough to repent his arrogance.* It was psychological warfare, Gifford vs. Gifford, reason vs. faith.

In the end reason lost. I was jittery, off balance, demoralized. The most astonishing people were coming out in support of Thomas the Proclaimer, and I felt increasingly isolated, a man of ice, heart of stone, the village atheist scowling at Christmas wreaths. Up until the final moment I wasn't sure what I was going to do, but then the hour struck and I found myself in my study, alone, door locked, safely apart from wife and children —who had already, all of them, somewhat defiantly announced their intentions of participating—and there I was on my knees, feeling foolish, feeling preposterous, my cheeks blazing, my lips moving, saying the words. *Saying the words.* Around the world the billions of believers prayed, and I also. I too prayed, embarrassed by my weakness, and the pain of my shame was a stone in my throat.

And the Lord heard us, and He gave a Sign. And for a day and a night (less 1×12^{-4} sidereal day) the Earth moved not around the sun, neither did it rotate. And the laws of momentum were confounded, as was I. Then Earth again took up its appointed course, as though nothing out of the ordinary had occurred. Imagine my chagrin. I wish I knew where to find those Irish boys. I have some apologies to make.

Four

Thomas Preaches in the Marketplace

I hear what you're saying. You tell me I'm a prophet. You tell me I'm a saint. Some of you even tell me I'm the Son of God come again. You tell me I made the sun stand still over Jerusalem. Well, no, I didn't do that, the Lord Almighty did that, the Lord of Hosts. Through His divine Will, in response to your prayers. And I'm only the vehicle through which your prayers were channeled. I'm not any kind of saint, folks. I'm not the Son of God reborn, or any of the other crazy things you've been saying I am. I'm only Thomas.

Who am I?

I'm just a voice. A spokesman. A tool through which His will was made manifest. I'm not giving you the old humility act, friends, I'm trying to make you see the truth about me.

Who am I?

I'll tell you who I was, though you know it already. I was a bandit, I was a man of evil, I was a defiler of the law. A killer, a liar, a drunkard, a cheat! I did what I damned pleased. I was a law unto myself. If I ever got caught, you bet I wouldn't have whined for mercy. I'd have spit in the judge's face and taken my punishment with my eyes open. Only I never got caught, because my luck was running good and because this is a time when a really bad man can flourish, when the wicked are raised high and the virtuous are ground into the mud. Outside the law, that was me! Thomas the criminal! Thomas the brigand, thumbing his nose! Doing bad was my religion, all the time—when I was down there in Brazil with those flamethrowers, or when I was free-lancing your pockets in our cities, or when I was ringing up funny numbers on the big computers. I belonged to Satan if ever a man did, that's the truth, and then what happened? The Lord came along to Satan and said to him, Satan, give me Thomas, I have need of him. And Satan handed me over to Him, because Satan is God's servant too.

And the Lord took me and shook me and knocked me around and said, Thomas, you're nothing but trash!

And I said, I know that, Lord, but who was it who made me that way?

And the Lord laughed and said, You've got guts, Thomas, talking back to me like that. I like a man with guts. But you're wrong, fellow. I made you with the potential to be a saint or a sinner, and you chose to be a sinner, yes, your own free will! You think I'd bother to create people to be wicked? I'm not interested in creating puppets, Thomas, I set out to make me a race of *human beings*. I gave you your options and you opted for evil, eh, Thomas? Isn't that the truth?

And I said, Well, Lord, maybe it is; I don't know.

And the Lord God grew annoyed with me and took me again and shook me again and knocked me around some more, and when I picked myself up I had a puffed lip and a bloody nose, and He asked me how I would do things if I could live my life over again from the start. And I looked Him right in the eye and said,

Well, Lord, I'd say that being evil paid off pretty well
for me. I lived a right nice life and I had all my hap-
pies and I never spent a day behind bars, oh, no. So tell
me, Lord, since I got away with everything the first
time, why shouldn't I opt to be a sinner again?

And he said, Because you've done that already,
and now it's time for you to do something else.

I said, What's that, Lord?

He said, I want you to do something important for
me, Thomas. There's a world out there full of people
who've lost all faith, people without hope, people
who've made up their minds it's no use trying any more,
the world's going to end. I want to reach those people
somehow, Thomas, and tell them that they're wrong.
And show them that they can shape their own destiny,
that if they have faith in themselves and in me they can
build a good world.

I said, That's easy, Lord. Why don't You just appear in the sky and say that to them, like You just did to
me?

He laughed again and said, Oh, no, Thomas, that's
much too easy. I told you, I don't run a puppet show.
They've got to *want* to lift themselves up out of despair.
They've got to take the first step by themselves. You
follow me, Thomas?

Yes, Lord, but where do I come in?

And He said, You go to them, Thomas, and you
tell them all about your wasted, useless, defiant life,
and then tell them how the Lord gave you a chance to
do something worthwhile for a change, and how you
rose up above your evil self and accepted the opportunity. And then tell them to gather and pray and re-
store their faith, and ask for a Sign from on high.
Thomas, if they listen to you, if they pray and it's sincere prayer, I promise you I *will* give them a Sign, I

will reveal myself to them, and all doubt will drop like scales from their eyes. Will you do that thing for me, Thomas?

Friends, I listened to the Lord, and I discovered myself shaking and quivering and bursting into sweat, and in a moment, in the twinkling of an eye, I wasn't the old filthy Thomas any more, I was somebody new and clean, I was a man with a high purpose, a man with a belief in something bigger and better than his own greedy desires. And I went down among you, changed as I was, and I told my tale, and all of you know the rest of the story, how we came freely together and offered up our hearts to Him, and how He vouchsafed us a miracle these two and a half weeks past, and gave us a Sign that He still watches over us.

But what do I see now, in these latter days after the giving of the Sign? What do I see?

Where is that new world of faith? Where is that new dream of hope? Where is mankind shoulder to shoulder, praising Him and working together to reach the light?

What do I see? I see this rotting planet turning black inside and splitting open at the core. I see the cancer of doubt. I see the virus of confusion. I see His Sign misinterpreted on every hand, and its beauty trampled on and destroyed.

I still see painted fools dancing and beating on drums and screaming that the world is going to be destroyed at the end of this year of nineteen hundred and ninety-nine. What madness is this? Has God not spoken? Has He not told us joyful news? God is with us! God is good! Why do these Apocalyptists not yet accept the truth of His Sign?

Even worse! Each day new madnesses take form! What are these cults sprouting up among us? Who are these people who demand of God that He return and spell out His intentions, as though the Sign wasn't enough for them? And who are these cowardly blasphemers who say we must lie down in fear and weep piteous tears, because we have invoked not God but Satan, and destruction is our lot? Who are these men of empty souls who bleat and mumble and snivel in our midst? And look at your lofty churchmen, in their priestly robes and glittering tiaras, trying to explain away the Sign as some accident of nature! What talk is this from God's own ministers? And behold the formerly godless ones, screeching like frightened monkeys now that their godlessness has been ripped from them! What do I see? I see madness and terror on all sides, where I should see only joy abounding!

I beg you, friends, have care, take counsel with your souls. I beg you, think clearly now if you ever have thought at all. Choose a wise path, friends, or you will throw away all the glory of the Day of the Sign and lay waste to our great achievement. Give no comfort to the forces of darkness. Keep away from these peddlers of lunatic creeds. Strive to recapture the wonder of that moment when all mankind spoke with a single voice. I beg you—how can you have doubt of Him now?—I beg you—faith—the triumph of faith—let us not allow—let us—not allow—not—allow—

(Jesus, my throat! All this shouting, it's like swallowing fire. Give me that bottle, will you? Come on, give it here! The wine. The wine. Now. Ah. Oh, that's better! Much better, oh, yes. No, wait, give it back—good, good—stop looking at me like that, Saul. Ah. *Ah.*)

And so I beseech you today, brothers and sisters in the Lord—brothers and sisters (what was I saying, Saul? what did I start to say?)—I call upon you to rededicate yourselves—to pledge yourselves to—to (is that it? I can't remember)—to a new Crusade of Faith, that's what we need, a purging of all our doubts and all our hesitations and all our (oh, Jesus, Saul, I'm lost, I don't remember where the hell I'm supposed to be. Let the music start playing. Quick. That's it. Good and louder. Louder.) Folks, let's all sing! Raise your voices joyously unto Him!

> *I shall praise the Lord my God,*
> *Fountain of all power . . .*

That's the way! Sing! Everybody sing!

Five

Ceremonies
of Innocence

Throughout the world the quest for an appropriate response to the event of June 6 continues. No satisfactory interpretation of that day's happenings has yet been established, though many have been proposed. Meanwhile passions run high; tempers easily give way; a surprising degree of violence has entered the situation. Clearly the temporary slowing of the earth's axial rotation must have imposed exceptional emotional stress on the entire global population, creating severe strains that have persisted and even intensified in the succeeding weeks. Instances of seemingly motiveless crimes, particularly arson and vandalism, have greatly increased. Government authorities in Brazil, India, the United Arab Republic, and Italy have suggested that clandestine revolutionary or counterrevolutionary groups are behind much of this activity, taking advantage of the widespread mood of uncertainty to stir discontent. No evidence of this has thus far been made public. Much hostility has been directed toward the organized religions, a phenomenon for which there is as yet no generally accepted explanation, although several sociologists have asserted that this pattern of violent anticlerical behavior is a reac-

tion to the failure of most established religious bodies
as of this time to provide official interpretations of the
so-called miracle of June 6. Reports of the destruction
by mob action of houses of worship of various faiths,
with accompanying injuries or fatalities suffered by ecclesiastical personnel, have come from Mexico, Den-
mark, Burma, Puerto Rico, Portugal, Hungary, Ethi-
opia, the Philippines, and, in the United States, Alabama,
Colorado, and New York. Statements are promised
shortly by leaders of most major faiths. Meanwhile a
tendency has developed in certain ecclesiastical quarters
toward supporting a mechanistic or rationalistic causa-
tion for the June 6 event; thus on Tuesday the Archbishop of York, stressing that he was speaking as a private citizen and not as a prelate of the Church of
England, declared that we should not rule out entirely
the possibility of a manipulation of the Earth's movements by superior beings native to another planet, in-
tent on spreading confusion preparatory to conquest.
Modern theologians, the Archbishop said, see no in-
herent impossibility in the doctrine of a separate act of
creation that brought forth an intelligent species on
some extraterrestrial or extragalactic planet, nor is it
inconceivable, he went on, that it might be the Lord's
ultimate purpose to cause a purging of sinful mankind
at the hands of that other species. Thus the slowing of
the Earth's rotation may have been an attempt by these
enemies from space to capitalize on the emotions generated by the recent campaign of the so-called prophet
Thomas the Proclaimer. A spokesman for the Coptic
Patriarch of Alexandria, commenting favorably two
days later on the Archbishop's theory, added that in the
private view of the Patriarch it seems less implausible
that such an alien species should exist than that a divine
miracle of the June 6 sort could be invoked by popular

demand. A number of other religious leaders, similarly speaking unofficially, have cautioned against too rapid acceptance of the divine origin of the June 6 event, without as yet going so far as to embrace the Archbishop of York's suggestion. On Friday Dr. Nathan F. Scharf, President of the Central Conference of American Rabbis, urgently appealed to American and Israeli scientists to produce a computer-generated mathematical schema capable of demonstrating how a unique but natural conjunction of astronomical forces might have resulted in the June 6 event. The only reply to this appeal thus far has come from Ssu-ma Hsiang-ju, Minister of Science of the People's Republic of China, who has revealed that a task force of several hundred Chinese astronomers is already at work on such a project. But his Soviet counterpart, Academician N. V. Posilippov, has on the contrary called for a revision of Marxist-Leninist astronomical theory to take into account what he terms "the possibility of intervention by as yet undefined forces, perhaps of supernatural aspect, in the motions of the heavenly bodies." We may conclude, therefore, that the situation remains in flux. Observers agree that the chief beneficiaries of the June 6 event at this point have been the various recently founded apocalyptic sects, who now regard the so-called Day of the Sign as an indication of the imminent destruction of life on Earth. Undoubtedly much of the current violence and the other irrational behavior can be traced to the increased activity of such groups. A related manifestation is the dramatic expansion in recent weeks of older millenarian sects, notably the Pentecostal churches. The Protestant world in general has experienced a rebirth of the Pentecostal-inspired phenomenon known as glossolalia, or "speaking in tongues," a technique for penetrating to revelatory or prophetic levels by means of unreined ecstatic outbursts *illalum gha ghollim ve illalum ghollim ghaznim kroo! Aiha! Kroo illalum nildaz sitamon ghaznim* of seemingly random syllables in no language known to the speaker; the value of this practice has *mehigioo camaleelee honistar zam* been a matter of controversy in religious circles for many centuries.

Six

The Woman Who
Is Sore at Heart
Reproaches Thomas

I knew he was in our county and I had to get to see him
because he was the one who made all this trouble for
me. So I went to his headquarters, the place where the
broadcasts were being made that week, and I saw him
standing in the middle of a group of his followers. A
very handsome man, really, somewhat too dirty and
wild-looking for my tastes, but you give him a shave
and a haircut and he'd be quite attractive in my esti-
mation. Big and strong he is, and when you see him you
want to throw yourself into his arms, though of course
I was in no frame of mind to do any such thing just
then and in any case I'm not that sort of woman. I went
right toward him. There was a tremendous crowd in the
street, but I'm not discouraged easily, my husband likes
to call me his "little bulldog" sometimes, and I just
bulled my way through that mob, a little kicking and
some elbowing and I think I bit someone's arm once
and I got through. There was Thomas and next to him
that skinny little man who's always with him, that Saul
Kraft, who I guess is his press agent or something. As

I got close, three of his bodyguards looked at me and
then at each other, probably saying oh-oh, here comes
another crank dame, and they started to surround me
and move me away, and Thomas wasn't even looking at
me, and I began to yell, saying I had to talk to Thomas,
I had something important to say. And then this Saul
Kraft told them to let go of me and bring me forward.
They checked me out for concealed weapons and then
Thomas asked me what I wanted.

I felt nervous before him. Such a famous man.
But I planted my feet flat on the ground and stuck my
jaw up the way Dad taught me, and I said, "You did
all this. You've wrecked me, Thomas. You've got me
so I don't know if I'm standing on my head or right side
up."

He gave me a funny sideways smile. "I did?"

"Look," I said, "I'll tell you how it was. I went to
Mass every week, my whole family, Church of the Re-
deemer on Wilson Avenue. We put money in the plate,
we did everything the fathers told us to do, we tried to
live good Christian lives, right? Not that we really
thought much about God. Whether He was actually up
there listening to me saying my paternoster. I figured
He was too busy to worry much about me, and I
couldn't be too concerned about Him, because He sur-
passes my understanding, you follow? Instead I prayed
to the fathers. To me Father McDermott was like God
Himself, in a way, not meaning any disrespect. What
I'm trying to say is that the average ordinary person,
they don't have a very close relationship with God, you
follow? With the church, yes, with the fathers, but not
with God. Okay. Now you come along and say the
world is in a mess, so let's pray to God to show Himself
like in the olden times. I ask Father McDermott about
it and he says it's all right, it's permitted even though it

isn't an idea that came from Rome, on such-and-such day we'll have this world moment of prayer. So I pray, and the sun stands still. June 6, you made the sun stand still."

"Not me. *Him*." Thomas was smiling again. And looking at me like he could read everything in my soul.

I said, "You know what I mean. It's a miracle, anyway. The biggest miracle since, I don't know, since the Resurrection. The next day we need help, guidance, right? My husband and I, we go to church. *The church is closed*. Locked tight. We go around back and try to find the fathers. Nobody there but a housekeeper and she's scared. Won't open up. Why is the church shut? They're afraid of rioters, she says. Where's Father McDermott? He's gone to the Archdiocese for a conference. So have all the other fathers. Go away, she says. Nobody's here. You follow me, Thomas? Biggest miracle since the Resurrection, *and they close the church the next day*."

Thomas said, "They got nervous, I guess."

"Nervous? Sure they were nervous. That's my whole point. Where were the fathers when we needed them? Conferring at the Archdiocese. The Cardinal was holding a special meeting about the crisis. *The crisis*, Thomas! God Himself works a miracle, and to the church it's a crisis! What am I supposed to do? Where does it leave me? I need the church, the church has always been telling me that, and all of a sudden the church locks its doors and says to me, Go figure it out by yourself, lady, we won't have a bulletin for a couple of days. The church was scared! I think they were afraid the Lord was going to come in and say we don't need priests any more, we don't need churches, all this organized-religion stuff hasn't worked out so well anyway, so let's forget it and move right into the Millennium."

"Anything big and strange always upsets the people in power," Thomas said, shrugging. "But the church opened again, didn't it?"

"Sure, four days later. Business as usual, except we aren't supposed to ask any questions about June 6 yet. Because they don't have The Word from Rome yet, the interpretation, the official policy." I had to laugh. "Three weeks, almost, since it happened, and the College of Cardinals is still in special consistory, trying to decide what position the church ought to take. Isn't that crazy, Thomas? If the Pope can't recognize a miracle when he sees one, what good is the whole church?"

"All right," Thomas said, "but why blame me?"

"Because you took my church away from me. I can't trust those people any more. I don't know what to believe. We've got God right here beside us, and the church isn't giving any leadership. What do we do now? How do we handle this thing?"

"Have faith, my child," he said, "and pray for salvation, and remain steadfast in your righteousness." He said a lot of other stuff like that too, rattling it off like he was a computer programmed to deliver blessings. I could tell he wasn't sincere. He wasn't trying to answer me, just to calm me down and get rid of me.

"No," I said, breaking in on him. "That stuff isn't good enough. *Have faith. Pray a lot.* I've been doing that all my life. Okay, we prayed and we got God to show Himself. What now? What's your program, Thomas? Tell me that. What do you want us to do? You took our church away—what will you give us to replace it?"

I could tell he didn't have any answers.

His face turned red and he tugged on the ends of his hair and looked at Saul Kraft in a sour way, almost like he was saying I-told-you-so with his eyes. Then he looked back at me and I saw either sorrow or fear in his face, I don't know which, and I realized right then that this Thomas is just a human being like you and me, a scared human being, who doesn't really understand what's happening and doesn't know how to go on from this point. He tried to fake it. He told me again to pray, never underestimate the power of prayer, et cetera, et cetera, but his heart wasn't in his words. He was stuck. *What's your program, Thomas?* He doesn't have any. He hasn't thought things through past the point of getting the Sign from God. He can't help us now. There's your Thomas for you, the Proclaimer, the prophet. He's scared. We're all scared, and he's just one of us, no different, no wiser. And last night the Apocalyptists burned the shopping center. You know, if you had asked me six months ago how I'd feel if God gave us a Sign that He was really watching over us, I'd have told you that I thought it would be the most wonderful thing that had ever happened since Jesus in the manger. But now it's happened. And I'm not so sure how wonderful it is. I walk around feeling that the ground might open up under my feet any time. I don't know what's going to happen to us all. God has come, and it ought to be beautiful, and instead it's just scary. I never imagined it would be this way. Oh, God. God I feel so lost. God I feel so empty.

Seven

An Insight of Discerners

Speaking before an audience was nothing new for me, of course. Not after all the years I've spent in classrooms, patiently instructing each season's hairy new crop of young in the mysteries of tachyon theory, anterior-charge particles, and time-reversal equations. Nor was this audience a particularly alien or frightening one: it was made up mainly of faculty people from Harvard and M.I.T., some graduate students, and a sprinkling of lawyers, psychologists, and other professional folk from Cambridge and the outskirts. All of us part of the community of scholarship, so to speak. The sort of audience that might come together to protest the latest incident of ecological rape or of preventive national liberation. But one aspect of my role this evening was unsettling to me. This was in the truest sense a religious gathering; that is, we were meeting to discuss the nature of God and to arrive at some comprehension of our proper relationship to Him. And I was the main speaker, me, old Bill Gifford, who for nearly four decades had regarded the Deity as an antiquated irrelevance. I was this flock's pastor. How strange that felt.

"But I believe that many of you are in the same

predicament," I told them. "Men and women to whom
the religious impulse has been something essentially foreign. Whose lives were complete and fulfilled although
prayer and ritual were wholly absent from them. Who
regarded the concept of a supreme being as meaningless and who looked upon the churchgoing habits of
those around them as nothing more than lower-class
superstitiousness on the one hand and middle-class pie-
tism on the other. And then came the great surprise of
June 6—forcing us to reconsider doctrines we had
scorned, forcing us to reexamine our basic philosophical constructs, forcing us to seek an acceptable explanation of a phenomenon that we had always deemed
impossible and implausible. All of you, like myself, suddenly found yourselves treading very deep metaphysical
waters."

The nucleus of this group had come together on an
ad hoc basis the week after It happened, and since then
had been meeting two or three times a week. At first
there was no formal organizational structure, no organizational name, no policy; it was merely a gathering of intelligent and sophisticated New Englanders who
felt unable to cope individually with the altered nature
of reality and who needed mutual reassurance and rein-
forcement. That was why I started going, anyway. But
within ten days we were groping toward a more positive
purpose: no longer simply to learn how to *accept* what
had befallen humanity, but to find some way of turning it to a useful purpose. I had begun articulating some
ideas along those lines in private conversation, and abruptly I was asked by several of the leaders of the
group to make my thoughts public at the next meeting.

"An astonishing event has occurred," I went on.
"A good many ingenious theories have been proposed
to account for it—as, for example, that the Earth was

brought to a halt through the workings of an extrasensory telekinetic force generated by the simultaneous concentration of the entire world population. We have also heard the astrological explanations—that the planets or the stars were lined up in a certain once-in-a-universe's-lifetime way to bring about such a result. And there have been the arguments, some of them coming from quite surprising places, in favor of the notion that the June 6 event was the doing of malevolent creatures from outer space. The telekinesis hypothesis has a certain superficial plausibility, marred only by the fact that experimenters in the past have never been able to detect even an iota of telekinetic ability in any human being or combination of human beings. Perhaps a simultaneous world-wide effort might generate forces not to be found in any unit smaller than the total human population, but such reasoning requires an undesirable multiplication of hypotheses. I believe that most of you here agree with me that the other explanations of the June 6 event beg one critical question: Why did the slowing of the Earth occur so promptly, in seemingly direct response to Thomas the Proclaimer's campaign of global prayer? Can we believe that a unique alignment of astrological forces just happened to occur the day after that hour of prayer? Can we believe that the extragalactic fiends just happened to meddle with the Earth's rotation on that particular day? The element of coincidence necessary to sustain these and other arguments is fatal to them, I think.

"What are we left with, then? Only with the explanation that the Lord Almighty, heeding mankind's entreaties, performed a miracle so that we should be confirmed in our faith in Him.

"So I conclude. So do many of you. But does it necessarily follow that mankind's sorry religious his-

tory, with all its holy wars, its absurd dogmas, its
childish rituals, its fastings and flagellations, is thereby
justified? Because you and you and you and I were
bowled over on June 6, blasted out of our skepticism
by an event that has no rational explanation, should we
therefore rush to the churches and synagogues and
mosques and enroll immediately in the orthodoxy of
our choice? I think not. I submit that our attitudes of
skepticism and rationalism were properly held, although
our aim was misplaced. In scorning the showy, trivial
trappings of organized faith, in walking past the
churches where our neighbors devoutly knelt, we erred
by turning away also from the matter that underlay their
faith: the existence of a supreme being whose divine
plan guides the universe. The spinning of prayer wheels
and the mumbling of credos seemed so inane to us that,
in our revulsion for such things, we were led to deny
all notions of a higher order, of a teleological universe,
and we embraced the concept of a wholly random cos-
mos. And then the Earth stood still for a day and a
night.

"How did it happen? We admit it was God's doing,
you and I, amazed though we are to find ourselves saying so. We have been hammered into a posture of belief
by that inexplicable event. But what do we mean by
'God'? Who is He? An old man with long white whiskers? Where is He to be found? Somewhere between the
orbits of Mars and Jupiter? Is He a supernatural being,
or merely an extraterrestrial one? Does He too acknowledge a superior authority? And so on, an infinity
of new questions. We have no valid knowledge of His
nature, though now we have certain knowledge of His
existence.

"Very well. A tremendous opportunity now exists
for us the discerning few, for us who are in the habit of

intellectual activity. All about us we see a world in frenzy. The Apocalyptists swoon with joy over the approaching catastrophe, the glossolaliacs chatter in maniac glee, the heads of entrenched churchly hierarchies are aghast at the possibility that the Millennium may really be at hand; everything is in flux, everything is new and strange. New cults spring up. Old creeds dissolve. And this is our moment. Let us step in and replace credulity and superstition with reason. An end to cults; an end to theology; an end to blind faith. Let it be our goal to relate the events of that awesome day to some principle of reason, and develop a useful, dynamic, *rational* movement of rebirth and revival—not a religion per se but rather a cluster of belief, based on the concept that a divine plan exists, that we live under the authority of a supreme or at least superior being, and that we must strive to come to some kind of rational relationship with this being.

"We've already had the moral strength to admit that our old intuitive skepticism was an error. Now let us provide an attractive alternate for those of us who still find ritualistic orthodoxy unpalatable, but who fear a total collapse into apocalyptic disarray if no steps are taken to strengthen mankind's spiritual insight. Let us create, if we can, a purely secular movement, a nonreligious religion, which offers the hope of establishing a meaningful dialogue between Us and Him. Let us make plans. Let us find powerful symbols with which we may sway the undecided and the confused. Let us march forth as crusaders in a dramatic effort to rescue humanity from unreason and desperation."

And so forth. I think it was a pretty eloquent speech, especially coming from someone who isn't in the habit of delivering orations. A transcript of it got into the local paper the next day and was reprinted all over.

My "us the discerning few" line drew a lot of attention, and spawned an instant label for our previously unnamed movement. We became known as the Discerners. Once we had a name, our status was different. We weren't simply a group of concerned citizens any longer. Now we constituted a cult—a skeptical, rational, antisuperstitious cult, true, but nevertheless a cult, a sect, the newest facet of the world's furiously proliferating latter-day craziness.

Eight

An Expectation of Awaiters

I know it hasn't been fashionable to believe in God these last twenty thirty forty years people haven't been keeping His path much but I always did even when I was a little boy I believed truly and I loved Him and I wanted to go to church all the time even in the middle of the week I'd say to Mother let's go to church I genuinely enjoyed kneeling and praying and feeling Him near me but she'd say no Davey you've got to wait till Sunday for that it's only Wednesday now. So as they say I'm no stranger to His ways and of course when they called for that day of prayer I prayed with all my heart that he might give us a Sign but even so I'm no fool I mean I don't accept everything on a silver platter I ask questions I have doubts I test things and probe a little I'm not one of your ordinary country bumpkins that takes everything on faith. In a way I suppose I could be said to belong to the discerning few although I don't want any of you to get the idea I'm a Discerner oh no I have no sympathy whatever with that atheistic bunch. Anyway we all prayed and the Sign came and my first reaction was joy I don't mind telling you I wept for joy when the sun stood still feeling that all the faith of a lifetime had been confirmed and the godless had better shiver in their boots but then a day or so later I began to think about it and I asked myself how do we know that the Sign really came from God? How can we be sure that the being we have invoked is really on our side I asked myself and of course I had no good answer to that. For all I knew we had conjured up Satan the Accursed and what we imagined was a miracle was really a trick out of the depths of hell designed to lead us all to perdition. Here are these Discerners telling us that they repent their atheism because they know now that God is real and God is with us but how naïve they are they aren't even allowing for the possibility that the Sign is a snare and a delusion I tell you we can't be sure the thing is we absolutely *can't be sure.* The Sign might have been from God or from the Devil and we don't know we won't know until we receive a second Sign which I await which I believe will be coming quite soon. And what will that second Sign tell us? I maintain that that has not yet been decided on high it may be a Sign announcing our utter damnation or it may be a Sign welcoming us to the Earthly Paradise and we must await it humbly and prayerfully my friends we must pray and purify ourselves and prepare for the worst as well as for the best. I like to think that in a short while God Himself will present Himself to us not in any indirect way like stopping the sun but rather in a direct manifestation either as God the Father or as God the Son and we will all be saved but this will come about *only if we remain righteous.* If we succumb to error and evil we will bring it to pass that the Devil's advent will descend on us for as Thomas has said himself our destiny is in our hands as well as in His and I believe the first Sign was only the start of a process that will be decided for good or for evil in the days just ahead. Therefore I Davey Strafford call upon you my friends to keep the way of the faith for we must not waver in our hope that He Who Comes will be lovingly inclined toward us and I say that this is our time of supreme test and if we fail it we may discover that it is Satan who shows up to claim our souls. I say once more we cannot interpret the first Sign we can only have faith that it is truly from God and we must pray that this is so while we await the ultimate verdict of heaven therefore we have obtained the rental of a vacant grocery store on Coshocton Avenue which we have renamed the First Church of the Awaiters of Redemption and we will pray round the clock there are seventeen of us now and we will pray in three-hour shifts five of us at a time in rotation the numbers increasing as our expected rapid growth takes place I trust you will come to us and swell our voices for we must pray we've got to there's no other hope now just pray a lot in order that He Who Comes may be benevolent and I ask you to keep praying and have a trusting heart in this our time of waiting.

Nine

A Crying of Proclaimers

Kraft enters the room as Thomas puts down the telephone. "Who were you talking to?" Kraft asks.

"Gifford the Discerner, calling from Boston."

"Why are you answering the phone yourself?"

"There was no one else here."

"There were three apostles in the outer office who could have handled the call, Thomas."

Thomas shrugs. "They would have had to refer it to me eventually. So I answered. What's wrong with that?"

"You've got to maintain distance between yourself and ordinary daily routines. You've got to stay up there on your pedestal and not go around answering telephones."

"I'll try, Saul," says Thomas heavily.

"What did Gifford want?"

"He'd like to merge his group and ours."

Kraft's eyes flash. "To merge? *To merge?* What are we, some sort of manufacturing company? We're a movement. A spiritual force. To talk mergers is nonsense."

"He means that we should start working together,

Saul. He says we should join forces because we're both on the side of sanity."

"Exactly what is that supposed to mean?"

"That we're both anti-Apocalyptist. That we're both working to preserve society instead of to bury it."

"An oversimplification," Kraft says. "We deal in faith and he deals in equations. We believe in a Divine Being and he believes in the sanctity of reason. Where's the meeting point?"

"The Cincinnati and Chicago fires are our meeting point, Saul. The Apocalyptists are going crazy. And now these Awaiters too, these spokesmen for Satan—no. We have to act. If I put myself at Gifford's disposal—"

"At his *disposal?*"

"He wants a statement from me backing the spirit if not the substance of the Discerner philosophy. He thinks it'll serve to calm things a little."

"He wants to co-opt you for his own purposes."

"For the purposes of mankind, Saul."

Kraft laughs harshly. "How naïve you can be, Thomas! Where's your sense? You can't make an alliance with atheists. You can't let them turn you into a ventriloquist's dummy who—"

"They believe in God just as much as—"

"You have power, Thomas. It's in your voice, it's in your eyes. They have none. They're just a bunch of professors. They want to borrow your power and make use of it to serve their own ends. They don't want you, Thomas, they want your charisma. I forbid this alliance."

Thomas is trembling. He towers over Kraft, but his entire body quivers and Kraft remains steady. Thomas says, "I'm so tired, Saul."

"Tired?"

"The uproar. The rioting. The fires. I'm carrying

too big a burden. Gifford can help me. With planning, with ideas. That's a clever bunch, those people."

"I can give you all the help you need."

"No, Saul! What have you been telling me all along? That prayer is sufficient unto every occasion! Faith! Faith! Faith! Faith moves mountains! Well? You were right, yes, you channeled your faith through me and I spoke to the people and we got ourselves a miracle, but what now? What have we really accomplished? Everything's falling apart, and we need strong souls to build and rebuild, and you aren't offering anything new. You—"

"The Lord will provide for—"

"Will He? Will He, Saul? How many thousands dead already, since June 6? How much property damage? Government paralyzed. Transportation breaking down. New cults. New prophets. Here's Gifford saying, Let's join hands, Thomas, let's try to work together, and you tell me—"

"I forbid this," Kraft says.

"It's all agreed. Gifford's going to take the first plane west, and—"

"I'll call him. He mustn't come. If he does I won't let him see you. I'll notify the apostles to bar him."

"No, Saul."

"We don't need him. We'll be ruined if we let him near you."

"Why?"

"Because he's godless and our movement's strength proceeds from the Lord!" Kraft shouts. "Thomas, what's happened to you? Where's your fire? Where's your zeal? Where's my old swaggering Thomas who talked back to God? Belch, Thomas. Spit on the floor, scratch your belly, curse a little. I'll get you some wine. It shocks me

to see you sniveling like this. Telling me how tired you
are, how scared."

"I don't feel like swaggering much these days,
Saul."

"Damn you, swagger anyway! The whole world is
watching you! Here, listen—I'll rough out a new speech
for you that you'll deliver on full hookup tomorrow
night. We'll outflank Gifford and his bunch. We'll co-opt
him. What you'll do, Thomas, is call for a new act of
faith, some kind of mass demonstration, something sym-
bolic and powerful, something to turn people away from
despair and destruction. We'll follow the Discerner line
plus our own element of faith. You'll denounce all the
false new cults and urge everyone to—to—let me think
—to make a pilgrimage of some kind?—a coming together—a mass baptism, that's it, a march to the sea,
everybody bathing in God's own sea, washing away
doubt and sin. Right? A rededication to faith." Kraft's
face is red. His forehead gleams. Thomas scowls at him.
Kraft goes on, "Stop pulling those long faces. You'll do
it and it'll work. It'll pull people back from the abyss of
Apocalypticism. Positive goals, that's our approach.
Thomas the Proclaimer cries out that we must work
together under God. Yes? Yes. We'll get this thing
under control in ten days, I promise you. Now go have
yourself a drink. Relax. I've got to call Gifford, and
then I'll start blocking in your new appeal. Go on. And
stop looking so glum, Thomas! We hold a mighty power
in our hands. We're wielding the sword of the Lord.
You want to turn all that over to Gifford's crowd? Go.
Go. Get some rest, Thomas."

Ten

A Prostration of Propitiators

ALL PARISH CHAIRMEN PLEASE COPY AND DISTRIBUTE. The Reverend August Hammacher to his dearly beloved brothers and sisters in Christ, members of the Authentic Church of the Doctrine of Propitiation, this message from Central Shrine: greetings and blessings. Be you hereby advised that we have notified Elder Davey Strafford of the First Church of the Awaiters of Redemption that as of this date we no longer consider ourselves in communion with his church, on grounds of irremediable doctrinal differences. It is now forbidden for members of the Authentic Church to participate in the Awaiter rite or to have any sacramental contact with the instrumentalities of the Awaiter creed, although we shall continue to remember the Awaiters in our prayers and to strive for their salvation as if they were our own people.

The schism between ourselves and the Awaiters, which has been in the making for more than a week, arises from a fundamental disagreement over the nature of the Sign. It is of course our belief, greatly strengthened by the violent events of recent days, that the Author of the Sign was Satan and that the Sign foretells a coming realignment in heaven, the probable beneficiaries

of which are to be the Diabolical Forces. In expectation
of the imminent establishment of the Dark Powers on
Earth, we therefore direct our most humble homage to
Satan the Second Incarnation of Christ, hoping that
when He comes among us He will take cognizance of
our obeisance and spare us from the ultimate holocaust.

Now the Awaiters hold what is essentially an ag-
nostic position, saying that we cannot know whether the
Sign proceeds from God or from Satan, and that pending further revelation we must continue to pray as before to the Father and the Son, so that perhaps through
our devotions we may stave off the advent of Satan
entirely. There is one point of superficial kinship between their ideas and ours, which is an unwillingness to
share the confidence of Thomas the Proclaimer on the
one hand, and the Discerners on the other, that the Sign
is God's work. But it may be seen that a basic conflict
of doctrine exists between ourselves and the Awaiters,
for they refuse to comprehend our teachings concerning
the potential benevolence of Satan, and cling to an attitude that may be deemed dangerously offensive by
Him. Unwilling to commit themselves finally to one side
or the other, they hope to steer a cautious middle course,
not realizing that when the Dark One comes He will
chastise all those who failed to accept the proper meaning of the revelation of June 6. We have hoped to sway
the Awaiters to our position, but their attitude has
grown increasingly abusive as we have exposed their
doctrinal inconsistencies, and now we have no option
but to pronounce excommunication upon them. For
what does Revelation say? "I know thy works, that thou
art neither cold nor hot: I would thou wert cold or hot.
So then because thou art lukewarm, and neither cold
nor hot, I will spue thee out of my mouth." We cannot
risk being tainted by these lukewarm Awaiters who will

not bow the knee to the Dark One, though they admit
the possibility (but not the inevitability) of His Advent.

However, dearly loved friends in Christ, I am
happy to reveal that we have this day established preliminary communion with the United Diabolist Apocalyptic Pentecostal Church of the United States, the
headquarters of which is in Los Angeles, California. I
need not here recapitulate the deep doctrinal chasms
separating us from the Apocalyptist sects in general; but
although we abhor certain teachings even of this Diabolist faction, we recognize large areas of common belief
linking us, and hope to wean the United Diabolist
Apocalyptics entirely from their errors in the course of
time. This is by no means to be interpreted as presently
authorizing communicants of the Authentic Church of
the Doctrine of Propitiation to take part in Apocalyptist
activities, even those which are nondestructive, but I do
wish to advise you of the possibility of a deeper relationship with at least one Apocalyptist group even as
we sever our union with the Awaiters. Our love goes out
to all of you, from all of us at Central Shrine. We pros-
trate ourselves humbly before the Dark One whose triumph is ordained. In the name of the Father, the Son,
the Holy Ghost, and He Who Comes. Amen.

Eleven

The March to the Sea

It was the most frightening thing ever. Like an army invading us. Like a plague of locusts. They came like the locusts came upon the land of Egypt when Moses stretched out his hand. Exodus 10:15 tells it: *For they covered the face of the whole earth, so that the land was darkened; and they did eat every herb of the land, and all the fruit of the trees which the hail had left: and there remained not any green thing in the trees, or in the herbs of the field, through all the land of Egypt.* Like a nightmare. Lucy and me were the Egyptians and all of Thomas' people, they were the locusts.

Lucy wanted to be in the middle of it all along. To her, Thomas was like a holy prophet of God from the moment he first started to preach, although I tried to tell her back then that he was a charlatan and a dangerous lunatic with a criminal record. Look at his face, I said, look at those eyes! A lot of good it did me. She kept a scrapbook of him like he was a movie star and she was a fifteen-year-old girl instead of a woman of seventy-four. Pictures of him, texts of all his speeches. She got angry at me when I called him crazy or unscrupulous: we had our worst quarrel in maybe thirty years when she wanted to send him $500 to help pay for his television expenses and I absolutely refused.

Naturally after the Day of the Sign she came to look upon him as being right up there in the same exalted category as Moses and Elijah and John the Baptist, one of the true anointed voices of the Lord, and I guess I was starting to think of him that way too, despite myself. Though I didn't like him or trust him I sensed he had a special power. When everybody was praying for the Sign I prayed too, not so much because I thought it would come about but just to avoid trouble with Lucy, but I did put my heart into the prayer, and when the Earth stopped turning a shiver ran all through me and I got such a jolt of amazement that I thought I might be having a stroke. So I apologized to Lucy for all I had said about Thomas. I still suspected he was a madman and a charlatan, but I couldn't deny that he had something of the saint and prophet about him too. I suppose it's possible for a man to be a saint and a charlatan both. Anything's possible. I understand that one of these new religions is saying that Satan is actually an incarnation of Jesus, or the fourth member of the Trinity, or something like that. Honestly.

Well then all the riotings and burnings began when the hot weather came and the world seemed to be going crazy with things worse not better after God had given His Sign, and Thomas called for this Day of Rededication, everybody to go down to the sea and wash off his sins, a real old-time total-immersion revival meeting where we'd all get together and denounce the new cults and get things back on the right track again.

And Lucy came to me all aglow and said, Let's go, let's be part of it. I think there were supposed to be ten gathering-places all around the United States, New York and Houston and San Diego and Seattle and Chicago and I don't remember which else, but Thomas himself was going to attend the main one at Atlantic City, which is just a little ways down the coast from us, and the proceedings would be beamed by live telecast to all the other meetings being held here and overseas. She hadn't ever seen Thomas in person. I told her it was crazy for people our age to get mixed up in a mob of the size Thomas always attracts. We'd be crushed, we'd be trampled, we'd die sure as anything. Look, I said, we live right here by the seashore anyway, the ocean is fifty steps from our front porch; so why ask for trouble? We'll stay here and watch the praying on television, and then when everybody goes down into the sea to be purified we can go right here on our own beach and we'll be part of things in a way without taking the risks. I could see that Lucy was disappointed about not seeing Thomas in person but after all she's a sensible woman and I'm going to be eighty next November and there had already been some pretty wild scenes at each of Thomas' public appearances.

The big day dawned and I turned on the television and then of course we got the news that Atlantic City had banned Thomas' meeting at the last minute on the grounds of public safety. A big oil tanker had broken up off shore the night before and an oil slick was heading toward the beach, the mayor said. If there was a mass meeting on the beach that day it would interfere with the city's pollution-prevention procedures, and also the oil would endanger the health of anybody who went into the water, so the whole Atlantic City waterfront was being cordoned off, extra police brought in from out of town, laser lines set up, and so forth. Actually the oil slick wasn't anywhere near Atlantic City and was drifting the other way, and when the mayor talked about public safety he really meant the safety of his city, not wanting a couple of million people ripping up the boardwalk and breaking windows. So there was Atlantic

City sealed off and Thomas had this immense horde of people already collected, coming from Philadelphia and Trenton and Wilmington and even Baltimore, a crowd so big it couldn't be counted, five, six, maybe ten million people. They showed it from a helicopter view and everybody was standing shoulder to shoulder for about twenty miles in this direction and fifty miles in that direction, that's how it seemed, anyway, and about the only open place was where Thomas was, a clearing around fifty yards across with his apostles forming a tight ring protecting him.

Where was this mob going to go, since it couldn't get into Atlantic City? Why, Thomas said, everybody would just march up the Jersey coast and spread out along the shore from Long Beach Island to Sandy Hook. When I heard that I wanted to jump into the car and start heading for maybe Montana, but it was too late: the marchers were already on their way, all the mainland highways were choked with them. I went up on the sundeck with our binoculars and I could see the first of them coming across the causeway, walking seventy or eighty abreast, and a sea of faces behind them going inland on and on back toward Manahawkin and beyond. Well it was like the Mongol hordes of Genghis Khan. One swarm went south toward Beach Haven and the other came up through Surf City and Loveladies and Harvey Cedars in our direction. Thousands and thousands and thousands of them. Our island is long and skinny like any coastal sandspit, and it's pretty well built up both on the beach side and on the bay side, no open space except the narrow streets, and there wasn't *room* for all those people. But they kept on coming, and as I watched through the binoculars I thought I was getting dizzy because I imagined some of the houses on the beach side were moving too, and then I realized that the houses *were* moving, some of the flimsier ones, they were being pushed right off their foundations by the press of humanity. Toppling and being ground underfoot, entire houses, can you imagine? I told Lucy to pray, but she was already doing it, and I got my shotgun ready because I felt I had to try at least to protect us, but I said to her that this was probably going to be our last day alive and I kissed her and we told each other how good it had been, all of it, fifty-three years together. And then the mob came spilling through our part of the island. Rushing down to the beach. A berserk crazy multitude.

And Thomas was there, right close to our place. Bigger than I thought he'd be, and his hair and beard were all tangled up, and his face was red and peeling some from sunburn—he was that close, I could see the sunburn—and he was still in the middle of his ring of apostles, and he was shouting through a bullhorn, but no matter how much amplification they gave him from the copter-borne speakers overhead it was impossible to understand anything he was saying. Saul Kraft was next to him. He looked pale and frightened. People were rushing into the water, some of them fully clothed and some stark naked, until the whole shoreline was packed right out to where the breakers begin. As more and more people piled into the water the ones in front were pushed beyond their depth, and I think this was when the drownings started. I know I saw a number of people waving and kicking and yelling for help and getting swept out to sea. Thomas remained on shore, shouting through the bullhorn. He must have realized it was all out of control, but there was nothing he could do. Until this point the thrust of the mob was all forward, toward the sea, but now there was a change in the flow: some of those in the water tried to force their way back up onto land, and smashed head on into those going the other way. I thought they were coming up out of the water to avoid being drowned, but then I saw the black smears on their clothing and I thought, *the oil slick!* and yes, there it was, not down by Atlantic City but up here by us, right off the beach and moving shoreward. People in the water were getting bogged down in it, getting it all over their hair and faces, but they couldn't reach the shore because of the rush still heading in the opposite direction. This was when the tramplings started as the ones coming out of the water, coughing and choking and blinded with oil, fell under the feet of those still trying to get into the sea.

I looked at Thomas again and he was like a maniac. His face was wild and he had thrown the bullhorn away and he was just screaming, with angry cords standing out on his neck and forehead. Saul Kraft went up to him and said something and Thomas turned like the wrath of God, turned and rose up and brought his hands down like two clubs on Saul Kraft's head, and you know Kraft is a small man and he went down like he was dead, with blood all over his face. Two or three apostles picked him up and carried him into one of the beach-front houses. Just then somebody managed to slip through the cordon of apostles and went running toward Thomas. He was a short, plump man wearing the robes of one of the new religions, an Awaiter or Propitiator or I don't know what, and he had a laser-hatchet in his hand. He shouted something at Thomas and lifted the hatchet. But Thomas moved toward him and stood so tall that the assassin almost seemed to shrink, and the man was so afraid that he couldn't do a thing. Thomas reached out and plucked the hatchet from his hand and threw it aside. Then he caught the man and started hitting him, tremendous close-range punches, slam slam

slam, all but knocking the man's head off his shoulders. Thomas didn't look human while he was doing that. He was some kind of machine of destruction. He was bellowing and roaring and running foam from his mouth, and he was into this terrible deadly rhythm of punching, slam slam slam. Finally he stopped and took the man by both hands and flung him across the beach, like you'd fling a rag doll. The man flew maybe twenty feet and landed and didn't move. I'm certain Thomas beat him to death. There's your holy prophet for you, your saint of God. Suddenly Thomas' whole appearance changed: he became terribly calm, almost frozen, standing there with his arms dangling and his shoulders hunched up and his chest heaving from all that hitting. And he began to cry. His face broke up like winter ice on a spring pond and I saw the tears. I'll never forget that: Thomas the Proclaimer all alone in the middle of that madhouse on the beach, sobbing like a new widow.

I didn't see anything after that. There was a crash of glass from downstairs and I grabbed my gun and went down to see, and I found maybe fifteen people piled up on the livingroom floor who had been pushed right through the picture window by the crowd outside. The window had cut them all up and some were terribly maimed and there was blood on everything, and more and more and more people kept flying through the place where the window had been, and I heard Lucy screaming and my gun went off and I don't know what happened after that. Next I remember it was the middle of the night and I was sitting in our completely wrecked house and I saw a helicopter land on the beach, and a tactical squad began collecting bodies. There were hundreds of dead just on our strip of beach. Drowned, trampled, choked by oil, heart attacks, everything. The corpses are gone now but the island is a ruin. We're asking the government for disaster aid. I don't know: is a religious meeting a proper disaster? It was for us. That was your Day of Rededication, all right: a disaster. Prayer and purification to bring us all together under the banner of the Lord. May I be struck dead for saying this if I don't mean it with all my heart: I wish the Lord and all his prophets would disappear and leave us alone. We've had enough religion for one season.

Twelve

The Voice from the Heavens

Saul Kraft, hidden behind nine thousand dollars' worth of security devices, an array of scanners and sensors and shunt-gates and trip-vaults, wonders why everything is going so badly. Perhaps his choice of Thomas as the vehicle was an error. Thomas, he has come to realize, is too complicated, too unpredictable—a dual soul, demon and angel inextricably merged. Nevertheless the Crusade had begun promisingly enough. Working through Thomas, he had coaxed God Almighty into responding to the prayers of mankind, hadn't he? How much better than that do you need to do?

But now. This nightmarish carnival atmosphere everywhere. These cults, these other prophets. A thousand interpretations of an event whose meaning should have been crystal-clear. The bonfires. Madness crackling like lightning across the sky. Maybe the fault was in Thomas. The Proclaimer had been deficient in true grace all along. Possibly any mass movement centered on a prophet who had Thomas' faults of character was inherently doomed to slip into chaos.

Or maybe the fault was mine, O Lord.

Kraft has been in seclusion for many days, perhaps

for several weeks; he is no longer sure when he began this retreat. He will see no one, not even Thomas, who is eager to make amends. Kraft's injuries have healed and he holds no grievance against Thomas for striking him: the fiasco of the Day of Rededication had driven all of them a little insane there on the beach, and Thomas' outburst of violence was understandable if not justifiable. It may even have been of divine inspiration, God inflicting punishment on Kraft through the vehicle of Thomas for his sins. The sin of pride, mainly. To turn Gifford away, to organize the Day of Rededication for such cynical motives—

Kraft fears for his soul, and for the soul of Thomas.

He dares not see Thomas now, not until he has regained his own spiritual equilibrium; Thomas is too turbulent, too tempestuous, emits such powerful emanations of self-will; Kraft must first recapture his moral strength. He fasts much of the time. He tries to surrender himself fully in prayer. But prayer will not come: he feels cut off from the Almighty, separated from Him as he has never been before. By bungling this holy Crusade he must have earned the Lord's displeasure. A gulf, a chasm, parts them; Kraft is earthbound and helpless. He abandons his efforts to pray. He prowls his suite restlessly, listening for intruders, constantly running security checks. He switches on his closed-circuit video inputs, expecting to see fires in the streets, but all is calm out there. He listens to news bulletins on the radio: chaos, turmoil, everywhere. Thomas is said to be dead; Thomas is reported on the same day to be in Istanbul, Karachi, Johannesburg, San Francisco; the Propitiators have announced that on the twenty-fourth of November, according to their calculations, Satan will appear on Earth to enter into his sovereignty; the Pope, at last breaking his silence, has declared that he has no idea what power might have been responsible for the startling happenings of June 6, but thinks it would be rash to attribute the event to God's direct intervention without some further evidence. So the Pope has become an Awaiter too. Kraft smiles. Marvelous! Kraft wonders if the Archbishop of Canterbury is attending Propitiator services. Or the Dalai Lama consorting with the Apocalyptists. Anything can happen now. Gog and Magog are let loose upon the world. Kraft no longer is surprised by anything. He feels no astonishment even when he turns the radio on late one afternoon and finds that God Himself seems to be making a broadcast.

God's voice is rich and majestic. It reminds Kraft somewhat of the voice of Thomas, but God's tone is less fervid, less evangelical; He speaks in an easy but serious-minded way, like a senator campaigning for election to his fifth term of office. There is a barely perceptible easternness to God's accent: He could be a senator from Pennsylvania, maybe, or Ohio. He has gone on the air, He explains, in the hope of restoring order to a troubled world. He wishes to reassure everyone: no apocalypse is planned, and those who anticipate the imminent destruction of the world are most unwise. Nor should you pay heed to those who claim that the recent Sign was the work of Satan. It certainly was not, God says, not at all, and propitiation of the Evil One is uncalled for. By all means let's give the Devil his due, but nothing beyond that. All I intended when I stopped the Earth's rotation, God declares, was to let you know that I'm here, looking after your interests. I wanted you to be aware that in the event of really bad trouble down there I'll see to it—

Kraft, lips clamped tautly, changes stations. The resonant baritone voice pursues him.

—that peace is maintained and the forces of justice are strengthened in—

Kraft turns on his television set. The screen shows nothing but the channel insignia. Across the top of the screen gleams a bright-green title:

ALLEGED VOICE OF GOD

and across the bottom, in frantic scarlet, is a second caption:

BY LIVE PICKUP FROM THE MOON

The Deity, meanwhile, has moved smoothly on to new themes. All the problems of the world, He observes, can be attributed to the rise and spread of atheistic socialism. The false prophet Karl Marx, aided by the Antichrist Lenin and the subsidiary demons Stalin and Mao, have set loose in the world a plague of godlessness that has tainted the entire twentieth century and, here at the dawn of the twenty-first, must at last be eradicated. For a long time the zealous godly folk of the world resisted the pernicious Bolshevik doctrines, God continues, His voice still lucid and reasonable; but in the past twenty years an accommodation with the powers of darkness has come into effect, and this has allowed spreading corruption to infect even such splendidly righteous lands as Japan, Brazil, the German Federal Republic, and God's own beloved United States of America. The foul philosophy of coexistence has led to a step-by-step entrapment of the forces of good, and as a result—

Kraft finds all of this quite odd. Is God speaking to every nation in English, or is He speaking Japanese to the Japanese, Hebrew to the Israelis, Croatian to the

Croats, Bulgarian to the Bulgars? And when did God become so staunch a defender of the capitalist ethic? Kraft recalls something about driving money-changers out of the temple, long ago. But now the voice of God appears to be demanding a holy war against communism. Kraft hears Him calling on the legions of the sanctified to attack the Marxist foe wherever the red flag flies. Sack embassies and consulates, burn the houses of ardent left-wingers, destroy libraries and other sources of dangerous propaganda, the Lord advises. He says everything in a level, civilized tone.

Abruptly, in midsentence, the voice of the Almighty vanishes from the airwaves. A short time later an announcer, unable to conceal his chagrin, declares that the broadcast was a hoax contrived by bored technicians in a satellite relay station. Investigations have begun to determine how so many radio and television stations let themselves be persuaded to transmit it as a public-interest item. But for many godless Marxists the revelation comes too late. The requested sackings and lootings have occurred in dozens of cities. Hundreds of diplomats, guards, and clerical workers have been slain by maddened mobs bent on doing the Lord's work. Property losses are immense. An international crisis is developing, and there are scattered reports of retribution against American citizens in several eastern European countries. We live in strange times, Kraft tells himself. He prays. For himself. For Thomas. For all mankind. Lord have mercy. Amen. Amen. Amen.

Thirteen

The Burial of Faith

The line of march begins at the city line and runs westward out of town into the suburban maze. The marchers, at least a thousand of them, stride vigorously forward even though a dank, oppressive heat enfolds them. On they go, past the park dense with the dark-green leaves of late summer, past the highway cloverleaf, past the row of burned motels and filling stations, past the bombed reservoir, past the cemeteries, heading for the municipal dumping-grounds.

Gifford, leading the long sober procession, wears ordinary classroom clothes: a pair of worn khaki trousers, a loose-fitting gray shirt, and old leather sandals. Originally there had been some talk of having the most important Discerners come garbed in their academic robes, but Gifford had vetoed that on the grounds that it wasn't in keeping with the spirit of the ceremony. Today all of the old superstitions and pomposities were to be laid to rest; why then bedeck the chief iconoclasts in hieratic costume as though they were priests, as though this new creed were going to be just as full of mummery as the outmoded religions it hoped to supplant?

Because the marchers are so simply dressed, the contrast is all the more striking between the plain garments they wear and the elaborate, rich-textured ecclesiastical paraphernalia they carry. No one is empty-handed; each has some vestment, some sacred artifact, some work of scripture. Draped over Gifford's left arm is a large white linen alb, ornately embroidered, with a dangling silken cincture. The man behind him carries a deacon's dalmatic; the third marcher has a handsome chasuble; the fourth, a splendid cope. The rest of the priestly gear is close behind: amice, stole, maniple, vimpa. A frosty-eyed woman well along in years waves a crozier aloft; the man beside her wears a mitre at a mockingly rakish angle. Here are cassocks, surplices, hoods, tippets, cottas, rochets, mozettas, mantellettas, chimeres, and much more: virtually everything, in fact, save the papal tiara itself. Here are chalices, crucifixes, thuribles, fonts; three men struggle beneath a marvelously carved fragment of a pulpit; a little band of marchers displays Greek Orthodox outfits, the rhason and the sticharion, the epitrachelion and the epimanikia, the sakkos, the epigonation, the zone, the omophorion; they brandish ikons and enkolpia, dikerotrikera and dikanikion. Austere Presbyterian gowns may be seen, and rabbinical yarmulkes and tallithim and tfilin. Farther back in the procession one may observe more exotic holy objects, prayer wheels and tonkas, sudras and kustis, idols of fifty sorts, things sacred to Confucianists, Shintoists, Parsees, Buddhists both Mahayana and Hinayana, Jains, Sikhs, animists of no formal rite, and others. The marchers have shofars, mezuzahs, candelabra, communion trays, even collection plates; no portable element of faith has been ignored. And of course the holy books of the world are well represented: an infinity of Old and New Testaments, the Koran, the Bhagavad-Gita, the Upanishads, the Tao Te Ching, the Vedas, the Vedanta Sutra, the Talmud, the Book of the Dead, and more. Gifford has been queasy about destroying books, for that is an act with ugly undertones; but these are extreme times, and extreme measures are required. Therefore he has given his consent even for that.

Much of the material the marchers carry was freely contributed, mostly by disgruntled members of congregations, some of it given by disaffected clergymen themselves. The other objects come mostly from churches or museums plundered during the civil disturbances. But the Discerners have done no plundering of their own; they have merely accepted donations and picked up some artifacts that rioters had scattered in the streets. On this point Gifford was most strict: acquisition of material by force was prohibited. Thus the robes and emblems of the newly founded creeds are seen but sparsely today, since Awaiters and Propritiators and their like would hardly have been inclined to contribute to Gifford's festival of destruction.

They have reached the municipal dump now. It is a vast flat wasteland, surprisingly aseptic-looking: there are large areas of meadow, and the unreclaimed regions of the dump have been neatly graded and mulched, in readiness for the scheduled autumn planting of grass. The marchers put down their burdens and the chief Discerners come forward to take spades and shovels from a truck that has accompanied them. Gifford looks up; helicopters hover and television cameras bristle in the sky. This event will have extensive coverage. He turns to face the others and intones, "Let this ceremony mark the end of all ceremonies. Let this rite usher in a time without rites. Let reason rule forevermore."

Gifford lifts the first shovelful of soil himself. Now the rest of the diggers set to work, preparing a trench three feet deep, ten to twelve feet wide. The topsoil comes off easily, revealing strata of cans, broken toys, discarded television sets, automobile tires, and garden rakes. A mound of debris begins to grow as the digging team does its task; soon a shallow opening gapes. Though it is now late afternoon, the heat has not diminished, and those who dig stream with sweat. They rest frequently, panting, leaning on their tools. Meanwhile those who are not digging stand quietly, not putting down that which they carry.

Twilight is near before Gifford decides that the trench is adequate. Again he looks up at the cameras, again he turns to face his followers.

He says, "On this day we bury a hundred thousand years of superstition. We lay to rest the old idols, the old fantasies, the old errors, the old lies. The time of faith is over and done with; the era of certainty opens. No longer do we need theologians to speculate on the proper way of worshiping the Lord; no longer do we need priests to mediate between ourselves and Him; no longer do we need man-made scriptures that pretend to interpret His nature. We have all of us felt His hand upon our world, and the time has come to approach Him with clear eyes, with an alert, open mind. Hence we give to the earth these relics of bygone epochs, and we call upon discerning men and women everywhere to join us in this ceremony of renunciation."

He signals. One by one the Discerners advance to the edge of the pit. One by one they cast their burdens in: albs, chasubles, copes, mitres, Korans, Upanishads, yarmulkes, crucifixes. No one hurries; the Burial of Faith is serious business. As it proceeds, a drum roll of dull distant thunder reverberates along the horizon. A storm on the way? Just heat lightning, perhaps, Gifford decides. The ceremony continues. In with the maniple. In with the shofar. In with the cassock. Thunder again: louder, more distinct. The sky darkens. Gifford attempts to hasten the tempo of the ceremony, beckoning the Discerners forward to drop their booty. A blade of

lightning slices the heavens and this time the answering
thunderclap comes almost instantaneously, *ka-thock*. A
few drops of rain. The forecast had been in error. A nuisance, but no real harm. Another flash of lightning. A
tremendous crash. That one must have struck only a few
hundred yards away. There is some nervous laughter.
"We've annoyed Zeus," someone says. "He's throwing
thunderbolts." Gifford is not amused; he enjoys ironies,
but not now, not now. And he realizes that he has become just credulous enough, since the sixth of June, to
be at least marginally worried that the Almighty might
indeed be about to punish this sacrilegious band of Discerners. A flash again. *Ka-thock!* The clouds now split
asunder and torrents of rain abruptly descend. In moments, shirts are pasted to skins, the floor of the pit turns
to mud, rivulets begin to stream across the dump.

And then, as though they had scheduled the storm
for their own purposes, a mob of fierce-faced people
in gaudy robes burst into view. They wield clubs, pitch-
forks, rake handles, cleavers, and other improvised
weapons; they scream incoherent, unintelligible slogans;
and they rush into the midst of the Discerners, laying
about them vigorously. "Death to the godless blasphemers!" is what they are shrieking, and similar
phrases. Who are they, Gifford wonders? Awaiters. Propitiators. Diabolists. Apocalyptists. Perhaps a coalition
of all cultists. The television helicopters descend to get a
better view of the melee, and hang just out of reach,
twenty or thirty feet above the struggle. Their powerful
floodlights provide apocalyptic illumination. Gifford
finds hands at his throat: a crazed woman, howling, grotesque. He pushes her away and she tumbles into the
pit, landing on a stack of mud-crusted Bibles. A frantic
stampede has begun; his people are rushing in all directions, followed by the vengeful servants of the Lord, who

wield their weapons with vindictive glee. Gifford sees his friends fall, wounded, badly hurt, perhaps slain. Where are the police? Why are they giving no protection? "Kill all the blasphemers!" a maniac voice shrills near him. He whirls, ready to defend himself. A pitchfork. He feels a strange cold clarity of thought and moves swiftly in, feinting, seizing the handle of the pitchfork, wresting it from his adversary. The rain redoubles its force; a sheet of water comes between Gifford and the other, and when he can see again, he is alone at the edge of the pit. He hurls the pitchfork into the pit and instantly wishes he had kept it, for three of the robed ones are coming toward him. He breaks into a cautious trot, tries to move past them, puts on a sudden spurt of speed, and slips in the mud. He lands in a puddle; the taste of mud is in his mouth; he is breathless, terrified, unable to rise. They fling themselves upon him. "Wait," he says. "This is madness!" One of them has a club. "No," Gifford mutters. "No. No. No. No."

Fourteen

The Seventh Seal

1. And when he had opened the seventh seal, there was silence in heaven about the space of half an hour.

2. And I saw the seven angels which stood before God; and to them were given seven trumpets.

3. And another angel came and stood at the altar, having a golden censer; and there was given unto him much incense, that he should offer it with the prayers of all saints upon the golden altar which was before the throne.

4. And the smoke of the incense, which came with the prayers of the saints, ascended up before God out of the angel's hand.

5. And the angel took the censer, and filled it with fire of the altar, and cast it into the earth: and there were voices, and thunderings, and lightnings, and an earthquake.

6. And the seven angels which had the seven trumpets prepared themselves to sound.

7. The first angel sounded, and there followed hail and fire mingled with blood, and they were cast upon the earth: and the third part of trees was burnt up, and all green grass was burnt up.

8. And the second angel sounded, and as it were a great mountain burning with fire was cast into the sea: and the third part of the sea became blood;

9. *And the third part of the creatures which were in the sea, and had life, died; and the third part of the ships were destroyed.*

10. *And the third angel sounded, and there fell a great star from heaven, burning as it were a lamp, and it fell upon the third part of the rivers, and upon the fountains of waters;*

11. *And the name of the star is called Wormwood: and the third part of the waters became wormwood; and many men died of the waters, because they were made bitter.*

12. *And the fourth angel sounded, and the third part of the sun was smitten, and the third part of the moon, and the third part of the stars; so as the third part of them was darkened, and the day shone not for a third part of it, and the night likewise.*

13. *And I beheld, and heard an angel flying through the midst of heaven, saying with a loud voice, Woe, woe, woe, to the inhabiters of the earth by reason of the other voices of the trumpet of the three angels, which are yet to sound!*

Fifteen

The Flight of
the Prophet

All, all over. Thomas weeps. The cities burn. The very
lakes are afire. So many thousands dead. The Apocalyptists dance, for though the year is not yet sped the end
seems plainly in view. The Church of Rome has pro-
nounced anathema on Thomas, denying his miracle: he
is the Antichrist, the Pope has said. Signs and portents
are seen everywhere. This is the season of two-headed
calves and dogs with cats' faces. New prophets have
arisen. God may shortly return, or He may not; revelations differ. Many people now pray for an end to all such
visitations and miracles. The Awaiters no longer Await,
but now ask that we be spared from His next coming;
even the Diabolists and the Propitiators cry, Come not,
Lucifer. Those who begged a Sign from God in June
would be content now only with God's renewed and
prolonged absence. Let Him neglect us; let Him dismiss
us from His mind. It is a time of torches and hymns.
Rumors of barbaric warfare come from distant conti-
nents. They say the neutron bomb has been used in
Bolivia. Thomas' last few followers have asked him to
speak with God once more, in the hope that things can
still be set to rights, but Thomas refuses. The lines of

communication to the Deity are closed. He dares not reopen them: see, see how many plagues and evils he has let loose as it is! He renounces his prophethood. Others may dabble in charismatic mysticism if they so please. Others may kneel before the burning bush or sweat in the glare of the pillar of fire. Not Thomas. Thomas' vocation is gone. All over. All, all, all over.

He hopes to slip into anonymity. He shaves his beard and docks his hair; he obtains a new wardrobe, bland and undistinguished; he alters the color of his eyes; he practices walking in a slouch to lessen his great height. Perhaps he has not lost his pocket-picking skills. He will go silently into the cities, head down, fingers on the ready, and thus he will make his way. It will be a quieter life.

Disguised, alone, Thomas goes forth. He wanders unmolested from place to place, sleeping in odd corners, eating in dim rooms. He is in Chicago for the Long Sabbath, and he is in Milwaukee for the Night of Blood, and he is in St. Louis for the Invocation of Flame. These events leave him unaffected. He moves on. The year is ebbing. The leaves have fallen. If the Apocalyptists tell us true, mankind has but a few weeks left. God's wrath, or Satan's, will blaze over the land as the year 2000 sweeps in on December's heels. Thomas scarcely minds. Let him go unnoticed and he will not mind if the universe tumbles about him.

"What do you think?" he is asked on a street corner in Los Angeles. "Will God come back on New Year's Day?"

A few idle loungers, killing time. Thomas slouches among them. They do not recognize him, he is sure. But they want an answer. "Well? What do you say?"

Thomas makes his voice furry and thick, and mumbles, "No, not a chance. He's never going to mess with us again. He gave us a miracle and look what we made out of it."

"That so? You really think so?"

Thomas nods. "God's turned His back on us. He said, Here, I give you proof of My existence, now pull yourselves together and get somewhere. And instead we fell apart all the faster. So that's it. We've had it. The end is coming."

"Hey, you might be right!" Grins. Winks.

This conversation makes Thomas uncomfortable. He starts to edge away, elbows out, head bobbing clumsily, shoulders hunched. His new walk, his camouflage.

"Wait," one of them says. "Stick around. Let's talk a little."

Thomas hesitates.

"You know, I think you're right, fellow. We made a royal mess. I tell you something else: we never should have started all that stuff. Asking for a Sign. Stopping the Earth. Would have been a lot better off if that Thomas had stuck to picking pockets, let me tell you."

"I agree three hundred percent," Thomas says, flashing a quick smile, on-off. "If you'll excuse me—"

Again he starts to shuffle away. Ten paces. An office building's door opens. A short, slender man steps out. *Oh, God! Saul!* Thomas covers his face with his hand and turns away. Too late. No use. Kraft recognizes him through all the alterations. His eyes gleam. "Thomas!" he gasps.

"No. You're mistaken. My name is—"

"Where have you been?" Kraft demands. "Everyone's searching for you, Thomas. Oh, it was wicked of you to run away, to shirk your responsibilities. You dumped everything into our hands, didn't you? But you were the only one with the strength to lead people. You were the only one who—"

"Keep your voice down," Thomas says hoarsely. No use pretending. "For the love of God, Saul, stop yelling at me! Stop saying my name! Do you want everyone to know that I'm—"

"That's exactly what I want," Kraft says. By now a fair crowd has gathered, ten people, a dozen. Kraft points. "Don't you know him? That's Thomas the Proclaimer! He's shaved and cut his hair, but can't you see his face all the same? There's your prophet! There's the thief who talked with God!"

"No, Saul!"

"Thomas?" someone says. And they all begin to mutter it. "Thomas? Thomas? Thomas?" They nod heads, point, rub chins, nod heads again. "Thomas? Thomas?"

Surrounding him. Staring. Touching him. He tries to push them away. Too many of them, and no apostles, now. Kraft is at the edge of the crowd, smiling, the little Judas! "Keep back," Thomas says. "You've got the wrong man. I'm not Thomas. I'd like to get my hands on him myself. I—I—" *Judas! Judas!* "Saul!" he screams. And then they swarm over him.

Going

One

In the early spring of 2095, with his one hundred thirty-sixth birthday coming on, Henry Staunt decided quite abruptly that the moment had arrived for him to Go. He would notify the Office of Fulfillment, get himself a congenial Guide, take a suite in one of the better Houses of Leavetaking. With the most pleasant season of the year about to unfurl, the timing would be ideal; he could make his farewells and renunciations during these cool green months and get decently out of the way before summer's blazing eye was open.

This was the first time that he had ever seriously considered Going, and he felt some surprise that the notion had stolen upon him so suddenly. Why, he wondered, was he willing to end it this morning, when he clearly had not been last week, last month, last year? What invisible watershed had he unknowingly crossed, what imperceptible valley of decision? Perhaps this was only a vagrant morning mood; perhaps by noon he would find himself eager to live another hundred years, after all. Eh? No, not likely. He was aware of the resolution, hard and firm, embedded, encapsulated, shining like a glittering pellet at the core of his soul. *Arrange for your Going, Henry.* Nothing equivocal about that. A tone of certainty. Of finality. Still, he thought, we must not hurry into this. First let me understand my own motives in coming to this decision. The unexamined death is not worth requesting.

He had heard that it was useful, when thoughts of

Going first came into one's mind, to consult that book of Hallam's—the handbook of dying, the anatomy of world-renunciation. Very well. Staunt touched a bright enameled control stud and the screen opposite the window flowered into color. "Sir?" the library machine asked him.

Staunt said, "Hallam's book. The one about dying."

"*The Turning of the Wheel: Departure as Consolation*, sir?"

"Yes."

Instantly its title page was on the screen. Staunt picked up the scanning rod and pressed it here and there and there, randomly, bringing this page and that into view. He admired the clarity of the image. The type was bold and elegant, the margins were wide; not for several moments did he begin paying attention to the text.

. . . essential that the decision, when it is made, be made for the proper reasons. Although sooner or later we must all turn the wheel, abandoning the world to those who await a place in it, nevertheless no one should leave in resentment, thinking that he has been driven too soon from the worldly sphere. It is the task of the civilized man to bring himself, in the fullness of time, to an acceptance of the knowledge that his life has been completed; Going should not be undertaken by anyone who is not wholly ready, and attaining that state of readiness should be our lifelong goal. Too often we delude ourselves into thinking we are truly ready, when actually we have not reached readiness at all, and choose Going out of unworthy or shallow motives. How tragic it is to arrive at the actual moment of Leavetaking and to realize that one has deceived oneself, that one's motivations are false, that one is, in fact, not in the least ready to Go!

There are many improper reasons for choosing to Go, but they all may be classified as expressions of the desire to escape. One who is experiencing emotional frustration, or difficulty with his work, or a deterioration of health, or intense fatigue, or disappointment of some kind, may, in a moment of dark whim, apply to a House of Leavetaking; but his real intention is a trivial one, that is, to punish the cruel world by escaping from it. One should never look upon Going as a way of getting even. I must point out again that Going is something more than mere suicide. Going is not a petulant, irrational, vindictive deed. It is a positive act, an act of willing renunciation, a deeply moral act; one does not enter into it lightly, solely to escape. One does not say: I loathe you, foul world, therefore I take my leave, and good riddance. One says: I love you, fair world, but I have experienced your joys to the fullest, and now remove myself so that others may know the same joys.

When one first considers Going, therefore, one must strive to discover if one has attained true readiness—that is, the genuine willingness to put aside the world for the sake of others—or if one is simply seeking to satisfy the ego through the gesture of suicide—

There was much more in that vein. He would read it some other time. He turned the screen off.

So. To find the motive for wanting to Go. Walking slowly through the cool, spacious rooms of his old suburban house, Staunt searched for his reasons. His health?

Perfect. He was tall, slender, still strong, with his own teeth and a full head of thick, close-cropped white hair. He hadn't had major surgery since the pancreas transplant nearly seventy years before. Each year he had his arteries retuned, his eyesight adjusted, and his metabolism enhanced, but at his age those were routine things; basically he was a very healthy man. With the right sort of medical care, and everyone nowadays had the right sort of medical care, his body would go on functioning smoothly for decades more.

What then? Emotional problems? Hardly. He had his friends; he had his family; his life had never been more serene than it was now. His work? Well, he rarely worked any longer: some sketches, some outlines for future compositions, but he knew he would never get around to finishing them. No matter. He had only happy thoughts about his work. Worries over the state of the world? No, the world was in fine shape. Rarely finer.

Boredom, perhaps. Perhaps. He had grown weary of his tranquil life, weary of being content, weary of his beautiful surroundings, weary of going through the motions of life. That could be it. He went to the thick clear window of the living room and peered out at the view that had given him so much delight for so many years. The lawn, still pale from winter, sloped evenly and serenely toward the brook, where stubby skunk cabbages clustered. The dogwoods held the first hints of color; the crocuses were not quite finished; the heavy buds of the daffodils would be bursting by Saturday. All was well outside. Lovely. As it always was, this time of year. Yet he was unmoved. It did not sadden him to think that he would probably not see another spring. There's the heart of it, Staunt thought: I must be ripe for Going, because I don't care to stay. It's that simple. I've done all I care to do, I've seen all I care to see; now I might just as well move along. The wheel has to turn. Others are waiting to fill my place. It is a far, far better thing I do, et cetera, et cetera.

"Get me the Office of Fulfillment," he told his telephone.

A gentle female face appeared on the small screen.

Staunt smiled. "My name's Henry Staunt, and I think I'm ready to Go. Would you send a Guide over as soon as you can?"

Two

An hour later, as Staunt stood by the studio window listening to one of his favorites among his own compositions, the string quartet of 2038, a green-blue copter descended and came fluttering to a halt on his lawn, resting on a cushion of air a short distance above the tips of the grass. It bore on its hull the symbol of the Office of Fulfillment—a wheel and a set of enmeshed gears. The hatch of the copter lifted and, to Staunt's surprise, Martin Bollinger got out. Bollinger was a neighbor, a friend of long standing, possibly the closest friend Staunt had these days; he often came over for visits; lately there had been some talk of Staunt's setting a group of Bollinger's poems to music; but what was Bollinger doing riding around in a Fulfillment Office copter?

Jauntily Bollinger approached the house. He was short, compact, buoyant, with sparkling brown eyes and soft, wavy hair. Staunt supposed he must be seventy or so, eighty at most. Still a young man. Prime of life. It made Staunt feel youthful just to have Bollinger around, and yet he knew that to Bollinger, Bollinger was no youngster. Staunt hadn't felt like a boy when *he* was eighty, either. But living to one hundred thirty-six changes your perspective about what's old.

From outside Bollinger said, "Can I come in, Henry?"

"Let him in," Staunt murmured. One of the sensors in the studio wall picked up the command and relayed it to the front door, which opened. "Tell him I'm in the studio," Staunt said, and the house guided Bollinger in. With a flick of two fingers Staunt cut down the volume of the music.

Bollinger, as he entered, nodded and said pleasantly, "I've always loved that quartet."

Staunt embraced him. "So have I. How good to see you, Martin."

"I'm sorry it's been so long. Two weeks, isn't it?"

"I'm glad you've come. Although—to be really honest—I'm not going to be free this afternoon, Martin. I'm expecting someone else."

"Oh?"

"In fact, someone from the very organization whose vehicle you seem to have borrowed. How do you happen to come here in one of their copters, anyway?"

"Why not?" Bollinger asked.

"I can't understand why you should. It makes no sense."

"When I come on official business, I use an official copter, Henry."

"Official business?"

"You asked for a Guide."

Staunt was shaken. "*You?*"

"When they told me who had called, I insisted I

be given the assignment, or I'd resign instantly. So I came. So here I am."

"I never realized you were with Fulfillment, Martin!"

"You never asked."

Staunt managed a baffled smile. "How long ago did you go into it?"

"Eight, ten years. A while ago."

"And why?"

"A sense of public duty. We all have to help out if the wheel's going to keep turning smoothly. Eh, Henry? Eh?" Bollinger came close to Staunt, looked up at him, staring straight into his eyes, and flashed an unexpectedly brilliant, somehow overpowering grin. Then he said in a crisp, aggressive tone, "What's all this about wanting to Go, Henry?"

"The idea came to me this morning. I was strolling around the house when suddenly I realized there was no further point in my staying here. I'm done: why not admit it? Turn the wheel. Clear a space."

"You're still relatively young."

Staunt laughed harshly. "Coming up on one hundred and thirty-six."

"I know men of one hundred sixty and one hundred seventy who haven't even dreamed of Going."

"That's their problem. I'm ready."

"Are you ill, Henry?"

"Never felt better."

"Are you in any kind of trouble, then?"

"None whatever. My life is unutterably tranquil. I have only the purest of motives in applying for Leavetaking."

Bollinger seemed agitated. He paced the studio, picked up and set down one of Staunt's Polynesian carvings, clasped his hands to his elbows, and said finally,

"We have to talk about this first, Henry. We have to talk about this!"

"I don't understand. Isn't it a Guide's function to speed me serenely on the way to oblivion? You sound as if you're trying to talk me out of Going!"

"It's the Guide's function," Bollinger said, "to serve the best interests of the Departing One, whatever those interests may be. The Guide may attempt to persuade the Departing One to delay his Going, or not to Go at all, if in his judgment that's the proper course to take."

Staunt shook his head. "There's a whole bustling world full of healthy young people out there who want to have more children, and who can't have them unless useless antiquities like myself get out of the way. I volunteer to make some space available. Are you telling me that you'd *oppose* my Going, Martin, if—"

"Maintaining the level of population at a consistent quantity is only one aspect of our work," Bollinger said. "We're also concerned with maintaining quality. We don't want useful older citizens taking themselves out of the world merely to make room for a newcomer whose capabilities we can't predict. If a man still has something important to give society—"

"I have nothing important left to give."

"If he does," Bollinger went on smoothly, "we will try to discourage him from Going until he's given it. In your case I think Going may be somewhat premature, and so I've wangled the assignment to be your Guide so that I can help you explore the consequences of what you propose to do, and perhaps—"

"What do you think I still can offer the world, Martin?"

"Your music."

"Haven't I written enough?"

"We can't be certain of that. You may have a masterpiece or two lurking in you." Bollinger began to pace again. "Henry, have you read Hallam's *Turning of the Wheel?*"

"I've glanced at it. This morning, in fact."

"Did you look at the section in which he explains why our society is unique in western civilization?"

"It may have slipped my mind."

Bollinger said, "Henry, ours is the first that accepts the concept of suicide as a virtuous act. In the past, you know, suicide was considered filthy and evil and cowardly; religions condemned it as an attack against the will of God, and even people who weren't religious tended to try to cover it up when a friend or a relative killed himself. Well, we're into a different concept. Since our medical skills are now so highly developed that almost no one ever dies naturally, even enlightened birth-limitation measures can't keep the world from filling up with people. So long as anyone is born at all, and no one dies, there's a constant and dangerous build-up of population, so that—"

"Yes, yes, but—"

"Let me finish. To cope with our population problem, we eventually decided to regard the voluntary ending of one's life as a noble sacrifice, and so forth. Hence the whole mystique of Going. Even so, we haven't entirely lost our old moral outlook on suicide. We still don't want valuable people to Go, because we feel *they have no right* to throw away their gifts, to deprive us of what they have to give. And so one of the functions of the Office of Fulfillment is to lead the old and useless toward the exit in a civilized and gentle way, but another of our functions is to keep the old and useful from Going too soon. Therefore—"

"I understand," Staunt said softly. "I agree with

the philosophy. I merely deny that I'm useful any more."

"That's open to question."

"Can it be, Martin, that you're letting personal factors interfere with your judgment?"

"What do you mean? That I'd keep you from Going because I prize your friendship so dearly?"

"I mean my promise to set your poems to music."

Bollinger reddened faintly. "That's absurd. Do you believe that my ego is so bound up in those poems that I'd meddle with your Going, simply so that you'd live to— No. I like to think that my judgment is objective."

"You could be wrong. You might disqualify yourself from being my Guide. Simply on the chance that—"

"No. I'm your Guide."

"Are we going to fight, then, over whether I'll be allowed to Go?"

"Of course not, Henry. We just want you to understand the significance of the step you've asked to take."

"The significance is that I'll die. Is that such a complicated thing to understand?"

Bollinger looked disturbed by Staunt's blunt choice of words. One tried not to connect Going and dying. One was supposed to resort to the euphemisms.

He said, "Henry, I just want to follow orderly procedure."

"Which is?"

"We'll get you into a House of Leavetaking. Then we'll ask you to examine your soul and see if you're as truly ready to Go as you think you are. That's all. The final decision about when you Go will remain in your hands. If you insisted, you could Go this evening; we wouldn't stop you. Couldn't. But of course such haste would be unseemly."

"As you say."

"The House of Leavetaking I recommend for you," Bollinger said, "is known as Omega Prime. It's in Arizona—beautiful desert country rimmed with mountains —and the staff is superb. I could show you brochures on several others, but—"

"I'll trust your judgment."

"Fine. May I use the phone?"

It took less than a minute for Bollinger to book the reservation. For the first time, Staunt felt a sense of inexorability about the course of events. He was on his way out. There would be no turning back now. He would never have the audacity to cancel his Going once he had taken up residence at Omega Prime. But why, he wondered, was he showing even these faint tremors of hesitation? Had Bollinger already begun to undermine his resolution?

"There," Bollinger said. "They'll have your suite ready in an hour. Would you like to leave tonight?"

"Why not?"

"Under our procedures," Bollinger said, "your family will be notified as soon as you've arrived there. I'll do it myself. A custodian will be appointed for your house; it'll be sealed and placed under guard pending transfer of your property to your heirs. At the House of Leavetaking you'll have all the legal advice you'll require, assistance in making a distribution of assets, et cetera, et cetera. There'll be no loose ends left dangling. It'll all go quite smoothly."

"Splendid."

"And that completes the official part of my visit. You can stop thinking of me as your Guide for a while.

Naturally, I'll be with you a good deal of the time at the House of Leavetaking, handling any queries you may have, doing whatever I can to make things easier for you. For the moment, though, I'm here simply as your friend, not as your Guide. Would you care to talk? Not about Going, I mean. About music, politics, the weather, anything you like."

Staunt said, "Somehow I don't feel very talkative."

"Shall I leave you alone?"

"I think that would be best. I'm starting to think of myself as a Departing One, Martin. I'd like a few hours to get accustomed to the idea."

Bollinger bowed awkwardly. "It must be a difficult moment for you. I don't want to intrude. I'll come back just before dinnertime, all right?"

"Fine," Staunt said.

Three

Afterward, feeling adrift, Staunt wandered aimlessly through his house, wondering how soon it would be before he changed his mind. He put no credence in Bollinger's flattering, hopeful hypothesis that he might yet have important works of art to give the world; Staunt knew better. If he had ever owed a debt of creativity to mankind, that debt had long since been paid in full, and civilization need not fear it would be losing anything significant by his Going. Even so, he might find it difficult, after all, to remove himself from all he

loved. Would the sight of his familiar possessions shake
his decision? Here were the memorabilia of a long,
comfortable life: the African masks, the Pueblo pots,
the Mozart manuscript, the little Elizabethan harpsi-
chord, the lunar boulder, the Sung bowl, the Canopic
jars, the Persian miniatures, the dueling pistols, the
Greek coins, all the elegant things that had collected
him in his years of traveling. Once it had seemed un-
bearable to him that he might ever be parted from these
precious objects. They had taken on life for him, so
that when a clumsy cleaning machine knocked a Cyp-
riote statuette to the floor and smashed it, he had wept
not for the monetary loss, but for the pain he imagined
the little clay creature was suffering, for the humiliation it must feel at being ruined. He imagined it hurl-
ing bitter reproaches at him: *I survived four thousand
years so that I might become yours, and you let me get
broken!* As a child might pretend that her dolls were
alive, and talk to them, and apologize to them for
fancied slights. It was, he had known all along, a foolish,
sentimental, even contemptible attitude, this attach-
ment he had to his inanimate belongings, this solemn
fond concern for their "comfort" and "feelings," this
way of speaking of them as "he" or "she" instead of
"it," of worrying about whether some prized piece was
receiving a place of display that was properly satisfying
to its ego. He acknowledged the half-submerged notion that he had created a family, a special entity, by
assembling this hodgepodge of artifacts from a hundred
cultures and a hundred eras.

Now, though, he deliberately confronted himself
with ugly reality: when he had Gone, his "family"
would be scattered, his beloved things sold or given
away, some of them surely lost or broken in transit,
some ending up on the dusty shelves of ignorant people,

none of them ever again to know the warmth of owner-
ship he had lavished on them. And he did not care. Except in the most remote, abstract way, he simply did
not care. Today the life was gone out of them, and they
were merely masks and pots and bits of bone and pieces
of paper—objects, interesting and valuable and attractive, but lacking all feeling. Objects. They needed no
coddling. He was under no obligation to them to worry
about their welfare. Somehow, without his noticing it,
his possessions had ceased to be his pets, and he felt
no pain at the thought of parting from them. I must
indeed be ready to Go, he told himself.

Here, in the little alcove off the studio, was his
real family. A stack of portrait cubes: his wife, his son,
his daughter, his children's children, his children's children's children, each of them recorded in a gleaming
plastic box a couple of inches high. There were so
many of them—dozens! He had had only the socially
approved two children, and so had his own children,
and none of his grandchildren or great-grandchildren
had had more than three, and yet look at the clutter
of cubes! The multitude of them was the most vivid possible argument in favor of the idea of Going. One simply had to make room, or everyone would be overwhelmed by the tide of oncoming young ones. Of course
in a world where practically no one ever died except
voluntarily, and that only at a great old age, families
did tend to accumulate amazingly as the generations
came along. Even a small family, and these days there
was no other kind, was bound to become immense over
the course of eighty or ninety years through the com-
pounding progressions of controlled but persistent fertility. All additions, no subtractions. Or very few. And
so the numbers mounted. Look at all the cubes!

The cubes were clever things: computer-actuated

personality simulations. Everyone got himself cubed at least once, and those who were particularly hungry for the odd sort of immortality that cubing conferred, had new cubes made every few years. The process itself was a simple electronic transfer; it took about an hour to make a cube. The scanning machines recorded your voice and patterns of speech, your motion habits, your facial gestures, your whole set of standard reactions and responses. A battery of concise, cunningly perceptive personality tests yielded a character profile. This, too, went into the cube. They ended by having your soul in a box. Plug the cube into a receptor slot, and you came to life on a screen, smiling as you would smile, moving as you would move, sounding as you would sound, saying things you were likely to say. Of course, the thing on the screen was unreal, a mechanical mock-up, a counterfeit approximation of the person who had been cubed; but it was programmed to respond to conversation and to initiate its own conversational gambits without the stimulus of prior inputs, to absorb new data and change its outlook in the light of what it heard; in short, it behaved not like a frozen portrait but like a convincing imitation of the living person from whom it had been drawn.

Staunt studied the collection of cubes. He had five of his son, spanning Paul's life from early middle age to early old age; Paul faithfully sent his father a new cube at the beginning of each decade. Three cubes of his daughter. A number of the grandchildren. The proud parents sent him cubes of the young ones when they were ten or twelve years old, and the grandchildren themselves, when they were adults, sent along more mature versions of themselves. By now he had four or five cubes of some of them. Each year there were new cubes: an updating of someone's old one, or some great-

great-grandchild getting immortalized for the first time, and everything landing on the patriarch's shelf. Staunt rather liked the custom.

He had only one cube of his wife. They had developed the process about fifty years ago, and Edith had been dead since '47, forty-eight years back. Staunt and his wife had been among the first to be cubed; just as well, for her time had been short, though they hadn't known it. Even now, not all deaths were voluntary. Edith had died in a copter crash, and Staunt, close to ninety, had not remarried. Having the cube of her had been a great comfort to him in the years just after her death. He rarely played it now, mainly because of its technical imperfections; since the process was so new when her cube had been made, the simulation was only approximate, and her movements were jerky and awkward, not much like those of the graceful Edith he had known. He had no idea how long it had been since he had last played her. Impulsively, he slipped her cube into the slot.

The screen brightened, and there was Edith. Supple, alert, aglow. Long creamy-white hair, a purple wrap, her favorite gold pin clasped to her shoulder. She had been in her late seventies when the cube was made; she looked hardly more than fifty. Their marriage had lasted half a century. Staunt had only recently realized that the span of his life without her was now nearly as long as the span of his life with her.

"You're looking well, Henry," she said as soon as her image appeared.

"Not bad for an old relic. It's 2095, Edith. I'll be one hundred thirty-six."

"You haven't switched me on in a while, then. Not for five years, in fact."

"No. But it isn't that I haven't thought of you,

Edith. It's just that I've tended to drift away from everything I once loved. I've become a sleepwalker, in a way. Wandering through the days, filling in my time."

"Have you been well?"

"Well enough," Staunt said. "Healthy. Astonishingly healthy. I can't complain."

"Are you composing?"

"Very little, these days. Nothing, really. I've made some sketches for intended work, but that's all."

"I'm sorry. I was hoping you'd have something to play for me."

"No," he said. "Nothing."

Over the years, he had faithfully played each of his new compositions to Edith's cube, just as he had kept her up to date on the doings of their family and friends, on world events, on cultural fads. He had not wanted her cube to remain fixed forever in 2046. To have her constantly learning, growing, changing, helped to sustain his illusion that the Edith on the screen was the real Edith. He had even told her the details of her own death.

"How are the children?" she asked.

"Fine. I see them often. Paul's in fine shape, a tough old man just like his father. He's ninety-one, Edith. Does it puzzle you to be the mother of a son who's older than you are?"

She laughed. "Why should I think of it that way? If he's ninety-one, I'm one hundred twenty-five."

"Of course. Of course." If she wanted it like that.

"And Crystal's eighty-seven. Yes, that *is* a little strange. I can't help thinking of her as a young woman. Why, her children must be old themselves, and they were just babies!"

"Donna is sixty-one. David is fifty-eight. Henry is forty-seven."

"Henry?" Edith said, her face going blank. After a moment's confusion she recovered. "Oh, yes. The third child, the little accident. Your namesake. I forgot him for a moment." Henry had been born soon after Edith's death; Staunt had told her cube about him, but imprinting of post-cubing events never took as well as the original programming; she had lost the datum for a moment. As if to cover her embarrassment, Edith began asking him about all the other grandchildren, the great-grandchildren, the whole horde that had accumulated after her lifetime. She called forth names, assigned the right children to the right parents, scampered up and down the entire Staunt family tree, showing off to please him.

But he forced an abrupt switch of subject. "I want to tell you, Edith, that I've decided it's time for me to Go."

Again the blank look. "Go? Go where?"

"You know what I mean. *Going*."

"No, I don't. Really, I don't."

"To a House of Leavetaking."

"I still don't follow."

He struggled against being impatient with her. "I've explained the idioms to you. Long ago. They've been in use at least thirty or forty years. It's voluntary termination of life, Edith. I've discussed it with you. Everyone comes to it sooner or later."

"You've decided to die?"

"To Go, yes, to die, to Go."

"Why?"

"Because of the boredom. The loneliness. I've outlived most of my early friends. I've outlived my own talent. I've outlived *myself*, Edith. A hundred thirty-six years. And I could go on another fifty. But why bother? To live just for the sake of living?"

"Poor Henry. You always had such a wonderful capacity for being interested in things. The day wasn't long enough for you, with your collections, and your books, and your music, and traveling around the world, and your friends—"

"I've read everything I want to read. I've seen the whole world. I'm tired of collecting things."

"Perhaps I was the lucky one, then. A decent number of years, a happy life, and then out. Quickly."

"No. I've enjoyed living on like this, Edith. I kept my health, I didn't go senile—it's been good, all of it. Except for not having you with me. But I've stopped enjoying things. Quite suddenly I've realized that there's no point in staying any longer. The wheel has to turn. The old have to clear themselves away. Somewhere there are people waiting to have a child, waiting for a vacancy in the world, and it's up to me to create that vacancy."

"Have you told Paul and Crystal?"

"Not yet. I made the decision just today. But I'll notify them—or it'll be done for me. They'll have most of my property. I'll give my cube of you to Paul. Everything's handled very efficiently for a Departing One."

"How soon will you—Go?"

Staunt shrugged. "I don't know yet. A month, two months—there's no rush about it."

"You sound as though you don't really want to do it."

He shook his head. "I want to, Edith. But in a civilized way. Taking my leave properly. I've lived a long time; I can't let go in a single day. But I won't stay here much longer."

"I'll miss you, Henry."

He pondered the intricacies of that. The cube missing the living man. Chuckling, he said, "Paul will play my cube to you, and yours to me. We'll talk to each other through the machinery. We'll always be there for each other."

The image of Edith reached a hand toward him. He cursed the clumsiness of the simulation. Gently he touched his fingertips to the screen, making a kind of contact with her across the decades, across the barriers separating them. He blew a kiss to her. Then, quickly, before sentimentality overcame him, he pulled her cube from the slot and set it beside those of his son and daughter. In haste, nearly stumbling, he went on into his studio.

The big room held the tangible residue of his long career. Over here, the music itself, in recorded performance: disks and cassettes for the early works, sparkling playback cubes for the later ones. Here were the manuscripts, uniformly bound in red half-morocco, one of his little vanities. Here were the scrapbooks of reviews and the programs of concerts. Here were the trophies. Here were the volumes of his critical writings. Staunt had been a busy man. He looked at the titles stamped on the bindings of the manuscripts: the symphonies, the string quartets, the concerti, the miscellaneous chamber works, the songs, the sonatas, the cantatas, the operas. So much. So much. He had tried his hand at virtually every form. His music was polite, agreeable, conservative, even a bit academic, yet he made no apologies for it: he had followed his own inner voices wherever they led, and if he had not been led to rebellion and fulminations, so be it. He had given pleasure through his work. He had added to the world's small stock of beauty. It was a respectable life's accomplishment. If he had had more passion, more turbulence, more dynamism, perhaps, he would have shaken the world as Beethoven had, as Wagner. Well, the great gesture had never been his to brandish; yet he had done his best, and in his way he had achieved enough. Some men heal the sick, some men soothe the souls of the troubled, some men invent wondrous machines—and some make songs and symphonies, because they must, and because it is all they can do to enrich the world into which they had been thrust. Even now, with his life's flame burning low, with everything suddenly seeming pointless and hollow to him, Staunt felt no sense of having wasted his time filling this room with what it held. Never in the past hundred years had a week gone by without a performance of one of his compositions somewhere. That was sufficient justification for having written, for having lived.

He turned on the synthesizer and rested his fingers lightly on the keys, and of their own will they played the opening theme of his *Venus* symphony of 1989, his first mature work. How far away all that seemed now—the glittering autumn of triumphs as he conducted it himself in a dozen capitals, the critics agog, everyone from the disgruntled Brahms-fanciers to the pundits of the avant-garde rushing to embrace him as the savior of serious music. Of course, there had been a reaction to that hysterical overpraise later, when the modernists decided that no one so popular could possibly be good and the conservatives began to find him too modern, but such things were only to be expected. He had gone his own way. Eventually others had recognized his genius—a limited and qualified genius, a small and tranquil genius, but genius nevertheless. As the world emerged from the storms of the twentieth century's bitter second half, as the new society of peace and harmony took shape on the debris of the old, Staunt created the music a quieter era needed, and became its lyric voice.

Here. He pushed a cube into a playback slot. The sweet outcry of his wind quintet. Here: *The Trials of Job,* his first opera. Here: *Three Orbits for Strings and Stasis Generator.* Here: *Polyphonies for Five Worlds.* He got them all going at once, bringing wild skeins of sound out of the room's assortment of speakers, and stood in the middle, trembling a little, accepting the sonic barrage and untangling everything in his mind.

After perhaps four minutes he cut off the sound. He did not need to play the music; it was all within his head, whenever he wanted it. Lightly he caressed the smooth, glossy black backs of his scrapbooks, with all the documentation of his successes and his occasional failures neatly mounted. He ran his fingers along the rows of bound manuscripts. So much. So very much. Such a long productive life. He had no complaints.

He told his telephone to get him the Office of Fulfillment again.

"My Guide is Martin Bollinger," he said. "Would you let him know that I'd like to be transferred to the House of Leavetaking as soon as possible?"

Four

Bollinger, sitting beside him in the copter, leaned across him and pointed down.

"That's it," he said. "Omega Prime, right below."

The House of Leavetaking seemed to be a string of gauzy white tentlike pavilions, arranged in a U-shape around a courtyard garden. The late afternoon sun tinged the pavilions with gold and red. Bare fangs of purplish mountains rose on the north and east; on the other side of Omega Prime the flat brown Arizona desert, pocked with cacti and palo verde, stretched toward the dark horizon.

The copter landed silently. When the hatch opened, Staunt felt the blast of heat. "We don't modulate the outdoor climate here," Bollinger explained. "Most Departing Ones seem to prefer it that way. Contact with the natural environment."

"I don't mind," Staunt said. "I've always loved the desert."

A welcoming party had gathered by the time he emerged from the copter. Three members of Omega Prime's staff, in smocks monogramed with the Fulfillment insignia. Four withered oldsters, evidently awaiting their own imminent Going. A transport robot, with its wheelchair seat already in position. Staunt, picking his way carefully over the rough, pebble-strewn surface of the landing field, was embarrassed by the attention. He said in a low voice to Bollinger, "Tell them I don't need the chair. I can still walk. I'm no invalid."

They clustered around him, introducing themselves: Dr. James, Miss Elliot, Mr. Falkenbridge. Those were the staff people. The four Departing Ones croaked their names at him too, but Staunt was so astonished by their appearance that he forgot to pay attention. The shriveled faces, the palsied clawlike hands, the parchment skin—did he look like that, too? It was years since he had seen anyone his own age. He had the impression that he had come through his fourteen decades well preserved, but perhaps that was only an illusion born of vanity, perhaps he really was as much of a ruin as these four. Unless they were much older than he, one hundred seventy-five, one hundred eighty years old, right at the limits of what was now the human span of mortality. Staunt stared at them in wonder, awed and dismayed by their gummy grins.

Falkenbridge, a husky red-haired young man, apparently some sort of orderly, was trying to ease him into the wheelchair. Irritably Staunt shook him off, saying, "No. No. I'll manage. Martin, tell him I don't need it."

Bollinger whispered something to Falkenbridge. The young man shrugged and sent the transport robot away. Now they all began walking toward the House of Leavetaking, Falkenbridge on Staunt's right, Miss Elliot on his left, both of them staying close to him in case he should topple.

He found himself under unexpectedly severe strain. Possibly refusing the wheelchair had been foolish bravado. The fierce dry heat, the fatigue of his ninety-minute rocket journey across the continent, the coarse texture of the ground, all conspired to make his legs wobbly. Twice he came close to falling. The first time Miss Elliot gently caught his elbow and steadied him; the second, he managed to recover himself, after a short half-stumble that sent pain shooting through his left ankle.

Suddenly, all at once, he was feeling his age. In a single day he had begun to dodder, as though his decision to enter a House of Leavetaking had stripped him of all his late-staying vigor. No. No. He rejected the idea. He was merely tired, as a man his age had every right to be; with a little rest he'd be himself again. He walked faster, despite the effort it cost him. Sweat trickled down his cheeks. There was a stitch in his side. His entire left leg ached.

At last they reached the entrance to Omega Prime.

He saw now that what had seemed to be gauzy tents, viewed from above, were in fact sturdy and substantial plastic domes, linked by an intricate network of covered passageways. The courtyard around which they were grouped, contained elaborate plantings of desert flora: giant stiff-armed cacti, looping white-whiskered succulents, odd and angular thorny things. The plants had been grouped with remarkable grace and subtleness around an assortment of strange boulders and sleek stone slabs; the effect was one of extraordinary beauty. Staunt stood a moment contemplating it. Bollinger said gently, "Why not go to your suite first? The garden will still be here this evening."

He had an entire dome to himself. Interior walls divided it into a bedroom, a sitting room, and a kind of utility room; everything was airy and tastefully simple, and the temperature was twenty-five degrees cooler than outside. A window faced the garden.

The staff people and the quartet of Departing Ones vanished, leaving Staunt alone with his Guide. Bollinger said, "Each of the residents has a suite like this. You can eat here, if you like, although there's a community dining room under the courtyard. There are recreational facilities there too—a library, a theater, a game room—but you can spend all of your time perfectly happily right where you are."

Staunt lowered himself gingerly into a webfoam hammock. As his weight registered, tiny mechanical hands began to massage his back. Bollinger smiled.

"This is your data terminal," he said, handing Staunt a copper-colored rod about eight inches long. "It's a standard access unit. You can get any book in the library—and there are thousands of them—screened on request, and you can play whatever music you'd like, and it's also a telephone input. Ask it to connect you with anyone at all. Go on. Ask."

"My son Paul," Staunt said.

"Ask it," said Bollinger.

Staunt activated the terminal and gave it Paul's name and access number. Instantly a screen came to life just beside the hammock. Staunt's son appeared in its silvery depths. The screen could almost have been a mirror, a strange sort of time-softening mirror that was capable of taking the face of a very old man and reflecting it as that of a man who was merely old. Staunt beheld someone who was a younger version of himself, though far from young: cool gray eyes, thin lips, lean bony face, a dense mane of white hair.

Paul's face was deeply lined but still vigorous. At the age of ninety-one he had not yet retired from the firm of architects he headed. So long as a man's health was good and his mind was sound and he still found his career rewarding, there was no reason to retire; when mind or body failed or career lost its savor, that was the time to withdraw and make oneself ready to Go.

Staunt said, "I'm calling you from Omega Prime."

"What's that, Henry?"

"You've never heard of it? A House of Leavetaking in Arizona. It looks like a lovely place. Martin Bollinger brought me here this evening."

Paul looked startled. "Are you thinking of Going, Henry?"

"I am."

"You never told me you had any such thing in mind!"

"I'm telling you now."

"Are you in poor health?"

"I feel fine," Staunt said. "Everyone asks me that, and I say the same thing. My health is excellent."

"Then why—"

"Do I have to justify it? I've lived long enough. My life is over."

"But you've been so alert, so *involved*—"

"It's my decision to make. It's ungracious of you to quarrel with me over it."

"I'm not quarreling," Paul said. "I'm trying to adapt to it. You know, you've been part of my life for nine decades. I don't give a damn what the social conventions are: I can't simply smile and nod and say how sweet when my father announces he's going to die."

"To Go."

"To Go," Paul muttered. "Whatever. Have you told Crystal?"

"You're the first member of the family to know. Except for your mother, that is."

"My mother?"

"The cube," said Staunt.

"Oh. Yes. The cube." A thin, edgy laugh. "All right. I'll tell the others. I suppose I'll have to learn how to be head of the family, finally. You're not going to be doing this immediately, are you?"

"Naturally not. Where do you get such ideas? I'll have a proper Leavetaking. Graceful. Serene. A few weeks, a month or two—the usual thing."

"And we can visit you?"

"I'll expect you to," Staunt said. "That's part of the ritual."

"What about—pardon me—what about the legal aspects? Disposition of property, things like that?"

"It'll all be managed in the customary way. The

Office of Fulfillment is supposed to help me. Don't worry: you'll get everything that's coming to you."

"That isn't a kind way to phrase it, Henry."

"I don't have to be kind any more. I don't even have to make sense. I'm just a crazy old man getting ready to Go."

"Henry—Father—"

"All right. I'm sorry. Somehow this conversation hasn't worked right at all. Shall we start it over?"

"I'd like to," Paul said.

Staunt realized he was quivering. The muscles of his face were drawn taut. He made a deliberate attempt to relax, and after a moment, said quietly, "It's a perfectly normal, desirable step to take. I'm old and tired and lonely and bored. I'm no use to myself or to anybody else, and there's really no sense troubling my doctors to keep me functioning any longer. So I'm going to Go. I'd rather Go now, when I'm still reasonably healthy and clear-witted, instead of trying to hang on another few decades until I've slid into senility. I've moved to Omega Prime, and you'll all come to visit me before my Leavetaking, and it'll be a peaceful and beautiful Going, I hope. That's all. There's nothing to weep about. In forty or fifty years you'll understand all this a lot better."

"I understand it now," Paul said. "You caught me by surprise when you called, but I understand. Of course. Of course. We don't want to lose you, but that's only our selfishness talking. You've lived a full life, and, well, the wheel has to turn."

How smoothly he does it, Staunt thought. How easily he slips into the jargon. How readily he agrees with me, after his first reflexive moment of shock. *Yes, Henry, certainly, Henry, it's wise of you to Go, Henry, you've lived long enough.* Staunt wondered which was the fraud: Paul's initial resistance to the idea of his Going, or his philosophical acquiescence. And what difference did it make? Why, Staunt asked himself, should I be offended if my son thinks it's right for me to Go when I was offended two minutes earlier by his trying to talk me out of it?

He was beginning to be unsure of his own ground. Perhaps he *did* want to be talked out of it.

I must read Hallam shortly, he told himself.

He said to Paul, "I have a great deal to do this evening. I'll call you tomorrow. Or you call me."

The screen went blank.

Bollinger said, "He took it rather well, I thought. The children don't always accept the idea that a parent is Going. They accept the theory of Leavetaking, but they always assume that it's someone else's old folks who'll Go."

"They want their own parents to live forever, even if the parents don't feel like staying around any longer?"

"That's it."

"What if someone *does* feel like staying forever?" Staunt asked.

Bollinger shrugged. "We never try to force the issue. We hint a little, as subtly as we know how, if someone is one hundred forty or one hundred fifty or so, and really a wreck, but clinging to life anyway. For that matter, if he's eighty or ninety, even, and just going through the motions of living, held together by his doctors alone, we'll try to encourage Going. We have gentle ways of working through doctors or friends or relatives, trying to overcome the fear of dying in the ones who linger, trying to get across the idea that it's not only best for society for them to move on, it's best for themselves. If they don't take the hint, there's nothing we can do. Involuntary euthanasia just isn't part of our system."

"How old," Staunt asked, "are the oldest living people now?"

"I think the oldest ones known are something like one hundred seventy-five or one hundred eighty. Which means they were born in the early part of the twentieth century, around the time of the First World War. Anyone born before that simply spent too much of his life in the era of medieval medicine to hope for a really long span. But if you were born, say, in 1920, you were still only fifty-five or sixty when the era of organ transplants and computerized health services and laser surgery was beginning, and if you were lucky enough to be in good shape in the 1970's, the 1980's, why, you could be kept going just about indefinitely thereafter. Into the era of tissue regeneration and all the rest. A few from the early twentieth century did hang on into the era of total medicine, and some of them are still with us. Politely declining to Go."

"How much longer can they last?"

"Hard to say," Bollinger replied. "We just don't know what the practical limits of the human life-span are. Our experience with total medicine doesn't go back far enough. I've heard it said that two hundred or two hundred ten is the top figure, but in another twenty or thirty years we may have some people who've reached that figure, and we'll find that we can keep them going beyond it. Maybe there *is* no top limit, now that we can do the things we do to rebuild a decaying body. But how hideously antisocial it is of them to hang around for century after century just to test our medical skills!"

"But if they're making valuable contributions to society through all those hundreds of years—"

"*If*," Bollinger said. "But the fact is that ninety, ninety-five percent of all people never make any contributions to society, even when they're young. They just occupy space, do jobs that could really be done better by machines, sire children who aren't any more gifted than they are—and hang on, living and living and living. We don't want to lose anyone who's valuable, Henry; I've been through that with you already. But most people aren't valuable to begin with, and get less valuable as they go along, and there's no reason in the universe why they should live past one hundred or one hundred ten, let alone to two hundred or three hundred or whatever."

"That's a harsh philosophy. Cynical, even."

"I know. But read Hallam. The wheel's got to turn. We've reached an average life-span that would have seemed wild fantasy as late as the time when you were a child, Henry, but that doesn't mean we have to strive to make everyone immortal. Not unless people are willing to give up having children, and they aren't. It's a finite planet. If there's inflow, there has to be outflow, and I like to think that those flowing out are the ones who have the least to offer to the rest of us. The decrepit, the feeble, the slow-witted, the mean-souled. Thank God, most old folks agree. For every one who absolutely won't give up his grip on life, there are fifty who are glad to go once they've hit one hundred or so. And as the remainder get even older, they change their minds about staying, just as you've done lately. Not many want to go on past one hundred fifty. The few who do, well, we'll look on them as experiments in geriatrics, and let them be."

"How old are those four who met my copter?" Staunt asked.

"I couldn't tell you. One hundred twenty, one hundred thirty, something like that. Most of those who arrange for Leavetaking now are people born between 1960 and 1980."

"Of my generation, then."

"I suppose, yes."

"Do I look as bad as they do? They're a bunch of walking mummies, Martin. I'd have guessed they were fifty years older than I am."

"I doubt that very much."

"But I'm not like them, am I? I've got my teeth. My hair. My real eyes. I look old, but not ancient. Or am I fooling myself, Martin? Am I really a dried-up nightmare too? Is it just that I've grown accustomed to the way I look, I haven't noticed the changes, decade after decade as I get older and older?"

"There's a mirror," Bollinger said. "Answer your own questions."

Staunt stared at himself. Lines and wrinkles, yes: a contour map of time, the valleys and ravines of a long life. Blotches on the skin. The glittering eyes deeply recessed; the cheeks fleshless, revealing the sharp outlines of the skull beneath. An old face, tremendously old. But yet not like *their* faces. He was no mummy yet. He imagined that a man of the twentieth century would guess him to be no more than eighty or eighty-five, just as a man of the twentieth century would guess Paul to be in his late sixties and Martin Bollinger in his late fifties. Those others, those four, showed their true ages. It must take all the magic at their doctors' command to keep them together. And now, weary of cheating death, they've come here to Go and be over with the farce. Whereas I am still strong, whereas I could continue easily, if only I wanted to continue.

"Well?" Bollinger asked.

"I'm in pretty good shape," Staunt said. "I'm quitting while I'm ahead. It's the right way to do it." He picked up the data terminal again. "I wonder if they have any of my music in storage here," he said, and opened the access node and made a request; and the room flooded with the first chords of his Twelfth Symphony. He was pleased. He closed his eyes and listened. When the movement ended, he looked around the room, and found that Bollinger had gone.

Five

Dr. James came to see him a little while later, as night was enfolding the desert. Staunt was standing by the window, watching the brilliant stars appear, when the room annunciator told him of his visitor.

The doctor was a youngish man—forty, fifty, Staunt was no longer good at guessing ages—with a long fragile-looking nose and a gentle, faintly unctuous, I-want-you-to-have-a-lovely-Going sort of manner. His first words to Staunt were, "I've been looking through your medical file. I really must congratulate you on the excellent state of your health."

"There's something about music that keeps people in good shape," Staunt said.

"Are you a conductor?"

"A composer. But I've conducted my own works quite often. Waving the baton—it's obviously good exercise."

"I don't know much about music, I'm afraid. Some afternoon you must program some of your favorite pieces for me." The doctor grinned shyly. "The simpler ones. Music for an unsophisticated medic, if you've written any." He was silent a moment. Then he said,

"You really do have an excellent medical history. Your doctor's computer transferred your whole file to us this afternoon when your reservation was made. Naturally, while you're with us we want you to remain in perfect health and comfort. You'll receive the same kind of care here that you were getting at home—the muscle therapies, the ion-balance treatments, the circulatory clearances, and so forth. Including any special supportive therapy that may become necessary. Not that I anticipate someone like you to need a great deal of that."

"I could last another fifty years, eh?"

Dr. James looked abashed. His plump cheeks glowed. "That choice is entirely up to you, Mr. Staunt."

"Don't worry. I'm not about to change my mind."

"No one here will hurry you," the doctor said. "We've had people remain at Omega Prime for three, even four years. Each man's Leavetaking is the most important event in his life, after all; he's entitled to go about it at his own pace, to disengage himself from the world as gradually as he wants. You do understand that there is no cost to you for any part of your residence here. The government underwrites the whole business."

"I think Martin Bollinger explained that to me."

"Good. Let me discuss with you, then, some of your Leavetaking options. Many Departing Ones prefer to begin their withdrawal from the world by making a grand tour—a kind of farewell to all the great sights, the Pyramids, the Taj Mahal, Notre Dame, the Sahara, Antarctica, whatever. We can make any such travel arrangements you'd like. We have several organized tours, on which you'd travel with five or six or ten other Departing Ones and several Guides—a one-month tour of the most famous places, a two-month tour, or a three-month tour. These are packaged in advance, but we can make changes in itinerary by unanimous consent of the

Departing Ones. Or, if you prefer, you could travel alone, that is, just you and your Guide, to any part of the world that—"

Staunt looked at him in astonishment. Was this man a doctor or a travel agent?

And did he want to take any such tour? It was vaguely tempting. At government expense to see the temples of Chichén Itzá by moonlight, to float over the Andes and descend into Machu Picchu, to smell the scent of cloves on Zanzibar, to look up at a sequoia's distant blue-green crown, to see the hippos jostling in the Nile, to roam the crumbling dusty streets of Babylon, to drift above the baroque intricacies of the Great Barrier Reef, to see the red sandstone spires of Utah, to tramp along the Great Wall of China, to make his farewells to lakes and deserts and mountains and valleys, to cities and wastelands, to penguins, to polar bears—

But he had seen all those places. Why go back? Why bother to make a breathless pilgrimage, dragging his flimsy bones from place to place? Once was enough. He had his memories.

"No," he said. "If I had any desire to travel anywhere, I wouldn't have thought of Going in the first place. If you follow me. The flavor's gone out of everything, do you see? I don't have the motivation for hauling myself around. Not even to make sentimental gestures of farewell."

"As you wish, Mr. Staunt. Most Departing Ones do take advantage of the travel option. But you'll find no coercion here. If you feel no urge to travel, why, stay right where you are."

"Thank you. What are some of the other Leave-taking options?"

"It's customary for the Departing Ones to seek experiences they may have missed during their lifetimes, or to repeat ones that they found particularly rewarding. If there's some special type of food that you enjoy—"

"I was never a gourmet."

"Or works of music you want to hear again, masterpieces you'd like to live with one last time—"

"There are some," Staunt said. "Not many. Most of them bore me now. When Mozart and Bach and Beethoven begin to bore a man, he knows it's time to Go. Do you know, even Staunt has begun to seem less interesting to me lately?"

Dr. James did not smile.

He said, "In any event, you'll find that we're programmed for every imaginable work of music, and if there are any you know of that we don't have and ought to have, I hope you'll tell us. It's the same with books. Your screen can give you any work in any language— just put in the requisition. A number of Departing Ones use this opportunity at last to read *War and Peace,* or *Ulysses,* or *The Tale of Genji,* say."

"Or *The Encyclopaedia Britannica,*" Staunt said, "from 'Aardvark' to 'Zwingli.' "

"You think you're joking. We had a Departing One here five years ago who set out to do just that."

"How far did he get?" Staunt wanted to know. " 'Antimony'? 'Betelgeuse'?"

" 'Magnetism,' I think. He was quite dedicated to the job."

"Perhaps I'll do some reading, too, doctor. Not the *Britannica.* But Hallam, at least. Maybe Montaigne, and maybe Hobbes, and maybe Ben Jonson. For about sixty years I've been meaning to read my way through Ben Jonson. I suppose this is my last chance."

"Another option," Dr. James said, "is a memory jolt."

"Which is?"

"Chemical stimulation of the mnemonic centers. It stirs up the memories, awakens things you may not have thought about for eighty or ninety years, sends images and textures and odors and colors of past experiences through your mind in a remarkably vivid way. In a sense, it's a trip through your entire past. I don't know any Departing One who's done it and not come out of it in a kind of ecstasy, a radiant glow of joy."

Staunt frowned. "I'd guess that it could be a painful experience. Disturbing. Depressing."

"Not at all. Never. It's emotion recollected in tranquillity: the experiences may have been painful originally, but the replay of them never is. The jolt allows you to come to terms with all that you've been and done. I've known people to ask to Go within an hour of coming out of the jolt, and not because they were depressed; they simply want to take their leave on a high note."

"I'll think about it," Staunt said.

"Other than the things I've mentioned, your period of Leavetaking is completely unstructured. You write the script. Your family will come to see you, and your friends; I think you'll get to know some of the other Departing Ones here; there'll be Leavetaking parties as one by one they opt to Go, and then there'll be Farewell ceremonies for them, and they'll Go; and eventually, a month, six months, as you choose, you'll request your own Leavetaking party and Farewell ceremony, and finally you'll Go. You know, Mr. Staunt, I feel a tremendous sense of exhilaration here every day, working with these wonderful Departing Ones, helping to make their last weeks beautiful, watching the serenity with which they Go. My own time of Going is still ninety or a hundred years away, I suppose, and yet in a way I look forward to it now; I feel a certain impatience, knowing that the happiest hours of my life will come at the very end of it. To Go when still healthy, to step voluntarily out of the world in an atmosphere of peace and fulfillment, to know that you cap a long and successful life by the noblest of all deeds, letting the wheel turn, giving younger people an opportunity to occupy your place—how marvelous it all is!"

"I wish," Staunt said, "that I could orchestrate your aria. Shimmering tremolos in the strings—the plaintive wail of the oboes—harps, six harps, making celestial noises—and then a great crescendo of trombones and French horns and bassoons, a sort of Valhalla music welling up—"

Looking baffled, Dr. James said, "I told you, I don't really know much about music."

"I'm sorry. I shouldn't mock, not at my age. I'm sure it *is* beautiful and marvelous. I'm very happy to be here."

"A pleasure to have you," said Dr. James.

Six

Staunt did not feel up to having dinner in the community dining room; he had had a long journey, crossing several time zones, and his appetite was awry. He ordered a light meal, juice and soup and fruit, and it arrived almost instantaneously via a subterranean conveyor system. He ate sparingly. Before I Go, he promised himself, I will have steak au poivre again, and escargots, and a curry of lamb, and all the other things I never cared much for while I was young enough to digest them. James offers me a chance; why not take it? I will become a preposthumous gourmet. Even if it kills me. Better to Go like that than by drinking whatever tasteless potion it is they give you at the end.

After dinner he asked where Bollinger was.

"Mr. Bollinger has gone home," Staunt was told. "But he'll be back the day after tomorrow. He'll spend three days a week with you while you're here."

Staunt supposed it was unreasonable of him to expect his Guide to devote all his time to him. But Bollinger might at least have stayed around for the first night. Unless the idea was to have the Departing One make his own adaptation to life in the House of Leavetaking.

He toyed with his data terminal, testing its resources. For a while he amused himself by pulling obscure music from the machine: medieval organa, Hummel sonatas, eighteenth-century German opera, odd electronic things from the middle of the twentieth century. But it was impossible to win that game; apparently, if the music had ever been recorded, the computer had access to it. Staunt turned next to books, asking for Hobbes and Hallam, Montaigne and Jonson—not screenings but actual print-out copies of his own, and within minutes after he placed the requisitions, the fresh crisp sheaves of pages began arriving on the same conveyor that had brought his dinner. He put the books aside without looking through them. Perhaps some telephone calls, he thought: my daughter, maybe, or a friend or two. But everyone he knew seemed to live in the East or in Europe, and it was some miserable early hour of the morning there. Staunt gave up the idea of talking to anyone. He dropped into a dull leaden mood. Why had he come to these three little plastic rooms in the desert, giving up his fine well-tended house, his treasures of art, his dogwoods, his books? Surrendering everything for this sterile halfway station on the road to death? *I could call Dr. James, I suppose, and tell him I'd like to Go right now. Save the staff some trouble, save the taxpayers some money, save my family the bother of going through the Farewell rituals. How is Going managed, anyway?* He believed it was a drug. Something sweet and pleasant, and then the body goes to sleep. A tranquil death, like Socrates', just a chill climbing quickly through the legs toward the heart. *Tonight. Tonight. To Go tonight.*

No.

I must play the game properly. I must do my Going with style.

He turned to the terminal and said, "I'd like someone to show me down to the recreation center."

Miss Elliot, the nurse, appeared, as though she had been stored waiting in a box just outside his suite. So far as Staunt still had the capacity to tell, she was a handsome girl, golden-haired and buxom, with fine clear skin and large glossy blue eyes, but there was something remote and impersonal and mechanical about her; she could almost have been a robot. "The recreation center? Certainly, Mr. Staunt." She offered her arm. He gestured as if to refuse it, but then, remembering his earlier struggle to walk, took it anyway, and leaned heavily on her as they went out. *Thus I accept my mortality. Thus I speed my final decline.*

A dropshaft took them into an immense, brightly lit area somewhere far underground. There was a mov-

ing slidewalk here; Miss Elliot guided him onto it and
they trundled along a few hundred yards, to a step-off
turntable that fed him smoothly into the recreation
center.

It was a good-sized room, divided chapel-fashion
at its far end into smaller rooms. Staunt saw screens,
data terminals, playback units, and other access equip-
ment, all of it duplicating what every Departing One
had in his own suite. But of course they came here out
of loneliness; it might be more comforting to do one's
reading or listening in public, he thought. There also
were games of various kinds suitable for the very old,
nothing that required any great degree of stamina or
coordination: stochastic chess, polyrhythmers, double-
orbit, things like that. We slide into childhood on our
way to the grave.

There were about fifty Departing Ones in the center, he guessed. Most of them looked as old as the four
who had met his copter earlier in the day; a few, fright-
eningly, seemed even older. Some looked much younger,
no more than seventy or eighty. Staunt thought at first
they might be Guides, but he saw on their faces a certain
placid slackness that seemed common to all these Departing Ones, a look of dim mindless content, of resig-
nation, of death-in-life. Evidently, one did not have to
be heavily stricken in years to feel the readiness to Go.

"Shall I introduce you to some of the other Departing Ones?" Miss Elliot asked.

"Please. Yes."

She took him around. This is Henry Staunt, she
said again and again. The famous composer. And she
told him their names. He recognized none of them.
David Golding, Michael Green, Ella Freeman, Seymour
Church, Katherine Parks. Names. Withered faces. Miss
Elliot supplied no identifying tags for any of them, as

she had done for him; no "Ella Freeman, the famous
actress," no "David Golding, the famous astronaut," no
"Seymour Church, the famous financier." They had not
been actresses or astronauts or financiers. God alone
knew what they had been; Miss Elliot wasn't saying, and
Staunt found himself without the energy to ask. Ac-
countants, stockbrokers, housewives, teachers, pro-
grammers. Anything. Nothing. Just people. Ordinary
people. Survivors from previous geological epochs. So
old, so old, so old. In hardly any of them could Staunt
detect the glimmer of life, and he saw for the first time
how fortunate he had been to reach this great old age of
his intact. The walking dead. Seymour Church, the famous zombie. Katherine Parks, the famous somnam-
bulist. None of them seemed ever to have heard of him.
Staunt was not surprised at that; even a famous composer learns early in life that he will be famous only
among a minority of his countrymen. But still, those
blank looks, those unfocused eyes. Pleased to meet you,
Mr. Stout. How d'ye do, Mr. Stint. Hello. Hello. Hello.

"Have you met some interesting people?" Miss Elliot said, passing close to Staunt half an hour later.

"I'm more tired than I thought," Staunt said. "Perhaps you should take me back to my suite."

Already the names of the other Departing Ones
were slipping from his mind. He had had brief, fragmen-
tary conversations with six or seven of them, but they
could not keep their minds on what they were saying,
and neither, he discovered, could he. A terrible fatigue
that he had never known before was settling over him.
Senility must be contagious, he decided. Thirty minutes
among the Departing Ones and I am as they are. I must
get away.

Miss Elliot guided him to his room. Mr. Falkenbridge, the orderly, appeared unbidden, helped him un-

dress, and put him to bed. Staunt lay awake a long time in the unfamiliar bed, his tense mind ticking relentlessly. A time-zone problem, he thought. He was tempted to ask for a sedative, but as he searched for the strength to sit up and ring for Miss Elliot, sleep suddenly captured him and drew him down into a pit of darkness.

Seven

In the next few days he managed to get to know some of the others. It was a task he imposed on himself. Throughout his life Staunt had negotiated, sometimes with difficulty, the narrow boundary between reserve and snobbery, trying to keep to himself without seeming to reject the company of others, and he was particularly eager not to withdraw into self-sufficiency at this time of all times. So he sought out his fellow Departing Ones and did what he could to scale the barriers separating them from him.

It was late in life to be making new friends, though. He found it hard to communicate much about himself to them, or to draw from them anything of consequence beyond the bare facts of their lives. As he suspected, they were a dull lot, people who had never achieved anything in particular except longevity. Staunt did not hold that against them: he saw no reason why everyone had to bubble with creativity, and he had deeply loved many whose only gifts had been gifts of friendship. But these people, coming now to the end of their days, were

hollowed by time's erosions, and there was so little left
of them that even ordinary human warmth had been
worn away. They answered his questions perfunctorily
and rarely responded with questions of their own. "A
composer? How nice. I used to listen to music sometimes." He succeeded in discovering that Seymour
Church had been living in the House of Leavetaking for
eight months at his son's insistence but did not want to
Go; that Ella Freeman had had (or believed she had
had) a love affair, more than a century ago, with a man
who later became President; that David Golding had
been married six times and was inordinately proud of it;
that each of these Departing Ones clung to some such
trifling biographical datum that gave him a morsel of in-
dividual identity. But Staunt was unable to penetrate beyond that one identifying datum; either nothing else was
in them, or they could not or would not reveal themselves to him. A dull lot, but Staunt was no longer in a
position to choose his companions for their merits.

During his first week in Arizona most of the members of his family came to see him, beginning with Paul
and young Henry, Crystal's son. They stayed with him
for two days. David, Crystal's other son, arrived a little
later, along with his wife, their children, and one of their
grandchildren; then Paul's two daughters showed up,
and an assortment of youngsters. Everyone, even the
young ones, wore sickly-sweet expressions of bliss.
They were determined to look upon Staunt's Going as a
beautiful event. In their conversations with him they
never spoke of Going at all, only of family gossip, music,
springtime, flowers, reminiscences. Staunt played their
game. He had no more wish for emotional turmoil than
they did; he wanted to back amiably out of their lives,
smiling and bowing. He was careful, therefore, not to
imply in anything he said that he was shortly going to

end his life. He pretended that he had merely come to this place in the desert for a brief vacation.

The only one who did not visit him, aside from a few great-grandchildren, was his daughter Crystal. When he tried to phone her, he got no reply. His callers avoided any mention of her. Was she ill, Staunt wondered? Dead, even? "What are you trying to hide from me?" he asked his son finally. "Where's Crystal?"

"Crystal's fine," Paul said.

"That's not what I asked. Why hasn't she come here?"

"Actually she hasn't been entirely well."

"As I suspected. She's seriously ill, and you think the shock of hearing about it will harm me."

Paul shook his head. "It isn't like that at all."

"What's wrong with her?" Visions of cancer, heart surgery, brain tumors. "Has she had some kind of transplant? Is she in a hospital?"

"It isn't a physical problem. Crystal's simply suffering from fatigue. She's gone to Luna Dome for a rest."

"I spoke to her last month," Staunt said. "She looked all right then. I want the truth, Paul."

"The truth."

"The truth, yes."

Paul's eyes closed wearily for a moment, and in that moment Staunt saw his son for what he was, an old man, though not so old a man as he. After a pause Paul said in a flat, toneless voice, "The trouble is that Crystal hasn't accepted your Going very well. I called her about it, right after you told me, and she became hysterical. She thinks you're being hoodwinked, that your Guide is part of a conspiracy to do away with you, that your decision is at least ten or fifteen years premature. And she can't speak calmly about it, so we felt it was best to get her away where she wasn't likely to speak to you, to keep her from disturbing you. There. That's the story. I wasn't going to tell you."

"Silly of you to hide it."

"We didn't want to spoil your Going with a lot of carrying on."

"My Going won't spoil that easily. I'd like to talk to her, Paul. She may benefit from whatever help I can give her. If I can make her see Going for what it really is—if I can convince her that her outlook is unhealthy —Paul, set up a call to Luna Dome for me, will you? The Fulfillment people will pay. Crystal needs me. I have to make her understand."

"If you insist," Paul said.

Somehow, though, technical problems prevented the placing of the call that day, and the next, and the one after that. And then Paul left the House of Leavetaking. When Staunt phoned him at home to find out where on the moon Crystal actually was, he became evasive and said that she had recently transferred from one sanatorium to another. It would be a few more days, Paul said, before the call could be placed. Seeing his son's agitation, Staunt ceased pressing the issue. They did not want him to talk to Crystal. Crystal's hysterics would ruin his Going, they felt. They would not give him the chance to soothe her. So be it. He could not fight them. This must be a difficult time for the whole family; if they wished to think that Crystal would upset him so terribly, he would let the matter drop, for a while. Perhaps he could speak to her later. There would be time before his Going. Perhaps. Perhaps.

Eight

Every Monday, Wednesday, and Friday, Martin Bollinger came to him, usually in midafternoon, an hour or so after lunch. Generally Staunt received his Guide in his suite, although sometimes, on the cooler days, they strolled together through the garden. Their meetings invariably fell into three well-defined segments. First, Bollinger would display lively interest in Staunt's current activities. What books are you reading? Have you been listening to music? Are there any interesting Departing Ones for you to talk with? Is the staff taking good care of you? Do your relatives visit you often enough? Has the urge to compose anything come over you? Is there anyone you'd especially like to see? Are you thinking of traveling at all? And so on and so on, the same questions surfacing frequently.

When the questions were over, Bollinger would glide into the second phase, a conversation with a quiet autumnal tone, a recollection of vanished days. Sometimes he spoke as though Staunt had already Gone; he talked of Staunt's compositions in the same way he might refer to those of some early master. The symphonies, Bollinger would say: what a testament, what a mighty cumulative structure, nothing like them since Mahler, surely. The quartets, obviously akin to Beethoven's, yet thoroughly contemporary, true expressions of their composer and his times. And Staunt would nod, solemnly accepting Bollinger's verdicts in curious, dreamy objectivity. They would talk of mutual friends in the same way, viewing them as closed books, as cubes rather than as living, evolving persons. Staunt saw that Bollinger was helping to place distance between him and the life he had lived. Already, he felt remote from that life. After several weeks in the House of Leavetaking, he was coming to look upon himself more as someone who had very carefully studied Henry Staunt's biography than as the actual living Staunt, the inhabitant of Staunt's body.

The third phase of each meeting saw Bollinger turn quite frankly to matters directly related to Staunt's Going. Constantly he pressed Staunt to examine his motives, and he avoided the false gentleness with which everyone else seemed to treat him. The Guide was pursuing truth. Do you truly wish to Go, Henry? If so, have you started to give thought to the date of your Leavetaking? Will you stay in the world another five weeks? Three months? Six? No, no one's rushing you. Stay a year, if you want. I merely wonder if you've looked realistically, yet, at what it means to Go. Whether you comprehend your purpose in asking for it. Get behind the euphemism, Henry. Going is dying. The termination of all. For you, the end of the universe. Is this what you want, Henry? Is it? Is it? Is it? I'm not trying to make it harder for you. I'm trying to make it more pure. A truly spiritual Going, the rarest kind. But only if you're ready. Are you aware that you can withdraw from the whole undertaking at any point? It isn't cowardly to turn away from Going. See Hallam: Going isn't suicide, it's a sweet renunciation, properly reserved only for those who fully understand their motives. Anyone can kill himself in a fit of gloom. A proper going requires spiritual strength. Some people enroll in a House of Leavetaking two, even three times before they can take that last step. Yes, they go through the entire ritual of Fare-

well, almost to the end—and then they say they want
to go home, and we send them home. We never push.
We are not interested in sending victims out of the
world. Only volunteers whose eyes are open. Have you
been reading Hallam, Henry? Our philosopher of death.
Look into yourself before you leap. Ask yourself, Is
this what I want?

"What I want is to Go," Staunt would reply. But he
could not tell Bollinger how long it would actually be
before he would find himself ready to take his leave.

There seemed to be some pattern in this thrice-
weekly pas de deux of conversation with his Guide.
Bollinger appeared to be maneuvering him patiently and
circuitously toward some sort of apocalyptic burst of
joyful insight, a radiant moment of comprehension in
which he would be able to say, feeling worthy of Hallam
as he did, "Now I shall Go." But the maneuvers did not
seem successful. Often, Staunt came away from Bollinger confused and depressed, less certain than ever of his
desire to Go.

By the fourth week, most of his time was being
given over to reading. Music had largely palled for him.
His family, having made the obligatory first round of
visits, had stopped coming; they would not return to the
House of Leavetaking until word reached them that he
was in the final phase of his Going and ready for his
Farewell ceremony. He had said all he cared to say to
his friends. The recreation center bored him and the
company of the other Departing Ones chilled him.
Therefore he read. At the outset, he went about it duti-
fully, mechanically, taking it up solely as a chore for the
improvement of his mind in its final hours. Like an old
pharaoh trying to repair his looks before he must be
delivered into the hands of the mummifiers, Staunt
meant to polish his soul with philosophy while he still

had the chance. It was in that spirit that he plodded through Hobbes, whose political ideas had set him ablaze when he was nineteen, and who merely seemed crabbed and sour now. *It may seem strange to some man, that has not well weighed these things; that nature should thus dissociate, and render men apt to invade, and destroy one another: and he may therefore, not trusting to this inference, made from the passions, desire perhaps to have the same confirmed by experience. Let him therefore consider with himself, when taking a journey, he arms himself, and seeks to go well accompanied; when going to sleep, he locks his doors; when even in his house he locks his chests; and this when he knows there be laws, and public officers, armed, to revenge all injuries shall be done him; what opinion he has of his fellow-subjects, when he rides armed; of his fellow citizens, when he locks his doors; and of his children, and servants, when he locks his chests. Does he not there as much accuse mankind by his actions, as I do by my words?* Growing up in a tense, bleak world of peace that was really war, Staunt had found it easy to accept Hobbes' dark teachings. Now he was not so sure that the natural condition of mankind was a state of conflict, every man at war with every other man. Something had changed in the world, it seemed. Or in Staunt. He put Hobbes away in displeasure.

He was almost afraid to turn to Montaigne, fearing that that other great guide of his youth might also have soured over the long decades. But no. Instantly the old charm claimed him. *I cannot accept the way in which we fix the span of our lives. I have observed that the sages hold it to be much shorter than is commonly supposed. "What!" said the younger Cato to those who would prevent him from killing himself, "am I now of an age to be reproached with yielding up my life too soon?" And yet he was but forty-eight years of age. He thought that age very ripe and well advanced, considering how few men reach it. Yes. Yes. And: Wherever your life ends, it is all there. The profit of life is not in its length but in the use we put it to: many a man has lived long, who has lived little; see to it as long as you are here. It lies in your will, not in the number of years, to make the best of life. Did you think never to arrive at a place you were incessantly making for? Yet there is no road but has an end. And if society is any comfort to you, is not the world going the selfsame way as you? Yes.* Perfect. Staunt read deep into the night, and sent for a bottle of Château d'Yquem from the House of Leavetaking's well-stocked cellars, and solemnly toasted old Montaigne in his own sleek wine, and read on until morning. *There is no road but has an end.*

When he was done with Montaigne, he turned to Ben Jonson, first the familiar works, *Volpone* and *The Silent Woman* and *The Case is Altered,* then the black, explosive plays of later years, *Bartholomew Fair* and *The New Inn* and *The Devil Is an Ass.* Staunt had always felt a strong affinity for the Elizabethans, and particularly for Jonson, that crackling, hissing, scintillating man, whose stormy, sprawling plays blazed with a nightmarish intensity that Shakespeare, the greater poet, seemed to lack. As he had always vowed he would, Staunt submerged himself in Jonson, until the sound and rhythm of Jonson's verse echoed and reechoed like thunder in his overloaded brain, and the texture of Jonson's mind seemed inlaid on his own. *The Magnetic Lady, Cynthia's Revels, Catiline his Conspiracy*—no play was too obscure, too hermetic, for Staunt in his gluttony. And one afternoon during this period he found himself doing an unexpected thing. From his data terminal he requested a print-out of the final pages of *The*

New Inn's first act, with an inch of blank space between each line. At the top of the sheet he wrote carefully, *The New Inn, an Opera by Henry Staunt, from the play of Ben Jonson*. Then, turning to Lovel's long speech, "O thereon hangs a history, mine host," Staunt began to pencil musical notations beneath the words, idly at first, then with sudden earnest fervor as the proper contours of the vocal line suggested themselves to him. Within minutes he had turned the entire speech into an aria and had even scribbled some preliminary marginal notes to himself about orchestration. The style of the music was strange to him, a spare, lean, angular sort of melodiousness, thorny and complex, with a curiously archaic flavor. It was the sort of music Alban Berg might have written during an extended visit to the early seventeenth century. It did not sound much like Staunt's own kind of thing. My late style, he thought. Probably the aria was impossible to sing. No matter: this was how the muse had called it forth. It was the first sustained composing Staunt had done in years. He stared at the completed aria in wonder, astonished that music could still flow from him like that, welling up without conscious command from the gushing spring within.

For an instant he was tempted to feed what he had written into a synthesizer and get back a rough orchestration. To hear the sound of it, with the baritone riding tensely over the swooping strings, might carry him on to set down the next page of the score, and the next, and the next. He resisted. The world already had enough operas that no one listened to. Shaking his head, smiling sadly, he dated the page, initialed it in his customary way, jotted down an opus number—by guesswork, for he was far from his ledgers—and, folding the sheet, put it away among his papers. Yet the music went on unfolding in his mind.

Nine

In his ninth week at the House of Fulfillment, finding himself stranded in stagnant waters, Staunt sought Dr. James and applied for the memory-jolt treatment. It seemed to be the only option left, short of Going, and he rarely contemplated Going these days. He was done with Jonson, and the impulse to request other books had not come to him; he peeked occasionally at his single page of *The New Inn,* but did not resume work on it; he was guarded and aloof in his conversations with Bollinger and with his occasional visitors; he realized that he was sliding imperceptibly into a deathlike passivity, without actually coming closer to his exit. He would not return to his former life, and he could not yet surrender and Go. Possibly the memory jolt would nudge him off dead center.

"It'll take six hours to prepare you," Dr. James said, his long nose twitching with enthusiasm for Staunt's project. "The brain has to be cleared of all fatigue products, and the autonomic nervous system needs a tuning. When would you like to begin?"

"Now," Staunt said.

They cleansed and tuned him, and took him back to his suite and put him to bed, and hooked him into his metabolic monitor. "If you get overexcited," Dr. James explained, "the monitor will automatically adjust the intensity of your emotional flow downward." Staunt was willing to take his chances with the intensity of his emotional flow, but the medic was insistent. The monitor stayed on. "It isn't psychic pain we're worried about," Dr. James said. "There's never any of that. But sometimes—an excess of remembered love, do you know?—a burst of happiness—it could be too much, we've found." Staunt nodded. He would not argue the point. The doctor produced a hypodermic and pressed its ultrasonic snout against Staunt's arm. Briefly Staunt wondered whether this was all a trick, whether the drug would really send him to his Going rather than for a trip along his time-track, but he pushed the irrational notion aside, and the snout made its brief droning sound and the mysterious dark fluid leaped into his veins.

Ten

He hears the final crashing chords of *The Trials of Job*, and the curtain, a sheet of dense purple light, springs up from the floor of the stage. Applause. Curtain calls for the singers. The conductor on stage, now, bowing, smiling. The chorus master, even. Cascades of cheers. All about him swirl the glittering mobile chandeliers of the Haifa Opera House. Someone is shouting incomprehensible jubilant words in his ear: the language is Hebrew, Staunt realizes. He says, Yes, yes, thank you so very much. They want him to stand and acknowledge the applause. Edith sits beside him, flushed with excitement, her eyes sparkling. His mind supplies the date: September 9, 1999. "Let them see you," Edith whispers through the tumult. A hand claps his shoulder.

Wild eyes blazing into his own: Mannheim, the critic. "The opera of the century!" he cries. Staunt forces himself to rise. They are screaming his name. *Staunt! Staunt! Staunt!* The audience is his. Two thousand berserk Israelis, his to command. What shall he say to them? *Sieg! Heil! Sieg! Heil!* He chokes on his own appalling unvoiced joke. In the end he can do nothing but wave and grin and topple back into his seat. Edith rubs his arm lovingly. His glowing bride. His night of triumph. To write an opera at all these days is a mighty task; to enjoy a premiere like this is heavenly. Now the audience wants an encore. The conductor at his station. The curtain fades. Job alone on stage: his final scene, the proud bass voice crying, "Behold, I am vile," and the voice of the Lord replying to him out of a thousand loudspeakers, filling all the world with sound: "Deck thyself now with majesty and excellency." Staunt weeps at his own music. If I live a hundred years, I will never forget this night, he tells himself.

Eleven

"The copter went down so suddenly, Mr. Staunt. They had it on the stabilizer beam all through the storm, but you know it isn't always possible—"

"And my wife? And my wife?"

"We're so sorry, Mr. Staunt."

Twelve

He sits at the keyboard fretting over the theory and harmony. His legs are not yet long enough to reach the piano's pedals: a nuisance, but temporary. He closes his eyes and strikes the keyboard. This is the key of C major, the easy one. The tonic chord. The dominant. Why did they wait so long to tell him about these things? He builds chord after chord. *I will now moderate into the key of D minor. Modulate. I do this and this and this.* He is nine years old. All this long hot Sunday afternoon he has explored this wondrous other language of sounds. While his family sits frozen by the television set. "Henry? Henry, they're going to be coming out of the module any minute!" He shrugs. What does the moon-walk matter to him? The moon is dead and far away. And this is the world of D minor. He has his own exploring to do today. "Henry, he's out! He came down the ladder!" Fine. Tonic. Dominant. And the diminished seventh. The words are strange. But how easy it is to go deeper and deeper into the maze of sound.

Thirteen

"The faculty and students take great pleasure, Mr. Staunt, to present you on the occasion of your one-hundredth birthday with this memorial of a composer who shared your divine productivity if not your blessed longevity: the original manuscript of Mozart's 'Divertimento in B,' Köchel number—"

Fourteen

"A boy, yes. We're calling him Paul, after Edith's father. And what an odd feeling it is to tell myself I have a son. You know, I'm forty-five years old. More than half my life gone, I suppose. And now a son."

Fifteen

The sun is huge in the sky, and the beach is ablaze with shimmering heat-furies, and beyond the crescent of pink sand the green Caribbean rests against its bed like water in a quiet tub. These are the hours when he remains under cover, in some shady hammock, reading, perhaps making notes for an essay or his next composition. But there is the girl again, crouched by the shore, gently poking at the creatures of the tidal pool, the shy anemones and the little sea-slugs and the busy hermit crabs. So he must expose his vulnerable skin, for tomorrow he will fly back to New York, and this may be his last chance to introduce himself to her. He has watched her through this whole week of vacation. Not a girl, exactly. Surely at least twenty-five years old. Very much her own person: self-contained, coolly precise, alert, elegant. Tempting. He has rarely felt so drawn toward anyone. Preserving his bachelorhood has been no chore for him; he glides as easily from woman to woman as he does from city to city. But there is something about the eyes of this Edith, something about her smile, that pulls him. He knows he is being foolish. All this is pure fantasy: he has no idea what she is like, where her interests lie. That look of intelligence and sympathy may be all his own invention; the girl inside the face may in truth be drab and empty, some programmer on holiday, her soul a dull haze of daydreams about glamorous holovision stars. Yet he must approach. The sun pounds his sensitive skin. She looks up, smiling, from the tidal pool. A purple sea-slug crawls lightly across her palm. He kneels beside her. She offers him the sea-slug, and he lets it crawl on his hand, and they laugh, and she points out limpets and periwinkles and barnacles for him, until there is a kind of contact between them through the creatures of this salty pond, and at last he says, feeling clumsy about it, "We haven't even introduced ourselves. I'm Henry Staunt."

"I know," Edith says. "The composer."

And it all becomes so much easier.

Sixteen

"—and the gold medal for the outstanding work in extended symphonic form by a student under sixteen years of age goes, as I'm sure everyone has already realized, to Henry Staunt, who—"

Seventeen

"And my wife? And my wife?"

"We're so sorry, Mr. Staunt."

Eighteen

"As long as we're getting into that end of the evening, Henry, I'll allow myself the prilivege of delivering a little analysis, too. Do you know what the real trouble with you is? With your music, with your soul, with everything? You don't suffer. You've never been touched by pain, or, if you have, it doesn't sink in. Look, you're forty years old, and you've never known anything but success, and your music is played everywhere, an incredible achievement for a living composer, and you could pass for thirty. Or even twenty-seven. Time doesn't claw you. I don't recommend suffering, mind you, but I do say it tempers an artist's soul; it adds a richness of texture that—forgive me—you lack, Henry. You know, you could live to be a very old man, considering the way you don't seem to age, and someday, when you're ninety-seven or one hundred five or something like that, you may realize that you've never really intersected reality, that you've kept yourself insulated, and that in a sense you haven't really lived at all or created anything at all or—forgive me, Henry. I take it all back, even if you are still smiling. Not even a friend should say things like that. Not even a friend."

Nineteen

"The Pultizer Prize for Music for the year 2002—"

Twenty

"I Edith do take thee Henry to be my lawful wedded husband—"

Twenty-One

"It isn't as if she was a bride, Henry. God knows it's terrible to lose her that way, but she was yours for fifty years, Henry, *fifty years,* the kind of marriage most people hardly dare to dream of having, and if she's gone, well, be content that you had the fifty, at least."

"I wish we had crashed together, though."

"Don't be childish. You're—what?—eighty-five, eighty-seven years old? You've got fifteen or twenty healthy and productive years ahead of you. More, if you're lucky. People live to fantastic ages nowadays. You might see one hundred ten or one hundred fifteen."

"Without Edith, what good is that?"

Twenty-Two

"Put your hands in the middle of the keyboard. Spread the fingers out as wide as you can. Wider. Wider. That's the boy! Now, Henry, this is what we call middle C—"

Twenty-Three

In haste, stumbling, he goes on into his studio. The big room holds the tangible residue of his long career. Over here, the music itself, in recorded performance: disks and cassettes for the early works, sparkling playback cubes for the later ones. Here are the manuscripts, uniformly bound in red half-morocco, one of his little vanities. Here are the scrapbooks of reviews and the programs of concerts. Here are the trophies. Here are the volumes of his critical writings. Staunt has been a busy man. He looks at the titles stamped on the bindings of the manuscripts: the symphonies, the string quartets, the concerti, the miscellaneous chamber works, the songs, the sonatas, the cantatas, the operas. So much. So much. Staunt feels no sense of having wasted his time, though, filling this room with what it holds. Never in the past hundred years has a week gone by without a performance of one of his compositions somewhere. That is sufficient justification for having written, for having lived. And yet, one hundred thirty-six years is such a long time.

He pushes cubes into playback slots, getting three of his works going at once, bringing wild skeins of sound out of the room's assortment of speakers, and stands in the middle, trembling a little, accepting the sonic barrage. After perhaps four minutes he cuts off the sound and orders his telephone to ring up the Office of Fulfillment.

"My Guide is Martin Bollinger," he says. "Would you let him know that I'd like to be transferred to the House of Leavetaking as soon as possible?"

Twenty-Four

Dr. James had told him, long before, that Departing Ones invariably came out of memory jolts in a state of ecstasy, and that frequently they were in such raptures that they insisted on Going immediately, before the high could ebb. Emerging from the drug, Staunt searched in vain for the ecstasy. Where? He was wholly calm. For some hours past, or maybe just a few minutes—he had no idea how long the memory jolt has lasted—he had tasted morsels of his past, scraps of conversation, bits of scenery, random textures of contact, a stew of incidents, nonchronological, unsorted. His music and his wife. His wife and his music. A pretty thin gruel for one hundred thirty-six years of life. Where were the storms? Where were the tempests? A single great tragedy, yes, and otherwise everything tranquil. Too orderly a life, too sane, too empty, and now, permitted to review it, he found himself with nothing to grasp but applause, which slipped through his fingers, and his love of Edith, and even that had lost its magic. Where was that excess of remembered love that Dr. James had said could be dangerous? Perhaps they had monitored him too closely, tuning down the intensity of his spirit. Or perhaps it was his spirit that was at fault. Old and dry, pale and lean.

Unlike the others he had heard about, he did not request immediate Going after his voyage. Without that terminal ecstasy, why Go? He felt not exactly depressed but certainly lowered; his tour of his yesterdays had thrust him into a sort of stasis, a paralysis of the will, that left him hung up as before, enmeshed by the strands of his own quiet past.

But if Staunt remained unready to Go, not so with others. "You are invited to the Farewell ceremony of David Golding," Miss Elliot told him the day after his memory jolt.

Golding was the man who had had six wives—outliving some, divorcing some, being divorced by some. His heroic husbandry was no longer apparent: now he was small and gnarled and fleshless, and because he was nearly blind, his pinched ungenerous face was disfigured by the jutting cones of two optical transducers. They said he was one hundred twenty-five years old, but to Staunt he looked at least two hundred. For the Farewell ceremony, though, the technicians of the House of Leavetaking had transformed the little old man into something sublime. His face gleamed with make-up that obliterated the crevices of decades; he held himself buoyantly upright, no doubt inflated into a semblance of his ancient virility by some drug; he was clad in a radiant,

shimmering gown. Scores of relatives and friends surrounded him in the Chambers of Farewell, a brightly
decorated underground suite opposite the recreation
center. Staunt, as he entered, was dismayed by the size
of the crowd. So many, so young, so noisy.

Ella Freeman sidled up to him and touched her
shriveled hand to Staunt's arm. "Look there: two of his
wives. He hadn't seen one in sixty years. And his sons.
All of them, his sons. Two or three by each wife!"

The ceremony, conducted by the relatively young
man who was Golding's Guide, was elegiac in tone,
brief, sweet. Standing under the emblem of the Office of
Fulfillment, the wheel and the gears, the Guide spoke
briefly of the philosophy of making room for others, of
the beauty of a willing departure. Then he praised the
Departing One in vague, general terms; one of his
sons delivered a more specific eulogy; lastly, Seymour
Church, chosen to represent Golding's companions at
the House of Leavetaking, croaked out a short, almost
incoherent speech of farewell. To this the Departing
One, who seemed transfigured with joy and already at
least halfway into the next world, made reply in a few
faint syllables, blurrily expressing gratitude for his long
and happy life. Golding barely appeared to comprehend
what was going on; he sat beaming in a kind of throne,
dreamy, distant. Staunt wondered if he had been
drugged into a stupor.

When the speeches were done, refreshments were
served. Then, accompanied only by his closest kin,
fifteen or twenty people, Golding was ushered into the
innermost room of the Chambers of Farewell. The door
slid shut behind him, and in his absence the Leavetaking
party proceeded merrily.

There were four such events in the next five weeks
At two of them—the Goings of Michael Green and

Katherine Parks—Staunt was asked to give the speech of farewell. It was a task that he performed gracefully, serenely, and, he thought, with a good deal of eloquence. He spoke for ten minutes about Michael Green, for close to fifteen about Katherine Parks, talking not so much about the Departing Ones, whom he had scarcely come to know well, but about the entire philosophy of Going, the beauty and wonder of the act of world-renunciation. It was not customary for the giver of the speech of farewell to manage such sustained feats, and his audience listened in total fascination; if the occasion had permitted it, Staunt suspected, they would have applauded.

So he had a new vocation, and several Departing Ones whom he did not know at all accelerated their own Goings so that they would not fail to have Staunt speak at the rites. It was summer now, and Arizona was caught in glistening tides of heat. Staunt never went outdoors any longer; he spent much of his time mingling in the recreation center, doing research, so to speak, for future oratory. He rarely read these days. He never listened to music. He had settled into a pleasing, quiet routine. This was his fourth month at the House of Leavetaking. Except for Seymour Church, who still refused to be nudged into Going, Staunt was now the senior Departing One in point of length of residence. And at the end of July, Church at last took his leave. Staunt, of course, spoke, touching on the Departing One's slow journey toward Going, and it was difficult for him to avoid self-conscious references to his own similar reluctance. Why do I tarry here? Staunt wondered. Why do I not say the word?

Every few weeks his son Paul visited him. Staunt found their meetings difficult. Paul, showing signs of strain and anxiety, always seemed on the verge of blurting out, "Why don't you Go, already?" And Staunt

would have no answer, for he did not know the answer.
He had read Hallam four times. Philosophically and psychologically he was prepared to Go. Yet he remained.

Twenty-Five

In mid-August Martin Bollinger entered his suite, held out a sheet of paper, and said, "What's this, Henry?"

Staunt glanced at it. It was a photocopy of the aria from *The New Inn*. "Where did you find that?" he asked.

"One of the staff people came across it while tidying your room."

"I thought we were entitled to privacy."

"This isn't an inquisition, Henry. I'm just curious. Have you started to compose again?"

"That scrap is all I wrote. It was months ago."

"It's fascinating music," Bollinger said.

"Is it, now? I thought it was rather harsh and forced, myself."

"No. No. Not at all. You always talked about a Ben Jonson opera, didn't you? And now you've begun it."

"I was enlivening a dull day," said Staunt. "Mere scribbling."

"Henry, would you like to get out of this place?"

"Are we back to *that*?"

"Obviously you still have music in you. Perhaps a great opera."

"Which you mean to squeeze out of me, eh? Don't talk nonsense. There's nothing left in me, Martin. I'm here to Go."

"You haven't Gone, though."

"You've noticed that," Staunt said.

"It was made clear to you at the beginning that you wouldn't be rushed. But I've begun to suspect, Henry, that you aren't interested in Going at all, that you're marking time here, perhaps incubating this opera, perhaps coming to terms with something indigestible in your soul. Whatever. You don't *have* to Go. We'll send you home. Finish *The New Inn*. Think the thoughts you want to think. Reapply for Going next year or the year after."

"You want that opera out of me, don't you?"

"I want you to be happy," said Bollinger. "I want your Going to be *right*. The bit of music here is just a clue to your inner state."

"There won't be any opera, Martin. And I don't plan to leave Omega Prime alive. To have put my family through this ordeal, and then to come home, to tell them it's all been just a holiday lark out here—no. No."

"As you wish," Bollinger said. He smiled and turned away, leaving an unspoken question hanging like a sword between them: *If you want to Go, Henry, why don't you Go?*

Twenty-Six

Staunt realized that he had taken on the status of a permanent Departing One, a kind of curator emeritus of the House of Fulfillment. Here he was, enjoying this life of ease and dignity, accepting the soft-voiced attentions of those who meant to slide him gently from the world, playing his role of patriarch among the shattered hulks that were the other Departing Ones here. Each week new ones came; he greeted them solemnly, helped them blend with those already in residence, and, in time, presided over their Goings. And he stayed on. Why? Why? Surely not out of fear of dying. Why, then, was he making a career out of his Going?

So that he might have the prestige of being a hero of his time, possibly—an exponent of noble renunciation, a practitioner of joyful departure. Making much glib talk of turning the wheel and creating a place for those to come—a twenty-first-century Sydney Carton, standing by the guillotine and praising the far, far better thing that he will do, only he finds himself enjoying the part so much that he forgets to kneel and present his neck to the blade.

Or maybe he is only interrupting the boredom of a too-bland life with a feigned fling at dying. The glamour of becoming a Departing One injecting interesting complexities into a static existence. But diversion and not death his real object. Yes? If that's it, Henry, go home and write your opera; the holiday should have ended by now.

He came close to summoning Bollinger and asking to be sent home. But he fought the impulse down. To leave Omega Prime now would be the true cowardice. He owed the world a death. He had occupied this body long enough. His place was needed; soon he would Go. Soon. Soon. Soon.

Twenty-Seven

At the beginning of September there were four days in a row of rain, an almost unknown occurrence in that part of Arizona. Miss Elliot said that the Hopi, doing their annual snake dances on their mesas far to the north, had overdone things this year and sent rain clouds all through the state. Staunt, to the horror of the staff, went out each day to stand in the rain, letting the cool drops soak his thin gown, watching the water sink swiftly into the parched red soil. "You'll catch your death of cold," Mr. Falkenbridge told him sternly. Staunt laughed.

He requested another wide-spaced print-out of *The New Inn* and tried to set the opening scene. Nothing came. He could not find the right vocal line, nor could he recapture the strange color of the earlier aria. The tones and textures of Ben Jonson were gone from his head. He gave the project up without regret.

There were three Farewell ceremonies in eight days. Staunt attended them all, and spoke at two of them.

Arbitrarily, he chose September 19 as the day of his own Going. But he told no one about his decision,

and September 19 came and went with Staunt unchanged.

At the end of the month he told Martin Bollinger,
"I'm a fraud. I haven't gotten an inch closer to Going in
all the time I've been here. I never wanted to Go at all.
I still want to live, to see and do things, to experience
things. I came here out of desperation, because I was
stale, I was bored, I needed novelty. To toy with death,
to live a little scenario of dying—that was all I was after.
Excitement. An event in an eventless life: Henry Staunt
Prepares to Die. I've been using all you people as players
in a cynical charade."

Bollinger said quietly, "Shall I arrange for you to
go home, then, Henry?"

"No. No. Get me Dr. James. And notify my family
that my Farewell ceremony will be held a week from
today. It's time for me to Go."

"But if you still want to live—"

"What better time to Go?" Staunt asked.

Twenty-Eight

They were all here, close around him. Paul had come,
and Crystal, too, back from the moon and looking
feeble, and all the grandchildren and the great-grandchildren, and the friends, the conductors and the younger
composers and some critics, more than a hundred people
in all coming to see him off. Staunt, undrugged but already beginning to ascend, had moved coolly among

them, thanking them for attending his Leavetaking party, welcoming them to his Farewell ceremony. He was amazed at how calm he was. Seated now in the throne of honor, he listened to the final orations and endured without objection a scrambled medley of his most famous compositions, obviously assembled hastily by someone inexpert in such matters. Martin Bollinger, giving the main eulogy, quoted heavily from Hallam: "Too often we delude ourselves into thinking we are truly ready, when actually we have not reached readiness at all, and choose Going out of unworthy or shallow motives. How tragic it is to arrive at the actual moment of Leavetaking and to realize that one has deceived oneself, that one's motivations are false, that one is, in fact, not in the least ready to Go!"

How true, Staunt told himself. And yet how false. For here I am ready to Go and yet not in the least ready, and in my unreadiness lies my readiness.

Bollinger finished what he had to say, and one of the Departing Ones, a man named Bradford who had come to Omega Prime in August, began to fumble through the usual final speech. He stammered and coughed and lost the thread of his words, for he was one hundred forty years old and due for Going himself next week, but somehow he made it to the end. Staunt, paying little attention, beamed at his son and his daughter, his horde of descendants, his admirers, his doctors. He understood now why Departing Ones generally seemed detached from their own Farewell ceremonies: the dreary drone of the speeches launched them early into the shores of paradise.

And then they were serving the refreshments, and now they were about to wheel him into the innermost room. And Staunt said, "May I speak also?"

They looked at him, appalled, frightened, obviously

fearing he would wreck the harmony of the occasion with this unconventional, ill-timed intrusion. But they could not refuse. He had delivered so many eulogies for others—now he would speak for himself.

Softly Staunt said, making them strain their ears to hear it, "I accept the concept of the turning wheel, and I gladly yield my place to those who are to come. But let me tell you that this is not an ordinary Going. You know, when I came here I thought I was weary of the world and ready to Go, but yet I stayed, I held back from the brink, I delayed, I pretended. I even—Martin knows this—began another opera. I was told I could go home, and I refused. Hallam forgive me, but I refused. For his way is not the only way of Going. Because life still seems sweet, I give it up today. And so I take my final pleasure: that of relinquishing the only thing left to me worth keeping."

They were whispering. They were staring.

I have said all the wrong things, he thought. I have spoiled the day for them. But whose Going is it? Why should I care about them?

Martin Bollinger, bending low, murmured, "It's still not too late, Henry. We can stop everything right now."

"The final temptation," Staunt said. "And I withstand it. Bring down the curtain. I'm ready to Go."

They wheeled him to the innermost chamber. When they offered him the cup, he seized it, winked at Martin Bollinger, and drained it in a single gulp.

About the Author

ROBERT SILVERBERG was born in New York and graduated from Columbia University. He now lives near San Francisco. He is the author of countless short stories and many novels. He has also had a substantial career as a non-fiction writer specializing in archaeological and historical themes. He is a past president of the Science Fiction Writers of America and was American guest of honor at the World Science Fiction Convention in Heidelberg, 1970. He has won the Hugo twice and the Nebula Award three times. His hobbies are gardening and travel. When he has time, his special interests include contemporary literature and music, medieval geography, and the raising of fuchsias and cacti.